The Secret Files of Sherlock Holmes

The Secret Files of Sherlock Holmes

June Thomson

(with the assistance of
Aubrey B. Watson)

New York

This is a work of fiction. Names, characters, places, and incidents either are the product of the author's imagination or are used fictitiously. Any resemblance to actual events or persons, living or dead, is entirely coincidental.

First published in Great Britain by Constable & Company, Ltd, London.

Otto Penzler Books
129 W. 56th Street
New York, NY 10019
(Editorial Offices only)

Macmillan Publishing Company
866 Third Avenue
New York, NY 10022

Macmillan Publishing Company is part of the Maxwell Communication Group of Companies.

Library of Congress Cataloging-in-Publication Data
Thomson, June.
The secret files of Sherlock Holmes / June Thomson, with the assistance of Aubrey B. Watson.
p. cm.
ISBN 1-883402-36-0
1. Holmes, Sherlock (Fictitious character)—Fiction. 2. Private investigators—England—Fiction. I. Title.
PR6070.H679S43 1993 93-5150 CIP
823'.914—dc20

Otto Penzler Books are available at special discounts for bulk purchases for sales promotions, premiums, fund-raising, or educational use. For details, contact:

Special Sales Director
Macmillan Publishing Company
866 Third Avenue
New York, NY 10022

10 9 8 7 6 5 4 3 2 1

Printed in the United States of America

TO

H. R. F. KEATING

IN GRATITUDE FOR

ALL HIS EXPERT HELP

AND ADVICE

ACKNOWLEDGEMENTS

I should like to take this opportunity of expressing my thanks to June Thomson for her help in preparing this collection of short stories for publication.

Aubrey B. Watson LDS, FDS, D orth.

FOREWORD

Students of the Sherlock Holmes' canon will be familiar with the opening sentence of 'The Problem of Thor Bridge' in which Watson, Holmes's companion and chronicler of many of the great consulting detective's cases, states that:

> Somewhere in the vaults of the bank of Cox and Co.,* at Charing Cross, there is a travel-worn and battered tin dispatch box with my name, John H. Watson, M. D., Late Indian Army, painted upon the lid.

Watson goes on to explain that the dispatch box contains records of 'some of the curious problems' which, at various times, Holmes was called upon to investigate and which were never fully narrated, either because the final explanation was not forthcoming or in order to protect the secrets of certain families in 'exalted positions'.

It was this same battered tin dispatch box which my late uncle claimed came into his possession in 1939, and the contents of which – or rather his copies of the papers it contained – he later bequeathed to me.

The story of how he acquired the box is a curious one and I shall relate it exactly as it was told to me by my late uncle,

* In February 1990, it was reported that Lloyds Bank is reviving its former Cox and King's branch in Pall Mall, Dr John H. Watson's bank, as a private bank for Armed Forces officers and their families. (Aubrey B. Watson)

leaving it to the reader to form his or her own judgement as to its reliability.

My uncle was also Dr John Watson although, in his case, the middle initial was F, not H. He was, moreover, a Doctor of Philosophy, not medicine, and up to the time of his retirement he taught that subject at All Saints College, Oxford.

He was, of course, fully aware of the similarity between his name and that of the famous Dr John H. Watson. He could hardly be otherwise; it was the subject of much light banter among his fellow dons at High Table. Rather than let it be the cause of any personal embarrassment, he decided to turn the situation to his advantage.

Consequently, despite the demands of his own academic studies (he published several philosophical treatises, among them *In Praise of Anguish,* all of which, alas, are no longer in print) he read widely in the Holmes' canon and became an acknowledged expert. He even wrote a short monograph on his illustrious namesake which he had privately printed and distributed amongst his friends and fellow enthusiasts. Unfortunately, I have not been able to trace any copies of it.

He was also, in a modest way, a collector of Holmesian and Watsonian memorabilia and had in his possession copies of the original *Strand Magazine* in which Dr Watson's accounts of Holmes's adventures were first published.

It was, he told me, because of his reputation among students of the canon, and no doubt also the similarity of his name to the other Dr Watson's, that in July 1939, shortly before the outbreak of the Second World War, he received a visit in his college rooms from a lady, a certain Miss Adelina McWhirter, whom he described as elderly, respectable and of an impoverished, genteel appearance.

She was, Miss McWhirter claimed, related to Holmes's Dr Watson on his mother's side of the family and had acquired, although she declined to explain how, the doctor's tin dispatch box, together with its contents, which had been deposited at Cox and Co., and which she was anxious to sell to someone, as she put it, 'of proven academic scholarship who would appreciate its true value'.

The actual monetary value she placed on it was £500, a not inconsiderable sum in 1939. She hinted that her own straitened circumstances had forced her to part with this family heirloom.

Miss McWhirter's excessive gentility inhibited my uncle from pressing her for too many details about her exact situation or how the box had come into her possession in the first place. However, when he examined it and the papers it contained, he was convinced they were genuine and, the £500 having been paid over (in cash, on Miss McWhirter's insistence), both box and contents passed into his possession.

It was at this point that international events intervened.

The date, you will remember, was July 1939. War seemed imminent and my uncle, fearful for the safety of the Watson papers, decided to make copies of them which he kept in his rooms in Oxford, depositing the box and its contents, together with his editions of the *Strand Magazine* and other valuable Holmesian memorabilia, in the strong-room of the main branch of his own bank, City and County, in Lombard Street, London EC3.

It was an unwise decision.

While All Saints College escaped unscathed, the main branch of the City and County suffered a direct hit during the bombing of 1942 and, although the dispatch box was rescued from the ruins, its paint was so blistered by the heat that the name on the lid was totally obliterated while the papers inside it were reduced to a mass of indecipherable charred fragments.

My uncle was placed in a dilemma.

Although he still had his copies of the Watson papers, they were, of course, in his own handwriting and he had nothing to prove the existence of the originals apart from the fire-damaged box and its burnt contents, which, to those of a sceptical disposition, amounted to no proof at all.

Nor could he trace Miss Adelina McWhirter, despite strenuous efforts on his part to do so. She had given him her address in London, a small, residential hotel in South Kensington where she said she was living, but when he applied there, he was told that she had moved out in the summer of 1939 – not long, in fact, after she had visited my uncle in Oxford – and had left no forwarding address. Repeated appeals to her through the personal columns in *The Times* to contact him failed to elicit any response.

Because of this lack of evidence to prove the authenticity of the Watson archives, my uncle, careful of his reputation as a scholar, decided not to publish any of the material, and on his death at the age of 98 on 2 June 1982 – ironically, forty years to the exact day after the originals were destroyed – the copies he had made passed to me under the terms of his will.

By the way, I do not know what happened to the dispatch box and its charred contents. It stood in my uncle's rooms in All Saints until at least 1949 for I remember seeing it on his desk when, as a child, I visited him in Oxford. What happened to it subsequently, I have no idea. It was not found among his effects after his death and may have been thrown out, as so much rubbish, by the staff at the Eventide Nursing Home in Carshalton, Surrey, in which he spent his last years.

For the same reason that made my uncle hesitate to publish the Watson papers in his lifetime, I, too, have thought long and hard for several years about what to do with his copies of them.

However, as I have no one to whom I can in turn bequeath them and being by profession an orthodontist and therefore having, unlike my late uncle, no academic reputation to protect, I have decided to risk bringing down on my head the obloquy and derision of all serious students of Mr Sherlock Holmes and Dr Watson by offering them for publication.

I make no claims for their genuineness. They are, as I have said, not the originals, if indeed the originals themselves were authentic and not mere forgeries. I can only present the facts, such as they are, as they were told to me.

There is a large quantity of these copies, all in my uncle's handwriting: some full-length accounts to which my uncle, the late Dr John F. Watson, added his own footnotes; and some rough jottings which the original Dr Watson, if indeed it were he who made them, appeared to have recorded hastily, perhaps as a memorandum of the events which may – or may not – have occurred.

The first of these I have chosen is one of the full-length

accounts, concerning an apparently unsolved case undertaken by Sherlock Holmes and also referred to by Dr Watson at the beginning of 'The Problem of Thor Bridge'. It is the investigation into the sudden disappearance of Mr James Phillimore, who, 'stepping back into his own house to get his umbrella, was never more seen in this world'.

There is no indication of the year in which the events purported to have happened may have occurred nor when the account was written down, although, from internal evidence, I tentatively suggest that the case may be placed in the late 1880s or early 1890s, but certainly subsequent to the time when Watson, after his marriage to Miss Mary Morstan, moved out of the lodgings which he shared with Holmes at 221B Baker Street.

As the account is also unnamed, I have taken it upon myself to give it the title of 'The Case of the Vanishing Head-waiter.'

Aubrey B. Watson LDS, FDS, D orth.

THE CASE OF THE VANISHING HEAD-WAITER

Although elsewhere in the published accounts of my adventures with Sherlock Holmes I have referred in passing to the disappearance of Mr James Phillimore as one of Holmes's unsolved cases, I have to confess that this was a deception on my part, carried out on Holmes's instructions in order to protect the anonymity of Mr Phillimore's exact whereabouts.

Rather than reveal them, especially to one certain individual, Holmes, preferring not to betray Phillimore's trust, allowed the public to believe that, in this particular case, all his deductive powers were of no avail and that he had to admit himself defeated.

However, I have his permission to write an account of the mystery and, in the hope that at some future date he may agree to the story being published, I intend preserving it among my papers.

The adventure began one Friday morning in late May when I called at 221B Baker Street soon after the post had arrived. I found Holmes seated at the breakfast table in the first-floor sitting-room among the clutter of familiar objects, reading a letter which he passed to me with the comment, 'Well, Watson, what do you make of that?'

By that time, I had known Holmes for long enough to have acquired some of his skills of observation and I perused the letter carefully before replying.

It read:

To Mr Sherlock Holmes.
Dear Sir,

I should be most grateful if you would grant me an interview on Friday next at 11 a.m., in order that I may discuss with you the sudden disappearance of my friend, Mr James Phillimore, a head-waiter, who vanished last Tuesday morning at seven-thirty, practically in front of my eyes, and who has not been seen since.

I would not normally trouble you but the police are not willing to pursue inquiries.

As I have asked for leave of absence from my place of employment for Friday morning, I trust you can comply with my request for an interview. I remain, Sir, Your Obedient Servant, Charles Nelson.

I noticed that the writing-paper was a popular brand, available at most stationers', and that the script was the careful, round hand of a clerk while the address, Magnolia Terrace, Clapham, suggested that the correspondent was neither distinguished nor famous.

I said as much, adding, 'You won't accept the case, will you, Holmes? A missing head-waiter! It seems far too commonplace to do much to enhance your reputation. Surely it is best left to the police to solve?'

Holmes, who was lighting his after-breakfast pipe, raised his eyebrows at me.

'Come, Watson!' he chided gently but not without an amused twinkle in his grey eyes. 'I have told you before* that the status of a client is a matter of less moment to me than the interest of his case. And this case, even though it involves a head-waiter, is certainly a curious one. Mr James Phillimore has not merely disappeared. It would seem he has totally vanished without trace on a Tuesday morning in broad daylight and in the middle of Clapham, too! Besides, although the police have been informed, they appear not to be interested in following up

* Dr John H. Watson remarks on this quality of Mr Sherlock Holmes in 'The Adventure of Black Peter'. (Dr John F. Watson)

the mystery. I shall certainly see this Mr Charles Nelson when he arrives and hear the full story before deciding whether or not to take up the investigation. Will you be able to stay for the interview? Or have you a more pressing appointment with one of your patients?'

It so happened that my morning was free and, once Mrs Hudson had cleared the table, Holmes and I settled down to read the morning papers while awaiting the arrival of Mr Nelson, Holmes occasionally interrupting the silence to comment out loud on some item which had caught his attention in the daily press.

'I see share prices are still rising,' he remarked at one point. 'Now would seem the right time to sell one's investments.'

A little later, he again broke in to exclaim, 'By Jove, Watson! Another burglary in Knightsbridge, this time at the home of Lady Whittaker whose emeralds have been stolen. I am beginning to suspect a master-mind behind these thefts. It would not surprise me if one of these days we receive a visit from Inspector Lestrade of the Yard.'

Lestrade did not, in fact, call that morning although, sharp on the stroke of eleven, footsteps were heard ascending the stairs and, after a hesitant knock at the door, Mr Nelson, a tall, awkward man in his thirties, with thinning fair hair, entered the room. He was dressed in a respectable dark suit and carried a bowler hat which he twisted nervously between his hands as if awed at finding himself in the presence of the great consulting detective.

Unexpectedly, for his letter had made no reference to a companion, he was accompanied by a young woman in her mid-twenties; not unhandsome but a little too buxom and high-coloured to be considered beautiful and with a bold, imperious air about her. I could envisage her in a few years' time developing into a formidable and overbearing matron.

Mr Nelson introduced her as Miss Cora Page, the fiancée of his friend, Mr Phillimore.

'Miss Page', Nelson continued, giving Holmes an apologetic glance, 'insisted on coming with me.'

The reason for his diffidence was immediately apparent for,

no sooner had Holmes invited them to sit down, than Miss Page took charge of the interview.

'Charlie here will be able to tell you the facts, Mr Holmes,' she began, after casting a disapproving glance about her at the clutter of books, papers and scientific apparatus which occupied every flat surface in the room and had in places overflowed on to the floor. 'My main concern is finding my fiancé. We were due to be married next month. The church is booked, the cake ordered, the dressmaker has nearly finished my wedding gown, apart from some alterations to the bodice, that is. And now Jim has gone and disappeared! I can't believe he'd desert me practically on the altar steps. It's too humiliating!'

Her voice rose as she spoke, her cheeks flushing even brighter, and, as she fumbled in her reticule for a handkerchief with which to dab her eyes, Holmes turned to me.

'Miss Page is naturally distressed at the disappearance of her fiancé, Watson, and no doubt also fatigued by the journey here from Clapham. Such a long way to come! Be a dear fellow and escort her downstairs where I am sure Mrs Hudson will provide her with tea and biscuits.'

Taking the hint, I accompanied Miss Page to the ground floor where I installed her in the housekeeper's room and, having seen her supplied with the refreshments which Holmes had recommended, I returned upstairs.

With Miss Page's departure, Mr Nelson seemed more at ease and, as I re-entered the room, I found him leaning forward in his armchair in earnest tête-à-tête with Holmes, who, holding up a hand, cut short his prospective client's account.

'One moment, Mr Nelson, if you please. Now that my good friend Dr Watson has rejoined us, may I take the opportunity to recapitulate the facts of the case for his benefit?' Turning to me, he continued, 'Mr Nelson has been telling me that it is his custom to accompany his friend, Mr James Phillimore, every morning to Clapham Junction station in order to catch the eight-five train into Town where they both have their places of work, Mr Nelson as clerk at Murchison and Whybrow's, the solicitors in King William Street, Mr Phillimore at Gudgeon's in St

Swithin's Lane where he is employed as head-waiter. You have heard of Gudgeon's, of course, Watson?'

'Indeed I have,' I replied, seating myself in the chair which Miss Page had just vacated. 'It is a well-known restaurant in the City, much frequented, I believe, by bankers and members of the Stock Exchange.'

'Quite so. Now it seems that every morning, on the dot of half past seven, as Mr Nelson described it, he would walk from Magnolia Terrace where he has lodgings . . .'

'Just off Lavender Hill,' Mr Nelson broke in.

'. . . into Laburnum Grove where his old friend, Mr Phillimore, would be waiting for him at the gate of number seventeen. They would then set off together down Lavender Hill for the station. And then, three days ago . . .' He looked across at Mr Nelson, inviting him to resume his account at the point where, it seemed, it had been interrupted.

Mr Nelson was eager to pick up the story.

'Well, Mr Holmes, as I was saying, it was Tuesday morning. There was Jim – Mr Phillimore – standing at his gate as per usual. There was nothing out of the ordinary about him except, as I got close up to him, he said, 'I fancy I can smell rain in the air, Charlie. I'm just popping back into the house for my brolly. It's in the hall so I shan't be more than half a jiffy.' So he gets out his keys, walks back up the garden path, opens the front door and goes inside, leaving the door ajar. And that's the last I saw of him.'

'You waited, I assume?' Holmes asked.

'Of course I did, Mr Holmes. I hung about at the gate for a good five minutes, expecting him to come out of the house at any moment. Then, when he didn't appear, I went up to the house myself, thinking he'd been taken ill of a sudden. I pushed open the door and went into the hall, calling out his name. But there was neither sight nor sound of him in either of the downstairs rooms. It was while I was looking and calling that his housekeeper heard me and came out of the kitchen. When I explained what had happened, she went with me up the stairs to look in the bedrooms. It's only a small house, Mr Holmes, and I swear we searched every inch of it, under the beds, in the wardrobes, even the cupboard under the stairs. But we found nothing.'

'What about the garden? You searched that, too?'

'Oh, yes, Mr Holmes. It is only a few yards square but there was no one there neither. It was as if he'd vanished into thin air.'

'Could he have climbed into a neighbour's garden?' I put in.

'No, he couldn't, Dr Watson. The fence is too high as you'll see for yourself if you come to the house; that is, if Mr Holmes is willing to take up the case.'

He turned to look at Holmes in appeal but my old friend, puffing away imperturbably at his pipe, refused to be drawn and merely nodded in my direction to encourage me to continue my line of questioning which I did with some hesitation, anxious not to appear a fool nor to assume Holmes's role of detective.

'Then is there any other means of exit from the premises? A back garden gate, for instance?'

'No, sir, there isn't. The only other way Jim – Mr Phillimore – could have left was by a passage which runs along the side of the house to the back door. It's the tradesmen's entrance. But he didn't go out that way. As I explained, I was standing at the gate for a good five minutes and I would have noticed him if he'd left by that route. There's a few people about at that time in the morning, like me and Jim making their way to work, but I know every one of them by sight and there's not enough of them for him to have slipped away unnoticed. Nor did his housekeeper see him pass the kitchen window which he'd have to do if he went out that way. And, like I said, by the time I went into the house, he'd already vanished.'

I could think of no other questions to put to Mr Nelson and I was relieved when Holmes, leaning forward to knock out the ashes of his pipe into the coal-scuttle, resumed charge of the interview.

'Tell me a little about your friend. What type of man is he?'

'Oh, a very quiet, unassuming man, Mr Holmes. Very regular in his habits.'

'Not the sort to take it into his head suddenly to disappear?'

'Quite out of character. That's why I'm so worried about him. He's a steady, reliable fellow who I'd trust with my last shilling.'

'Any problems at his place of employment?'

'Quite the contrary. The management of Gudgeon's are as concerned as I am about his disappearance. When I called round there to explain the situation to them, they spoke most highly of him.'

'Then is he in any financial difficulties?'

'Not that I know of, Mr Holmes. He lived very modestly, never spending more than he earned which, seeing as he was a head-waiter, were decent wages, not to mention the tips he'd get as extras.'

'Tips!' Holmes exclaimed, as if he had never heard of the word.

Mr Nelson regarded him in surprise.

'Yes, Mr Holmes, tips; small gratuities which a satisfied customer offers for good service.'

'Yes, yes, of course. I understand that. Pray continue, Mr Nelson. When I interrupted you, you were speaking of your friend's modest style of living.'

'And so it was, sir. He didn't drink, didn't smoke, didn't gamble. His only extravagance was to treat himself occasionally to a seat in the upper circle at a music-hall. I know for a fact that he had over a hundred pound saved up. And he didn't have to find a weekly rent neither. There'd been a bit of money in the family. His parents had owned an eating-house in the City Road. In fact, it was there where Jim got his foot on the first rung of the catering ladder, so to speak. As a lad, he'd worked for them, waiting at table. But, in his quiet way, Jim's ambitious and gradually he moved on to higher things, eventually finishing up as head-waiter at Gudgeon's. After his father died, his mother sold up the business and with the proceeds bought the house in Laburnum Grove, partly to retire to and partly to give Jim a home. He was living in lodgings at the time. Then, when old Mrs Phillimore died last October, he inherited the house along with its contents.'

'Where, I assume, he intended setting up home with Miss Page after their marriage?'

Nelson gave Holmes another of his contrite glances.

'I'm sorry about her coming with me, Mr Holmes. I had hoped to speak to you in private. But once she heard I had written to you for an appointment, she wouldn't take no for an answer. She's a very determined young lady is Cora. And naturally, she's upset by Jim's disappearance. As she told you, they were due to be married next month. Jim had been putting the wedding off on account of Cora and his mother not seeing eye to eye and neither of them willing to share the same house with the other. Mrs Phillimore was a bit of a Tartar, between me and you; crippled with arthritis in her later years and as deaf as a post. But that didn't stop her getting her own way. It was on her account that Jim took on Mrs Bennet as a live-in housekeeper so there'd be someone to look after his mother when he was out at work. By the way, sir, I took the liberty of mentioning to Mrs Bennet that you might be calling at the house to make inquiries.'

He again looked appealingly at Holmes but when he failed to respond apart from nodding encouragement to the man to continue, Nelson resumed his account.

'Old Mrs Phillimore led him a terrible dance when she was alive. Boss him about! I've never heard the like of it. Not that Jim ever complained and he was a good son to her. Taught her and himself to lip-read so that the two of them could still have some means of communication. Anyway, once she died, Cora – Miss Page – insisted on Jim naming the day and the wedding was fixed for June 14th, reception afterwards in the private room over the Farriers' Arms and a honeymoon in Bournemouth.' Mr Nelson stared down gloomily into his bowler hat which he was nursing between his knees. 'It don't look as if it'll come off now, does it, Mr Holmes? Not with the bridegroom gone and vanished off the face of the earth.'

'It would seem highly unlikely,' Holmes agreed.

'So what do you say, sir?' Nelson continued eagerly. 'Will you take the case? I don't know who else to turn to. The police aren't interested. They say that as Jim is over-age and there's no sign of foul play, there's not much they can do. He might turn up. Or then again he might not. It's all very worrying and bothersome. He's been a good friend to me, has Jim, and I would be more than grateful if you would make a few inquiries. I don't know what your fees are but I have a bit of money put aside for a rainy day which I'm willing to part with for Jim's sake for, with him disappearing the way he did, I reckon that day has already arrived.'

Holmes seemed to come to a sudden decision for, springing to his feet, he held out his hand.

'I shall certainly take on the case, Mr Nelson. As for the fees . . .' He made a deprecatory gesture. 'Payment will be by results. If I fail to find your friend, Mr James Phillimore, then there will be no charge. That seems a fair arrangement.'

Before Mr Nelson could protest or even express his thanks, Holmes had ushered him out of the room and down the stairs to the ground floor where presumably Nelson found Miss Page for, a few minutes later, as Holmes and I stood at the window, we watched the two of them walking away down Baker Street, the lady clasping her tall, ungainly companion by the arm and talking vociferously while he listened, head bent, to her monologue.

Holmes chuckled sardonically.

'Unless Mr Nelson is very careful, he will find himself married off sooner or later to his friend's fiancée,' he remarked. 'As he himself described her, she won't take no for an answer. Well, what do you make of it, Watson? Not that particular relationship but the case of Mr James Phillimore, the vanishing head-waiter.'

'It is certainly very strange,' I replied. 'Phillimore seems a man from a respectable enough background . . .'

'Who also possessed a very keen sense of smell,' Holmes added in a jocular fashion. 'As I remember, Tuesday morning was particularly fine with not a cloud to be seen. And yet he assured Mr Nelson that he could smell rain and insisted on going back to the house for his umbrella. I think *I* detect a whiff of conspiracy. Come, Watson, get your hat. We are going out.'

He was already striding towards the door.

'Where to?' I demanded, snatching up my hat and stick and hurrying after him.

'Where else but seventeen Laburnum Grove, Clapham, to

examine the scene of Mr James Phillimore's extraordinary disappearing act?'

The house, as we discovered when the hansom cab deposited us at the gate, was a small, red-brick villa of the type erected in such areas as Clapham and Brixton for clerks, shop-assistants and minor tradesmen and their families. A narrow strip of front garden, just wide enough to accommodate two rose bushes and a tiny patch of lawn, separated it from the road where a few trees, too young yet to have developed beyond the sapling stage, grew out of the paving-stones between the gas lamp-standards.

The garden path, a mere few yards in length and paved with red and yellow tiles, led up to the front door where Holmes banged on the knocker.

The door was opened by an elderly, grey-haired woman, dressed in clean but shabby black, with tired, lined features – Mrs Bennet, the housekeeper, I assumed.

'Come in, sir,' she said, dropping a little bob of a curtsey. 'You must be Mr Sherlock Holmes, the famous detective. I've read about you in the illustrated papers. Mr Nelson said you might be calling on account of Mr Phillimore's disappearing. He said I was to answer any questions – Mr Nelson, that is.'

After Holmes had introduced me and Mrs Bennet had dropped another curtsey, a difficult manoeuvre in Phillimore's narrow hall, still further encumbered by a large hat-stand, she showed us into a small sitting-room which overlooked the back garden where she waited just inside the door, her work-worn hands folded on the front of her apron.

I have remarked elsewhere* on Holmes's skill at putting a humble witness at ease. It was so with Mrs Bennet. It is also worth recording his own ability to appear totally relaxed in whatever surroundings he may find himself, whether it be the splendours of a panelled library in a ducal mansion or the fetid basement of an opium den in Limehouse.

On this occasion, he drew out an upright chair and, seating

* Dr John H. Watson makes this comment in 'The Adventure of the Missing Three-Quarter'. (Dr John F. Watson)

himself upon it, crossed his legs as if perfectly at home in Mr Phillimore's cramped but tidy living-room, with its ugly furniture, too large for the space yet polished to a high gloss, its potted plants and its family photographs, most of them featuring a heavy-chinned, disagreeable-looking old lady who could only be the late Mrs Phillimore.

'There is no need to be nervous,' Holmes said, addressing Mrs Bennet and giving her one of his most cordial smiles, for when Holmes is in a good humour, there is no kinder nor more charming man in the whole world. 'I shall ask you a few simple questions, nothing more. First of all, I should like you to tell me in your own words exactly what Mr Phillimore did on Tuesday morning from the time he rose until he left the house.'

'Rose, sir?' Mrs Bennet seemed surprised that the great detective should have come all that way to question her about such trivial domestic happenings. 'The same as he always did. He got up at half past six as usual, washed and shaved – I took him up a can of hot water – dressed and came downstairs for his breakfast.'

'And then?'

'He put on his coat, called out goodbye to me and went out by the front door to wait at the gate for Mr Nelson.'

'Nothing else happened before he left? No post came? No messages?'

'Only the paper, sir, which he glanced at over his breakfast.'

'Ah, the morning newspaper!' Holmes seemed unwarrantedly pleased by this information. 'And which morning newspaper does Mr Phillimore subscribe to?'

'*The Times*, sir.'

I was surprised to hear this. It seemed an unusual choice of reading-matter for a head-waiter and one which I could only ascribe to Phillimore's contact with Gudgeon's City clients who no doubt had influenced his taste towards a more superior daily paper. Holmes himself, however, appeared not to find the information significant for, when I glanced at him to observe his response, apart from commenting 'Really?' in an uninterested voice, he passed on to other matters.

'Tell me what happened after Mr Phillimore left the house.'

'Why, nothing at all, sir, until I heard Mr Nelson in the hall calling out Mr Phillimore's name. I was in the kitchen, washing up the breakfast things and, when I went out to see what Mr Nelson wanted, he told me that five minutes before Mr Phillimore had come back into the house to get his umbrella and hadn't come out again. We looked all over and Mr Nelson searched the garden but there was no sign of him.'

'I see he did not, in fact, take his umbrella,' Holmes remarked. 'It is still in the hall-stand.'

'Is it, Holmes?' I interjected. 'I had not noticed.'

'He didn't take nothing!' Mrs Bennet burst out, her mouth beginning to tremble. 'He's left everything behind – every stitch of clothing he owned down to his winter overcoat and his best boots. Oh, sir, what's happened to him? And what's to happen to me and the house? My wages is paid up until the end of the month and the police have told me to stay on in case he turns up. I can't think where he can have gone to or why. He's never done anything like this before. He's so regular, I swear you could set Big Ben by him. He's not even so much as gone away on a holiday except for that week he spent in Margate after his mother died and the doctor ordered him a complete rest and a change of air.'

'Margate?' Holmes inquired. 'Do you happen to know whereabouts in Margate he stayed?'

'I couldn't say, sir, except it was a boarding-house with a funny, foreign-sounding name.'

'I see. And apart from his holiday in Margate, have there been any more recent changes in Mr Phillimore's routine?'

'Well, not really . . .'

Seeing her hesitate, Holmes asked quickly, 'But you have noticed something?'

'Only his wardrobe, sir. He took to locking it over the past few days. I noticed on Monday morning when I went to his room to hang up a coat I'd sponged and pressed for him.'

'But it is unlocked now?'

'Why, yes, sir, so it is!' Mrs Bennet exclaimed. 'How did you know that?'

'It seemed a possibility,' Holmes answered carelessly before continuing, 'There is one more question and then I shall not need to detain you any longer, Mrs Bennet. After Mr Phillimore left by the front door, did you notice anyone pass by the kitchen?'

'No, sir; I did not. I was stood by the sink in front of the window from the time Mr Phillimore left the house until Mr Nelson called out and not a blessed soul went past it. I'd take my Bible oath on that.'

'Thank you, Mrs Bennet,' Holmes said gravely. 'You have been most helpful.'

'Has she, Holmes?' I asked, after Mrs Bennet had left the room. 'I can't see she has added anything of significance to our knowledge of the case apart from reiterating the same information we have already learned from Mr Nelson.'

'You underestimate her contribution, Watson. There is the matter of the locked wardrobe.'

'Oh, that!'

'Never dismiss the smallest fact, however unimportant it may appear. It is the basis on which all successful deduction is founded.'

'Then what about *The Times*?' I asked eagerly. 'I thought, when Mrs Bennet mentioned it, it seemed an odd choice of paper for a head-waiter to read.'

'Ah, *The Times*! One should certainly never dismiss *The Times*. A most worthy publication,' Holmes remarked with an abstracted air. He had wandered across the room to examine a pair of french windows which led into the back garden before turning his attention to the two drawers of a large and ugly sideboard which occupied the adjoining wall. 'Ah! What have we here? Take a look at these, Watson.'

He handed me a small bundle of printed sheets.

'They're music-hall programmes,' I replied, glancing through them briefly. 'The Tivoli. Collins's. Oh, I say, Holmes! Look at this one. Lottie Lynne was playing at the Alhambra in February. I wish I had known. I might have gone to hear her. Such a delightful voice!'

'I have noticed before, Watson, that you have a predilection for small, blonde young ladies,' Holmes commented with an amused air, putting the programmes back into the drawer and shutting it. 'I myself prefer the acrobats. Well, I think I have seen all I need down here. I suggest we examine the rest of the house and then the garden.'

The house was so small that the search took a mere ten minutes, Holmes only pausing to open Phillimore's wardrobe, still containing his abandoned clothes, but apart from the brief remark 'Roomy, I see!', he made no other observation.

The garden was smaller even than the house, a mere few square yards of lawn bordered by narrow flower-beds, all neatly kept, and surrounded on all sides by an eight-foot-high fence which had additional two-foot lengths of trellis nailed to the top of it, making escape by that route impossible, as Mr Nelson had pointed out.

There was not even a potting-shed nor a decent-sized bush where a man might conceal himself. Nevertheless, Holmes stalked all round its perimeter before examining the passage which ran along the side of the house.

It was a narrow path, squeezed in between the building on one side and a continuation of the fence on the other. At the far end, it ran at an oblique angle to join the tiled path which led from the gate to the front door. At the near end, it opened out on to a small paved area outside the kitchen door where presumably tradesmen would make their deliveries.

We left number seventeen Laburnum Grove shortly afterwards, Holmes striding off so briskly down the road towards Lavender Hill that I was hard put to keep up with him. At the bottom of the hill, we turned into the main thoroughfare, where Holmes hailed a cab.

When Holmes had given instructions to the driver and the hansom had started off, he turned to me to ask unexpectedly, 'Tell me, Watson, what would you say would be the lifetime's ambition of a hotel or restaurant employee?'

'To retire, I should imagine, and never have to fold another napkin again.'

'But suppose, like Phillimore, he was the type who wished to rise in the world?'

'Well then, to own the establishment in which he'd worked and watch other people fold the napkins.'

'Exactly, Watson!' Holmes said with an air of satisfaction and, settling himself back against the upholstery, folded his arms and closed his eyes, his lean, aquiline features taking on an expression of such intense concentration that I knew better than to interrupt his train of thought.

The silence continued until, as we were rattling across Battersea Bridge, he roused himself to remark, 'You know, Watson, there are several unusual elements in this case but the one which strikes me as most extraordinary of all is the timing of Mr Phillimore's disappearance. Why Tuesday? Why not Monday or Friday? If one wished to vanish, it would seem more logical to choose either the beginning or the end of the week. As far as I can ascertain, nothing remarkable happened on Tuesday morning to make Phillimore decide it was time to disappear.'

'Perhaps he couldn't on Monday. Something may have happened to detain him.'

I saw Holmes's keen features suddenly light up.

'My dear old fellow!' he exclaimed. 'I believe you may have put your finger on the key to the whole mystery!'

'Have I, Holmes?' I asked, highly pleased, and was further gratified when Holmes continued, 'I should value your opinion on the case. Tell me, what aspect of it most intrigues you?'

'I must admit that I find Phillimore's motivation the most puzzling feature. A man of regular habits suddenly takes it into his head to vanish without a word of warning, abandoning not only his house, his job and his life's savings but his clothes . . .'

'Together with his fiancée,' Holmes reminded me with a smile. 'Perhaps Miss Cora Page was the reason for his disappearance. Phillimore would not be the first man who, faced with the imminent prospect of marriage, showed a clean pair of heels just before his wedding day. Should I ever find myself in such an unlikely and unfortunate situation, I should be strongly tempted to do the same. And, by the way, Watson, if we succeed in running Phillimore to earth, I want you to say nothing to him about the possibility of Miss Page's transferring her affections to Charlie Nelson.'

'Why?'

'My dear fellow, is it not obvious?'

'You mean he would be jealous?'

'I mean Phillimore, who appears a decent enough individual, might come out of hiding in order to save his friend from the same dreadful fate which nearly overtook him. "Greater love hath no man . . ." and all that. I have your word?'

'Of course, Holmes. So you think we shall find Phillimore?'

'I believe there is a very good chance of our doing so. You remarked a little earlier on Phillimore's regularity of habits and I think that it is in this aspect of his personality that we shall find the answer to his secret. But first I want to return to Laburnum Grove at the same hour of the morning in which Phillimore disappeared. Although Charlie Nelson and Mrs Bennet both swore they saw nothing unusual, I am convinced something must have occurred but so ordinary that neither of them noticed it. Whenever there is an apparent mystery, one should always look to the commonplace in order to solve it. But few people do. They prefer the mystery to its solution. It is this tendency on the part of human nature on which depends the success of the stage magician or illusionist.' He gave me an oblique glance as if inviting my comment but, as I did not then understand the significance of his remark, I said nothing and, after a brief silence, he continued, 'Will you be free early tomorrow, Watson? I propose taking a cab to Clapham and observing for myself exactly what occurs in Laburnum Grove at half past seven in the morning.'

'I shall be delighted to accompany you, provided it won't take too long. I have an appointment at ten o'clock with a patient.'

'A patient!' Holmes exclaimed, throwing up his hands in mock surprise. 'This is such a rare occurrence, Watson, that I shall make myself personally responsible for seeing that you are returned to your consulting room in good time.'

The following morning, I again presented myself at 221B Baker Street where I joined Holmes for an early breakfast. A hansom had been ordered for seven o'clock and we set off once more in the direction of Clapham, through half-empty streets, looking clean and dazzling-bright in the morning sunshine after an overnight shower which had laid the dust and left the leaves on the trees glistening as if newly washed.

As we turned into Laburnum Grove, Holmes instructed the driver to draw up on the opposite side of the road to number seventeen and a little distance from it, from which position we had an excellent view not only of Phillimore's garden gate but a good stretch of the street as well.

Several people passed down the road in the direction of Lavender Hill, by their appearance and attire mostly clerks and shop-assistants on their way to their respective places of employment and, after a few minutes' wait, we were rewarded by the sight of Charlie Nelson turning the corner from Magnolia Terrace, at precisely half past seven.

I saw him hesitate at the gate of number seventeen and glance across at the house, as if reminding himself of his erstwhile companion's extraordinary disappearance and then, on drawing level with our hansom, cast another glance in its direction, surprised no doubt at the presence of a cab in the area at that hour of the morning. But I comforted myself with the thought that Holmes and I were sitting too far back inside the vehicle for him to see us.

It was as this idea struck me that I heard Holmes give an involuntary exclamation but not, as I first thought, at Nelson's interest in our cab. His gaze was fixed on another vehicle which had come slowly plodding into view on the opposite side of the road.

It was a baker's van, drawn by a tired-looking pony, not the type of conveyance to attract anyone's attention and yet Holmes was watching with keen interest as the bread delivery man, a tall youth of about eighteen or so, dressed in a cap and a long white apron, climbed down off his seat and, taking his basket from the rear of the vehicle, opened the gate to Phillimore's house, walked down the path and disappeared from sight into the passage which ran along the side of the building.

Meanwhile, the pony, well used, it seemed, to this morning routine, ambled slowly along the street to a gate a few doors along where it waited for its driver.

Within a few moments, the delivery man had reappeared but,

before I could comment on Holmes's evident interest in the man's activities, Holmes had leapt out of the cab and, ordering the driver to take me to my address in Paddington,* called out as the cab drove off, 'You must not be late for your appointment, Watson. I shall expect you at Baker Street for luncheon. Twelve o'clock sharp!'

Rather than arriving late, I was a good hour and a half too early and I spent the intervening time until my patient arrived musing over the strange case of Mr Phillimore's disappearance although I could make little of it.

A locked wardrobe? A bread delivery man? A head-waiter who read *The Times* and had a liking for an occasional visit to a music-hall?

None of it seemed to point to Mr Phillimore's present whereabouts and I looked forward impatiently to the time when I could return to Baker Street and question Holmes over luncheon.

On this occasion, luncheon was a simple meal of cold meat, bread and pickles which Holmes urged me to eat quickly as time was short.

'Now look here, Holmes,' I protested as I seated myself at the table. 'You and I have shared many adventures and you have always taken me into your confidence. Do you or do you not know where Mr Phillimore is hiding and, if you do, how have you arrived at your conclusion?'

'My dear old fellow,' Holmes replied, carving away energetically at the cold beef. 'I had no intention of keeping you in the dark. I myself was not sure of all the facts until this morning. But I am now fairly confident that I can find our vanishing head-waiter.'

'How?'

'From my observations of human nature; a most worthwhile subject, Watson, which every aspiring detective should make his lifetime's study. I have frequently noticed that even the

* After his marriage to Miss Mary Morstan, Dr John H. Watson moved out of 221B Baker Street and took up private practice, first in Paddington, later in Kensington. (Dr John F. Watson)

most hardened and experienced criminal has a particular routine or pattern of behaviour which, if only one can discover it, will lead to his arrest. Remember Harry Beecham, the notorious forger? He was constantly moving his equipment from one back street workshop to another so that the police had the deuce of a job keeping up with him. I eventually ran him to earth because he always went to the same barber in Shadwell to have his hair cut; had done for years and could not, it seemed, shake off the habit. Now, how much more likely is that precept to apply to Mr James Phillimore, *par excellence* a man of regular routines to whom familiarity of surroundings would be essential? He may have disappeared in Clapham but he has most certainly reappeared in some environment where he will feel almost as much at home.'

'Oh, I see, Holmes!' I exclaimed. 'The boarding-house in Margate where he spent his week's convalescence!'

'Exactly!'

'But how do you propose finding him? Margate is a popular seaside resort. It must contain hundreds of boarding-houses. Do you intend inquiring at each and every one of them? It could take days.'

'Not days, Watson; merely a matter of a few hours. Mrs Bennet mentioned that the establishment had a foreign-sounding name. I suggest "Mon Repos" is a distinct possibility. I have noticed before that it is a favourite with seaside landladies although why they choose that particular nomenclature, when to run such businesses must be anything but restful, is beyond my comprehension. I cannot believe it is meant ironically. Landladies are not usually renowned for their sense of humour. We shall also look for a boarding-house which has a neat garden and a freshly-whitened front doorstep. I believe Mr Phillimore's inclinations may very well run in those directions. Now do eat up, Watson. I have ordered a cab to take us to Victoria Station to catch the one-fifteen to Margate.'

We caught the train, Holmes passing the journey by chatting amiably about many different subjects – French literature, the quality of the acoustics in St James's Hall, the best fish-restaurant in London; anything but the case in hand – until the train arrived at Margate.

We took a four-wheeler from the rank outside the station, Holmes instructing the cabby to drive us to any boarding-house in the resort with the name of 'Mon Repos'.

There were nine, the man informed us.

At the first two, Holmes got out and rang the bell, returning after a few minutes with a shake of the head, indicating that they were not the one he was seeking.

At the third, a dingy house with dirty lace curtains and a 'Vacancy' sign hanging in the window, he did not even trouble to alight. After giving it a cursory glance, he ordered the cabby to drive on.

The fourth 'Mon Repos' was a red-brick villa, not unlike Phillimore's house in Clapham only larger and standing detached in a decent-sized front garden in which brightly-coloured flowers were growing in neat beds.

'I believe we have found it, Watson!' Holmes exclaimed and, telling the cabby to wait, he leapt out and strode up the path to the front door.

His knock was answered by a short, pleasant-looking woman in her thirties with soft fair hair and a ready smile.

'I'm sorry, sir,' she began, 'but I have no vacancies. Every room has been taken.'

'It is not rooms my friend and I are inquiring about,' Holmes told her. 'My query concerns one of your lodgers, a Mr James Phillimore.'

As she put one hand to her mouth in sudden consternation, a door leading off the hall opened and a tall man with greying hair emerged. His long chin must have been inherited from his mother but not his general demeanour, which was agreeable and good-natured. He was comfortably dressed in shirt-sleeves and slippers but, despite the casual nature of his attire, he still retained the attentive and respectful manner of an upper servant or the more superior type of waiter.

'Mr Holmes, isn't it?' he inquired, advancing towards us. 'Mr Sherlock Holmes? I saw you through the window as you came up the path and I recognized your face from the pictures in the *Illustrated London News*. And your companion is Doctor Watson, I presume? I imagine my old friend Charlie Nelson put you on to finding me. It's the kind of action I might have expected of him. A good pal is Charlie Nelson, not the sort to leave any stone unturned, if you'll forgive the expression.' Turning to address the landlady who in a state of some distress had retreated into the hall, he added reassuringly, 'It's all right, Ellen. There's nothing to worry about. I propose that these gentlemen and me adjourn to the sitting-room to talk matters over. A pot of tea wouldn't go amiss, would it, sir?'

This time he addressed Holmes directly.

'Indeed it would not, Mr Phillimore,' Holmes assured him.

Together the three of us retired to the sitting-room, through the door of which Phillimore had just emerged. There, in comfortable and well-furnished surroundings, Phillimore installed Holmes and myself in a pair of armchairs, he himself choosing a seat facing us on the other side of the fireplace.

'Well, sir,' he said, looking across at us with a grave yet frank expression. 'So you have found me out.'

'Not entirely,' Holmes admitted, 'for, although I know the method by which you contrived your disappearance, I am still a little puzzled about your reasons. I spoke this morning to Sammy Webb, the young man who delivers the bread. This was after you left me, Watson, to attend your patient,' he broke off to explain for my benefit before turning back to Phillimore. 'He was reluctant to give you away but, on receiving my assurance that I was acting entirely for your benefit, Mr Phillimore, he explained how, on Tuesday morning, he walked round to your back door – part of his normal routine, incidentally – where he left on the doorstep a penny bag of bread-rolls, the usual order. You meanwhile, having returned to the house ostensibly to collect your umbrella, had gone quickly and quietly upstairs to your bedroom to retrieve a cap, a long white apron and a large basket of the type in which bread is carried, part of a simple but effective disguise, the props for which are easily obtained and which you kept concealed in your locked wardrobe. Thus attired and carrying the basket, you left the house through the sitting-room windows and walked round to the front of the house by means of the side passage, appearing to all the world as Sammy Webb, the bread delivery man. No one took any notice of you, not even Mrs Bennet who was washing-up at the sink by the kitchen window. I asked her this very morning if she had seen a delivery man but she had registered neither Webb's arrival nor his apparent departure, so accustomed is she to his routine. Even your friend, Charlie Nelson, waiting for you at the gate, failed to give you a second glance. He, too, is so used to seeing Webb make his deliveries that he swore he saw nothing unusual happen on Tuesday at the time of your disappearance. It wasn't until Dr Watson and I waited outside your house this morning in a cab that we realized the truth.'

It was generous of him to include me in this explanation when I had contributed nothing to the revelation but I really could not allow him to omit one very important factor.

'Wait a moment, Holmes!' I broke in. 'What happened to Sammy Webb, the real delivery man?'

'Simple, my dear fellow,' Holmes replied. 'Sammy Webb remained out of sight in the side-passage until Charlie Nelson, growing impatient at waiting for his friend to reappear, went into the house to find him. Webb then left by the front gate and sauntered off to rejoin his vehicle, Mr Phillimore having in the meantime climbed into the back of it among the loaves and halfpenny buns when there were no passers-by to witness his action. It was, you recall, Watson, a closed van. With Mr Phillimore concealed inside it, Webb then drove the vehicle away and resumed his normal round until they reached a quiet side street where Mr Phillimore, divested of his disguise, emerged and, no doubt, caught a train or omnibus to Victoria Station where he bought a single ticket to Margate. By the way,' he continued, turning back to Mr Phillimore, 'Sammy Webb explained his reasons for agreeing to help you. He is still most grateful for the two guineas you gave him to pay off the debts he had unfortunately accrued through playing cards.'

James Phillimore bowed his head in acknowledgement but said nothing, merely continuing to regard Holmes with that serious, attentive expression.

At this moment, the door opened and the pleasant, fair-haired landlady, whom Phillimore had addressed as Ellen, entered, carrying a tray loaded with tea-things and a freshly-baked seed-cake. Placing the tray on a low table in front of the hearth, she smiled tentatively at the three of us and then, passing behind Phillimore's chair, placed a hand briefly on his shoulder before leaving the room.

As the door closed behind her, Phillimore said in a low voice, 'You remarked a little earlier, Mr Holmes, that you did not fully understand my motives for disappearing. That's my reason – my Ellen, the best and kindest woman a man could ever wish to meet. I stayed here in this boarding-house last October, after the death of my mother, when the doctor ordered a rest and sea air. I am not by nature a romantic man, sir. All my life I have had to work hard and do my duty, serving other people. There has never been much time for day-dreams. But the moment I set eyes on Ellen, I knew she was the only woman for me. What could I do? I was engaged to Miss Page; a nice enough young lady although it was largely on her insistence that I agreed to becoming her fiancé. But compared to Ellen . . .'

He broke off, his grave features flushing with emotion.

'Yes, yes, of course! I quite understand,' Holmes said hastily before, turning to me, he urged, 'Pour the tea, my dear fellow. I think all of us are in need of refreshment.'

By the time I had filled and passed round the cups, together with slices of the excellent seed-cake, Phillimore had sufficiently recovered his composure to continue his account.

'I am sorry I have caused so much bother,' he said quietly. 'If I could have slipped away without troubling anyone, believe me, I would have done so. And it was always my intention to make up for any distress others have suffered on my account. I am making arrangements to have the house made over to Charlie Nelson. Like I said, he's always been a good friend and I would like him to have the benefit of it. I certainly have no further use for the place. He's living in lodgings at the moment and he's none too happy there. Then there's Mrs Bennet. She ought to have retired years ago but she's a widow and can't afford to stop working. I'm getting a solicitor to draw up an annuity for her which will pay her two pounds a week during her lifetime. As for Cora – Miss Page – well, I feel really bad about letting her down but better that than an unhappy marriage as I hope she will realize herself when she has had time to think about it.'

'She is not an unattractive young lady. She could quite easily find someone else to marry,' Holmes suggested, giving me a small glance to warn me to say nothing on the subject of Charlie Nelson and Miss Page.

'That's as maybe, Mr Holmes. All the same, I shall make over to her the hundred pounds or so I've got saved up, without, of course, letting her, or anyone else for that matter, know what's happened to me or where I'm living.'

'It sounds most generous,' Holmes murmured.

'It's the least I can do. You see, when I decided to disappear, I wanted to make a clean start and leave everything connected with my old life behind me – the house, my job, even my clothes.'

'But not your investments? Oh, please, Mr Phillimore!' Holmes expostulated as Phillimore started up in his chair. 'Pray don't distress yourself! I assure you I know nothing about any sums of money you may have put aside in a banking account apart from the fact that one must exist.'

'Then how did you find out about it?' Phillimore demanded.

'By a simple process of deduction combined with a knowledge of human nature. It is a very unusual man indeed who, having worked as hard as you have done all his life, turns his back entirely on all that he has achieved. I assumed it was so in your case. As a matter of fact, it was an inadvertent remark on the part of your friend Charlie Nelson which gave me the clue. He spoke of the "tips" you had received at Gudgeon's. Now a tip can be something more than a mere financial reward for good service. It can be a piece of advice, especially one involving monetary gain.

'I happen to know Gudgeon's. I have lunched there on several occasions and a very comfortable establishment it is, too; rightly popular with its select clientele which includes members of the Stock Exchange, who no doubt discuss their business affairs discreetly over an excellent luncheon of steak and kidney pudding accompanied by a glass or two of claret. A head-waiter, especially one who has taught himself to lip-read for the benefit of his deaf mother, might very easily pick up a good many tips on when to buy or sell certain shares. Am I not right, Mr Phillimore?'

'Indeed, you are, Mr Holmes,' Phillimore admitted with a rueful smile. 'I've been quietly investing any spare cash I could afford for years now.'

'And Monday was a good day to sell. I noticed in *The Times*, a paper which carries information on current share prices and to which you also subscribe, that the market was particularly buoyant. Hence your decision to disappear on Tuesday morning, once you had the opportunity to sell out on Monday. I hope you made a killing, as the 'Change would describe it?'

'Five thousand pounds, Mr Holmes; more than I've ever dreamed of owning and more than enough for Ellen and me to marry on, which we intend doing as soon as the banns can be read. After that, we're proposing to invest the money by buying a nice, comfortable hotel on the sea-front which has recently come on the market, Ellen and me running it and with other people to do the cooking and waiting at table for a change.'

'I wish you well,' Holmes observed. 'I am sure it will be a great success. However, when I asked you for the reason behind your disappearance, I meant not so much why you chose to vanish but what made you decide to do it in such a spectacular fashion. Why not simply walk out of the house, leaving a letter behind on the table for your housekeeper to find later? Am I right in thinking that Marvello the Great Magician, whom I noticed featured in all the music-hall programmes you left behind in the sideboard drawer and who must have been a particular favourite of yours, might have had some influence over your actions?'

Phillimore's face lit up.

'You've seen his act, have you, Mr Holmes? The little dog that disappears from its basket and reappears in his coat pocket? And the trick with his young lady assistant who vanishes from behind the opened umbrella? It was that turn which put the idea of the umbrella and disappearing into my head in the first place. He's rightly called Marvello for he is a marvel, sir; a veritable wonder. I've been to every music-hall where he's been on the bill and I have never failed to be amazed how he does it.'

'So you decided to emulate him?'

Phillimore looked a little embarrassed.

'There isn't much as escapes you, is there, Mr Holmes? You're quite right. When I made up my mind to disappear, I thought – why not vanish in style instead of creeping off like a thief in the night? I wanted – well, it's hard to explain but all my life I've never done anything that hasn't been routine and humdrum. But vanishing! Now that's something rare and out of the ordinary. As you'll know, Mr Holmes, being a devotee, Marvello ends his act by disappearing himself in a cloud of coloured smoke to a great roll of drum beats. I couldn't have the smoke and the drums . . .'

'But your vanishing act was none the less carried out with considerable panache. I am sure the Great Marvello himself would have applauded it,' Holmes remarked, getting to his feet and holding out his hand. 'Goodbye, Mr Phillimore. We have a four-wheeler waiting outside and with a little good fortune and some smart driving on the part of the cabby, we may be able to catch the five-ten to London. And rest assured, your secret is safe with us.'

As we climbed into the cab and it drove off towards the station, Holmes turned to me with a smile, cutting short the protest which I had been about to make, as if he had read my thoughts, a gift of mental prognosis which on several occasions I have had good reason to believe he may have possessed.

'Yes, my dear Watson, you may indeed write up the story of the vanishing head-waiter if you so wish. But on no account must it be published. If Miss Cora Page should discover Phillimore's present whereabouts, she would turn Margate inside out to find him and sue him for breach of promise. I have given him my word and, as far as the world at large is concerned, this investigation must remain one of those unsolved cases which proved too difficult even for my deductive powers.'

THE CASE OF THE AMATEUR MENDICANTS

It was not often I was able to bring a case to Holmes's notice* and it is with some misgivings I admit it was through my personal instigation that my old friend became involved in the following adventure.

It occurred in the year '87, not long after my marriage when, having returned to civil practice, I had moved out of my former lodgings in Baker Street, leaving Holmes in sole occupancy among his books, his papers and his scientific apparatus.

It was my habit when paying professional calls on patients in the immediate vicinity of my consulting-rooms to do so on foot, particularly if the weather was fine, and it was while on one of these excursions one afternoon in June that I ran into, almost literally, an old army acquaintance of mine, Major Adolphus (Dolly) Venables, whom I had last met while serving in India. Major Venables had been an officer in my own regiment, the Fifth Northumberland Fusiliers, to which I was attached as Assistant Surgeon before being transferred to the Berkshires and posted to the Afghan frontier.

On my arrival in India, Major Venables and his wife had been extremely kind to me, inviting me on several occasions to their bungalow for afternoon tea or a *chota peg*.

* Dr John H. Watson introduced Mr Sherlock Holmes to two other cases, that of Mr Hatherley, an account of which was published under the title of 'The Adventure of the Engineer's Thumb', and that of Colonel Warburton's madness, which so far has not found its way into print. (Dr John F. Watson)

They often spoke fondly of their son, Edward, known affectionately as Teddy, their only child who, as was the custom, had been sent back to England to be educated, in his case under the care of Mrs Venables' maiden sister, Miss Edith Warminster.

After I was wounded and was invalided out of the army, I lost touch with 'Dolly' Venables although from time to time I heard news of him through mutual acquaintances, learning with considerable distress of the death of his wife in India of yellow fever. She had been an unassuming, gentle-hearted woman.

It was not until that June afternoon when I met with Venables again so unexpectedly in the street after an interval of several years that I was able to renew the friendship.

I found him little changed. He still preserved his upright, military bearing and open kindliness of expression which had characterized him in India although his former vigorous manner, that of a man used to an active, outdoor life, was not as apparent as it had once been. He seemed sadder and more subdued, an alteration which at the time I assumed was caused by his wife's death.

Discovering that I lived not far from his own address in Dorset Court, he invited me to his house that evening, one of several such meetings which were to occur over the following months, usually at his place or the lounge-bar of some convenient hotel for, although my wife made him very welcome, he seemed a little inhibited in her company, perhaps comparing his own widowed state with our domestic happiness. It was also easier for us to reminisce about our army days together tête-à-tête in a totally masculine setting.

It was during these meetings that, little by little, I learned his story. Indeed, he seemed grateful to have someone in whom he could confide.

His main topic of conversation was his son, Teddy. As I have explained, the boy had been sent back to England to be educated at boarding school, spending the holidays with his maiden aunt at her home in Farnham.

Although no expense had been spared in his upbringing, it appeared that the effort had been largely wasted for the lad had proved troublesome both at school and at home. Indeed, he had been expelled from several boarding establishments for various escapades and misdemeanours.

Listening to Venables' account, it was not difficult to guess that the main cause of his indiscipline was the aunt, Miss Warminster, who, like her sister, Major Venables' late wife, was of a gentle, soft-hearted disposition and had failed to exercise that kind of control which a high-spirited youth requires.

Not to put too fine a point on it, the boy had been thoroughly spoilt.

On the death of Miss Warminster, when Teddy was sixteen, Major Venables had retired from the army on half-pay and had returned to England to supervise his son's education, there being no one else whom he could entrust with the task.

However, the damage had been done and Venables, who whilst serving in his regiment had found no difficulty in disciplining the men under his command, had found his son intractable.

To add to his problems, there were also financial worries. As I myself had discovered on first being invalided out of the army, it is not easy to live comfortably on half-pay and, in the Major's case, with school fees to pay and a growing lad to maintain, he had been hard put to it on occasions to meet all his bills. In fact, the house in Dorset Court where he was then living was a modest, rented dwelling, hardly bigger than an urban cottage, with two bedrooms only and very cramped living quarters on the ground floor which the Major had done his best to turn into a comfortable home for himself and his son by introducing various pieces of furniture in the way of rattan chairs and carved teak tables as well as a collection of Oriental knick-knacks which he had brought back with him from India.

He could not even afford a proper servant, being forced to rely on the services of a daily cleaning-woman only.

At the time of my meeting with him in the street, the Major had been living in Dorset Court for the past three years, providing a home for his son who was then nineteen and was studying medicine at my old hospital, Barts.

I met Teddy on only one occasion. He was leaving the house

just as I was about to ring at the doorbell and he brushed past me quite rudely without speaking as I stood on the step. A tall, good-looking young man, he had inherited his mother's fair hair and finely-drawn features but while hers had been infused with a gentle candour, his bore only the sulky petulance of an immature youth.

Through my contacts at Barts, especially with my former dresser, Stamford, I was able, by means of a few discreet inquiries, to learn a few more facts about young Venables that his father had either not thought fit to confide in me or had not known himself. All the information I received confirmed my worst fears.

The young man was often late for lectures, if he did not absent himself entirely, and, while intelligent, was lazy and lacked application. The standard of his work was frequently so unsatisfactory, according to Stamford, that there was a chance of his being dismissed before his course of studies was complete.

I come now to an evening in late December. My wife having gone to stay with her aunt* on a belated Christmas visit, I had, on her insistence, returned temporarily to my old lodgings in Baker Street where she felt I should be better cared for by Mrs Hudson than by our own unsatisfactory cook-general who was at the time serving out her notice.† It was also on my wife's suggestion that I took the opportunity for a few days' holiday myself, leaving a colleague in charge of my practice.

I had not seen the Major for two or three weeks, an earlier appointment to meet at the Criterion Bar having been cancelled by him on account of illness.

Holmes, who was engaged on a case at the time, had gone out on one of his mysterious errands connected with it and I

* This was the second time Mrs Watson had gone to see her aunt in 1887, an earlier visit having taken place in September. *Vide* 'The Five Orange Pips'. (Dr John F. Watson)

† Dr John H. Watson and his wife had problems with another domestic, Mary Jane, a 'clumsy and careless servant girl' who also had been served notice by Mrs Watson. *Vide* 'A Scandal in Bohemia'. (Dr John F. Watson)

was sitting alone by the fire, reading. It was a cold, wintry evening and there was no reason why I should not have remained indoors except that I was overcome by a sudden impulse to see my old army acquaintance. Although Holmes would have been amused at my fancy, putting it down to mere imagination or womanish intuition, I had a strong feeling that something was badly the matter and that the Major urgently needed my services.

It was only seven o'clock, not too late to pay him a call, and with no further ado, I got up from my seat by the fire, put on my heavy greatcoat and took a cab to his house.

There was a light burning in the hall of the Major's house so I knew someone was at home although it was several minutes before he answered my ring at the bell.

When he finally opened the door, I almost failed to recognize him. In the few short weeks since I had last seen him, he was shockingly changed, his features haggard, his shoulders bowed, his gait that of an old man.

'Are you ill, Venables?' I cried, distressed by his appearance.

'I have been, Watson,' he replied in a husky voice. 'But I am a little better now. It was kind of you to call and inquire after me. If you will forgive me, however, I am in no state to receive visitors.'

He seemed about to close the door but I refused to be dismissed.

'I am coming in,' I told him. 'Although you say you are no longer ill, as a doctor my professional obligations will not allow me to walk away and leave you in this condition.'

He acquiesced reluctantly, preceding me down the hall to the little sitting-room where in the brighter light of the gas lamps, I was able to observe him more closely.

He looked ghastly as he sat huddled in a chair by the remains of a coal fire, gaunt and famished with grey skin and trembling hands.

I made up the fire and, having fetched a tumbler from the sideboard, poured him a stiff whisky from my hip flask.

It was only when the glass was in his hand and I had

inquired, 'Now, my dear fellow, what is the matter with you?', that he found the strength or the courage to speak.

The story he had to tell was, I suppose, not altogether unexpected under the circumstances, especially in the light of what I had learned from Stamford.

Young Venables had been dismissed from Barts. And that was not all. For several months past, his conduct had caused his father far more concern than he had confided in me. The young man had been coming home later and later at night, sometimes the worse for drink. On occasions, he had not returned until the following day, dishevelled in appearance and refusing to give his father an account of where he had been and what he had been doing.

'Dolly' Venables had done his best to control his son's excesses, remonstrating with him, threatening to stop his allowance, pleading with him for his dead mother's sake to mend his ways. It was all to no avail. Young Venables had continued with his ill-disciplined behaviour.

One of the Major's chief concerns was Teddy's apparent access to money for, even after he had made good his threat and had cut off his son's allowance, the young man still managed to acquire funds from somewhere, continuing to stay out late at night and to indulge himself in drink and expensive new clothes such as silk cravats, dress shirts, even a pair of hand-made boots from Bellamy's of Piccadilly.

'Although God knows where he found the money,' the Major whispered, his hands clasped so tightly round his whisky glass that his knuckles showed white beneath the skin.

A final confrontation had taken place a week earlier. The young man had again returned home in an inebriated state in the early hours of the morning and, when his father had faced him on the stairs, a terrible quarrel had broken out in which Teddy had admitted he had been dismissed from Barts. On receiving a stern dressing-down from his father, the young man had lost his temper, shouted that he would not stay a moment longer to be treated like a child and, rushing into his room, had flung all his possessions into two valises before storming out of the house.

The Major had not seen or heard anything of him since and had no knowledge of his present whereabouts.

At this point in his account, Venables broke down.

It is a dreadful thing to see a grown man weep, especially someone of the Major's proud and reticent disposition. As a friend, I was deeply moved by his distress; as a doctor, I was concerned about both his mental and his physical condition.

'Now look here, Venables,' I said, drawing one of the rattan chairs close to his. 'There must be some action you can take to find out where your son is. Has he gone to stay with friends?'

It seemed that the Major had contacted all Teddy's known acquaintances but none of them had seen him. In fact, the young man appeared to have cut himself off from all his former school friends and fellow students at Barts.

'Then did he leave anything behind – a letter, say, or a diary – from which you might obtain a clue to his present address?'

'Only this,' Venables replied. 'I found it under the paper lining in his bureau drawer.'

Reaching up to the mantelpiece, he took down a small pasteboard oblong which he handed to me. It was a visiting card on which were engraved the following words:

COLONEL F. T. FORTESCUE-LAMB

Secretary

The Association for Maimed Soldiers

A. M. S. Head Office,
Buckmaster Buildings,
10–19 Titchbourne Street,
London, E 1.

I said, 'Does your son know this Colonel?'

'Not to my knowledge although I myself was acquainted with Fortescue-Lamb several years ago in India. He was serving then in the Seventh Inverskillen Bombardiers. But you see, Watson, the baffling part of it is that Fortescue-Lamb retired from the army before I did and I happen to know that he emigrated to

Australia to run a sheep farm. I remember joking with him about the suitability of his name for his new career. As I received a greetings card from him, postmarked Bollawanga, only this very Christmas, I assume he must still be there. You follow my point? If old Baa-Lamb, as we used to call him, is sheep-farming in Australia, what is he doing acting as secretary to this charity and why should my son have his card?'

'Could you not write or call at this address in Titchbourne Street and make inquiries?'

'I could indeed, Watson. I have hesitated to do so in case I caused any further bad feeling between Teddy and myself. He already resents my meddling in his affairs, as he calls it.'

'Yes; I can understand your reluctance. Then would you have any objections if I explained the situation to Sherlock Holmes and showed him this card? The circumstances are certainly very strange and could well interest him. As he is quite used to making this type of inquiry, you may rely on his discretion.'

In the course of our meetings, I had told Venables a little about my own history and background since I had retired from the army, including the fact that I had once shared lodgings in Baker Street with the famous consulting detective, Sherlock Holmes, with whose reputation Venables was already acquainted.

On my mentioning Holmes's name, Venables sat up, his haggard features alight with new hope.

'Would you ask him to take the case, Watson? I should be enormously relieved if Mr Holmes would agree. I feel Teddy is in some kind of trouble but I should much prefer to know the worst than remain in ignorance. What are Mr Holmes's fees? I am afraid the state of my present finances . . .'

He broke off, once more plunged into a state of despair.

To console him, I said airily, although I had no idea what Holmes might charge in this particular case, 'Oh, they are very small, Venables; a mere token sum,' intending, should they not be so, to make up the difference out of my own pocket rather than see my old army companion suffer any further distress. 'So that is decided,' I concluded, anxious to bring Venables to a decision. 'I shall place the facts before Sherlock Holmes tonight.'

In the event, I did not have the opportunity to discuss the case with Holmes that evening. Although I waited up for him until after midnight, he failed to return home until the early hours and it was not until the following morning over breakfast that I was able to give him the full story of Teddy Venables' disappearance and to show him the visiting-card.

Holmes listened attentively to my account, inquiring when I had finished, 'And you say that this Colonel Fortescue-Lamb is at present in Australia?'

'Yes; according to Venables. So you see, Holmes . . .'

'I do indeed, Watson. But the mystery can be quite easily solved. As soon as we have finished breakfast, we shall take a cab to the – ,' he consulted the card, ' – A. M. S. Head Office in Titchbourne Street and ask whoever is in charge there how Fortescue-Lamb manages to run two such widely separated ventures.'

'You will be discreet, will you not?' I asked. 'Venables would not wish his son to know that he has requested the inquiries.'

Holmes, who was in high spirits that morning, threw up his hands in mock horror.

'When am I ever not the soul of discretion, my dear fellow? But pray continue. I can tell from your expression that you have not completed all you wished to say.'

'About your fees – ?'

Putting down his cup, Holmes regarded me with an expression of quizzical kindliness before replying, 'For friends or friends of friends there are no charges. Besides, last night I completed a case on behalf of a wealthy client, an American peanut millionaire whose younger brother had formed an unfortunate attachment with a female midget. No, not another word, my good Watson. And now, if you have quite finished your kipper, we shall take a hansom to Titchbourne Street without any further delay.'

Titchbourne Street was a drab turning off Wapping Lane, not far from the river for, as we alighted from the cab, we could smell its muddy odour and could glimpse down the alley-ways which ran between the buildings the masts and rigging of the ships tied up at the wharves.

The street itself was lined with wholesalers' and importers' warehouses, their grimy brick edifices dwarfing a row of low, mean houses and a solitary public house, the Britannia, which stood on the corner.

To my surprise, number 10 to 19 was one of these warehouses, a four-storeyed premises with tiers of barred windows. A large board fastened across the façade announced in bold lettering the words: 'Geo. Buckmaster, Furniture Importers and Wholesalers'.

'This is very puzzling, Holmes,' I remarked. 'It is hardly the place where one would expect to find the headquarters of a charitable instittition.'

'But we have evidently found the correct address,' Holmes replied. He had approached a black-painted door, the only entrance along the whole length of the frontage, to which was affixed a small plaque which read: 'A. M. S. Head Office. Postal Inquiries Only'.

The door proved to be firmly locked for Holmes tried the handle in vain and, when persistent loud knocking failed to rouse anyone inside the building, he turned back towards the Britannia public house, remarking, 'If I am not mistaken, there should be a way through to a rear entrance where goods are unloaded. Ah, I thought so, Watson! Here is an alley-way which leads along the side of the tavern and which should take us to it.'

Holmes was right. The alley opened into a broad cobblestoned lane, which ran parallel to Titchbourne Street and was entirely enclosed on both sides by the tall rear walls of the various wholesale establishments, all of which were supplied with ramps and double doors where goods could be despatched or delivered.

Indeed, as we approached the back of Buckmaster's premises, we could see that a large covered van was standing outside such a pair of doors which were flung wide open, a boy holding the horses' heads, while three men in sacking aprons unloaded furniture from the interior of the vehicle.

A short, stout man, wearing a billycock hat and with a large silver watch-chain looped across the front of his waistcoat, appeared to be in charge.

He listened to Holmes's inquiry, his head cocked on one side so that he could still keep an eye on the men's activities.

'The A. M. S.?' said he. 'I can't tell you much about it; or even what it is, come to that, except it's some institution or other as uses the premises for an accommodation address. A young man calls round every other day to collect any letters that have been delivered. You'll have to ask the manager, Mr Littlejohn.'

He broke off to shout at the men who were lifting a large mahogany wardrobe off the van. 'Careful with that! You'll smash them mirrors in the doors!' before, turning back to Holmes, he continued, 'If you'll excuse me, gentlemen, I've got work to do. Go and see Mr Littlejohn at the main office in Grace Street, that's my advice.'

'Would you have any objection if I looked briefly inside the building?' Holmes inquired and, when the man appeared to hesitate, there was a chink as coins exchanged hands; at which the foreman winked, touched one finger to the brim of his hat and, having cocked his head this time in the direction of the interior of the warehouse, sauntered off in a deliberately nonchalant manner.

Taking this elaborate pantomime as permission, Holmes and I also strolled off as casually towards the double wooden doors, which were fitted with an extra entrance by way of a small wicket opening and which led into a broad stone passage.

As we entered, I noticed Holmes lift his head to sniff the air as if he had detected some peculiar aroma in the atmosphere. For my part, I could smell nothing more than the musty scent of old plaster and a damp cellar odour which seemed to come seeping up the stone steps from some basement or lower vault below the building.

The stairs in question led off to our right, one flight ascending to the upper floors, another leading downwards, this set of steps being closed off from the passage by means of a tall iron grille, secured by a padlock and chain.

Alongside the staircases ran a shaft fitted with ropes, its

purpose being, I supposed, to serve as a hoist for raising or lowering heavier items of furniture to and from the upper storeys. Another gate, this time only knee-high, barricaded off the opening to this shaft in order to prevent anyone falling accidentally down it.

At the far end of the passage was a second door, fitted with glass panels, which was locked, as Holmes discovered when he tried the handle.

It led into a small vestibule which must have given access to the front entrance in Titchbourne Street for, when I joined Holmes to peer through the dusty glass, I could see the street door with its letter-box facing us and several envelopes lying below it on a strip of matting which partly covered the bare floor-boards.

The vestibule looked unused, the paintwork grimy, the ceiling festooned with old cobwebs.

The men had begun to carry the furniture from the van into the warehouse and, taking it as a sign that it was time to depart, we left, Holmes nodding to the foreman as we passed him.

Once out of earshot, he remarked, 'Strange, Watson!'

'What was, Holmes?'

'The odour of cigar smoke.'

When I confessed I had not noticed it, Holmes, whose senses were keener than those of any other man I knew, raised his eyebrows.

'Did you not? It was stale but still strong and unmistakably from a good havana. As you know, I have made a study of the various tobaccos and the different types of ash they leave behind.* Their aromas are also quite distinctive. I cannot imagine even the foreman smoking such an expensive brand. And look at this!'

He extended the long index finger of his right hand, on the tip of which was a small dark stain.

'Oil,' he explained briefly before wiping it away with fastidious care on his pocket handkerchief. 'It was from the padlock

* Mr Sherlock Holmes had published a monograph on the subject, entitled 'Upon the Distinction between the Ashes of the Various Tobaccos', which is referred to in *The Sign of Four*. (Dr John F. Watson)

on the grille which barred off the basement stairs. I am becoming more and more interested in the case you have laid before me, my dear fellow. A missing medical student and a secretary to a charitable institution who contrives simultaneously to run an Australian sheep-farm! And now cigar smoke and a freshly oiled padlock! The investigation has begun to develop most satisfactorily.'

Although I was gratified by Holmes's remark, I was becoming curious about our destination for he was walking ahead of me so rapidly and purposefully that I was forced to lengthen my own stride in order to keep up with him.

When I inquired, 'Where are we going now?', he replied over his shoulder, 'To Grace Street, of course, to interview the manager, Mr Littlejohn.'

'Should we not ask directions, Holmes? The district is quite unfamiliar to me.'

'But not to me,' he replied carelessly. 'I know this area particularly well. An old acquaintance of mine lives only a few streets away – Ikey Morrison, a former pickpocket and a good one, too, who turned respectable when he married a widow, the proprietress of a second-hand clothes shop. Ikey now runs the business. He is a most useful fellow to me in a variety of ways.'

By that time, I had known Holmes for long enough not to be entirely surprised at anything he might tell me about himself.

At the end of the lane by the Britannia public house, Holmes turned off, plunging confidently into a series of narrow byways and alleys, thus demonstrating his familiarity with the neighbourhood, until we eventually emerged into a busy thoroughfare, full of shops and businesses, which he announced was Grace Street.

Buckmaster's premises were half-way down on the left, a small, rather shabby establishment, consisting of an almost bare front office, minimally furnished with one chair and a deal counter behind which a solitary clerk was on duty.

On Holmes's request to see the manager, we were shown into a back room where a plump, moist-faced young man was seated at a desk.

Littlejohn, for so the man proved to be, had an outward air of smiling affability, an open, hail-fellow-well-met manner which was belied by the wary expression in his eyes and by a looseness about his lower lip suggesting greed and self-indulgence.

On the way there, Holmes had warned me how he proposed conducting the interview and I was therefore prepared when he introduced me as Mr Sullivan, himself as Mr Chadwick, partners in a firm importing Benares brassware, and announced that we were looking for a warehouse in the district in which to store our goods.

'I have been advised,' Holmes continued, 'that Buckmaster's owns large premises and that, as manager, you might be willing to lease out some of the floor space.'

Mr Littlejohn smiled apologetically.

'Unfortunately, I cannot accommodate you, Mr Chadwick. All our available space is needed for the storage of our own goods.'

'Are there not even a few square feet to spare?' Holmes persisted. 'Or even a basement which is available for rent?'

'There is a lower vault,' Mr Littlejohn conceded. 'However, it is too damp to be used.'

'Benares brassware does not easily deteriorate. I might add that I am willing to pay above any fixed asking rent if you could oblige me.'

I saw Littlejohn pause at this offer of money in his own pocket, running his tongue over his lower lip so that it glistened greedily before his expression turned to one of regret.

'I am sorry, Mr Chadwick, but I really cannot help you.'

Holmes continued to press the point.

'Would it be worth my while to apply to Mr Buckmaster himself?'

At this, Mr Littlejohn dropped all pretence of joviality, his eyes growing hard and watchful, his voice coldly dismissive as he replied, 'Mr Buckmaster is an elderly gentleman who leaves the management of the business entirely in my hands. You will oblige me by refraining from contacting him, Mr Chadwick. It will be of no use. Good morning to you, sir!'

Outside in the street, Holmes began to chuckle but he gave no reason for his amusement, merely remarking, as he hailed a passing hansom, 'Highly satisfactory, Watson! A few more threads are in our hands.'

'What threads, Holmes?'

But the only reply I received was the enigmatic comment, 'To the cord which, like Ariadne's clew, will lead us to the heart of the labyrinth where no doubt we shall find young Teddy Venables.'

To my secret disappointment, on our return to Baker Street Holmes made no further reference to the case, instead devoting the rest of the morning to reading the newspapers, leaving me to speculate on what exactly he had meant by his reference to threads.

It was only after luncheon had been served and cleared away that he turned his attention again to the inquiry.

Going into his bedroom, he emerged carrying a large cardboard box, the contents of which he spread out on the table. They comprised a collection of locks of different types and a bunch of what I took to be small metal rods, pointed at one end and of varying thicknesses.

Drawing up a chair, he proceeded to set aside one of the locks and to select a metal rod from among the others with great care and deliberation.

Overcome with curiosity, I put down the *Morning Chronicle* and looked over his shoulder.

'What on earth are you doing, Holmes?'

'Is it not obvious, Watson? I am making sure that my lock-picking skills* have not quite deserted me. One has to keep in practice, you know, and I shall need all my expertise tonight.'

'Tonight? For what reason?'

'When I break into Buckmaster's premises,' he replied coolly.

'But isn't that against the law?'

* Mr Sherlock Holmes's skill at house-breaking and opening locks was put to use in several cases, including 'The Adventure of the Illustrious Client' and 'The Adventure of the Retired Colourman'. (Dr John F. Watson)

'Of course it is, my dear fellow. If you can suggest a more legitimate method of entering the building, I shall be delighted to hear it. However, I fear I am left with no choice except to make an unauthorized entry. You wish to discover young Venables' whereabouts, do you not?'

'Of course I do, Holmes. But breaking and entering . . .!'

'If I am to solve the mystery, then I have to acquire those letters we saw lying in the front vestibule in Buckmaster's warehouse. I am convinced that they are crucial evidence to whatever lies behind young Venables' recent activities and his sudden departure from home. I can, of course, proceed no further with the case, if that is what you prefer. Indeed, I ought to warn you that there is every chance that the Major's son is involved in some unlawful affair. The data you laid before me suggest that this is so. The fact that he had money to spend, that he returned home late on many occasions in an inebriated condition and has since disappeared would indicate some illicit connection.'

A little apprehensive for Venables' sake, I asked, 'What do you think it can be, Holmes?'

He shrugged.

'It is impossible to tell at this stage of the inquiry. But whatever the nature of the activity, it is certainly centred at Buckmaster's premises. The letters, the cigar smoke and the newly-oiled padlock all point in that direction. Doubtless the manager, Littlejohn, has some knowledge of it. It was he who permitted the place to be used as an accommodation address and no doubt handed over keys to the premises so that the post could be collected. Moreover, you must have noticed how anxious he was not to lease out the vault to me even though I offered him a bribe and how concerned he became when I suggested I should speak to Buckmaster about it. Well, Watson? What is your decision? Shall I put away my picklocks or shall I continue with the case?'

I was silent for several moments, thinking of Venables weeping in that small rented house.

It was a difficult decision to make and I am not certain even now that I chose the right one. However, recalling Venables' remark that he would rather know the worst than remain in ignorance of his son's whereabouts, I finally made up my mind.

'I think we should proceed, Holmes.'

'You say "we", Watson, although if you prefer not to be involved that is again a matter for your choosing. No, my dear fellow, do not answer me now. Wait until you have heard my plans for this evening before deciding. Firstly, I propose to take a cab to Ikey Morrison's second-hand clothes shop in Cutlers' Row, where I shall disguise myself as a street-loafer. Morrison's is one of several such premises I use on these occasions.* Suitably disguised, I shall then proceed to Buckmaster's warehouse where I shall gain entry through the wicket opening in the large double doors at the back of the building. It has a spring catch similar to this one,' he added, indicating one of the locks which were laid out on the table. 'Once inside, I shall open the inner door which leads into the vestibule by the same method, purloin two or three of the letters we saw lying on the mat, and return to Ikey Morrison's with them where I shall steam them open. Having read them and made notes of any names, addresses and details of their contents worth recording, I shall then reseal them, return to Buckmaster's to post them back through the letter-box and, having removed my disguise, I shall take a cab home. I do not anticipate being inside Buckmaster's warehouse for longer than ten minutes at most. So, Watson, shall you accompany me? Or would you prefer to remain here by the fire and await my return?'

On this occasion, I had no hesitation in coming to a decision although, as events were to prove, Holmes's arrangements for the evening were to be seriously disrupted and we were, owing to circumstances quite unforeseen at the time, to be detained at Buckmaster's premises a great deal longer than my old friend had planned.

'Of course I shall come with you,' I said warmly. 'As the case

* In 'The Adventure of Black Peter', Dr John H. Watson refers to 'five small refuges in different parts of London in which he (Mr Sherlock Holmes) was able to change his personality'. (Dr John F. Watson)

involves the son of a friend, I have no intention of letting you undertake it on your own.'

There was a mischievous light in Holmes's eyes as he inquired, 'You are not concerned that, as a respectable married man and a doctor, you will be breaking the law?'

'Not if it is in a good cause.'

'Very well then, Watson!' said he. 'We shall commit the felony together.'

Later that evening, we set off by cab for Cutlers' Row, a narrow street, only a little wider than an alley-way, which evidently served as the locality for other such businesses as Ikey Morrison's for, as the hansom drove down it, I noticed a variety of signs advertising used goods for sale from furniture to boots and from books to kitchen utensils, while the three golden balls hanging above the pawnbrokers' were so numerous that they twinkled in the flaring light of the gas-jets like whole galaxies of planets.

Despite the lateness of the hour, for it was by then nearly eleven o'clock, most of the shops were open for business, including Ikey Morrison's which we entered through a narrow doorway into an ill-lit and malodorous interior, crammed full of second-hand clothes which lined the walls and even dangled from the ceiling, suspended on ropes.

As I hesitated at the door, reluctant to proceed any further, Holmes, who seemed perfectly at home in this unlikely setting, strode ahead towards the back of the shop, thrusting aside the hanging skirts and dresses, the dingy shirts and shabby coats, calling out Ikey's name.

A crack of yellow light showed at the back and the small figure of a man emerged, blinking at us suspiciously. Then, recognizing my companion, he came forward eagerly, hands outstretched, to meet him.

'Mr 'Olmes! This is a pleasure! Forgive me not welcomin' you straight off but I thought you was the rozzers come nosin' round. Gawd knows what's a-goin' on but they've been buzzin' about round 'ere like flies on a plate of cat's-meat for the past couple of nights. There's two of 'em posted right this very minute at the top of the Row, dressed up as beggars, only they don't fool no one.'

'Is there now?' Holmes asked with evident interest. 'I wonder why?'

We had followed our host into a small back room where in the brighter light of a gas-lamp I was able to observe him more closely.

He was a tiny, sharp-eyed man with the features of an intelligent gnome and swift, darting movements. Almost before we had finished shaking hands, he had whirled about and, whisking some piles of old clothes from two chairs, had waved us towards them. I could imagine him darting through a crowd of people with similar speed and dexterity, helping himself to purses and pocket-books before their owners were even aware of it. His hands, I noticed with interest, were small and long-fingered like the paws of an agile monkey.

There was no sign of Mrs Morrison and, when Holmes inquired after her, Morrison replied that she was down at the Castle having a wet, which I understood to mean she had gone to some local hostelry in search of alcoholic refreshment.

'And now, Mr 'Olmes,' Ikey Morrison continued, 'I take it you're 'ere on business?'

'Indeed we are, Ikey. My friend, Dr Watson, and I need two outfits which will give us the appearance of a pair of street-loafers. I should also be much obliged if, on our return in about quarter of an hour, a kettle of water could be boiling in readiness.'

'Nuffin' easier,' Ikey Morrison assured him, showing no surprise at Holmes's request although, in the event, the kettle was not to be needed.

Darting across to a battered steamer-trunk which stood against the far wall, Ikey Morrison lifted the lid and, having rummaged about inside, produced two sets of very old clothes, including tattered waistcoats, torn shirts and a pair of overcoats, of such a dirty and disreputable appearance that I shrank from putting them on.

Seeing my hesitation, Morrison said, 'They're all clean,

doctor. There ain't no lice in 'em, if that's what's botherin' you. I've 'ad 'em all steamed and frumigated.'

Despite this assurance, I declined to accept one of the caps, preferring to go bare-headed, and it was only on Holmes's insistence that I agreed to the boots which Ikey Morrison offered me.

We changed behind a hanging curtain, Holmes streaking our faces as well as our hands with grease from a candle stump and grime from the floor, of which there was a plentiful supply.

Thus transformed into a pair of low ruffians and with our mufflers close about our faces, the dark lanterns which we had brought with us concealed under our coats, we emerged from Ikey Morrison's shop and set off up Cutlers' Row in the direction of Buckmaster's warehouse, I taking care to slouch along, my hands in my pockets, as Holmes had instructed me.

Titchbourne Street was only a few turnings away and, as we passed the Britannia public house and entered the lane which ran behind it, Holmes touched my arm to draw my attention to a man who lay slumped in its doorway.

'One of Lestrade's men,' he murmured in my ear.

'Is he?' I asked. I had taken him to be a tramp sleeping off an excess of alcohol.

'You can tell by the boots. They are much too new. You see now, Watson, why I insisted on your changing yours?'

'But what are Lestrade's men doing in the area?'

Holmes raised his thin shoulders.

'It could be any number of reasons. The neighbourhood is notorious as a meeting-place for criminals. I could name three premises in Cutlers' Row alone which deal in stolen goods and that is not to take into account the numerous low "dives" and lodging-houses in the side-streets. But I rather think Lestrade's men will not interfere with our own activities.'

As he had been speaking, we had passed along the lane and had reached the rear entrance to Buckmaster's premises where Holmes halted and, having cast a glance up and down the turning to make sure that we were unobserved, drew me into the doorway.

It was a matter of a mere few seconds for him to take the

bunch of picklocks from his pocket, select the right one and, inserting it into the lock in the small wicket opening, give it a dexterous turn at which the spring catch yielded and we were able to enter the building.

Once inside, we closed the door and lit our dark lanterns by the light of which we could see to cross the passage towards the door which led into the vestibule.

My heart was already beating high at the adventure and at the thought of the illegality of our actions when, just as we reached the door and Holmes was preparing to open it, we had cause to stop short.

In the distance we could hear the sound of wheels rapidly approaching.

'I rather suspect,' Holmes remarked, 'that we are about to receive a visit from a certain gentleman who enjoys a good Havana cigar.'

There was no time for further explanation. Hardly had he finished speaking than the vehicle drew to a halt outside the building.

Motioning to me to do the same, Holmes extinguished his lantern, thrust it into his pocket and turned back towards the shaft, our nearest means of escape.

In the dim light filtering in through the glass panels in the door, I saw him seize the rope which dangled from the hoist and start to climb down it. A gesture of his head before it disappeared below floor level invited me to follow.

It was many years, not since my school-days, in fact, that I had climbed a rope and the wound I had received from the Jezail bullet on the Afghan frontier* made any vigorous exercise quite painful on occasions. Nevertheless, I copied his example, clambering over the low grille and lowering myself after him into the blackness of the shaft.

I found it a dizzying sensation, not knowing how deep it was

* There is some confusion as to where exactly Dr John H. Watson was wounded. In *A Study in Scarlet*, he states that he was struck in the shoulder. However, in *The Sign of Four*, he refers to his 'wounded leg'. (Dr John F. Watson)

or where it might end, and it was with considerable relief that at last I felt my feet touch solid ground and Holmes's hand stretched out to steady me.

I had emerged into a stone passage, similar to the one upstairs but smelling more strongly of damp and disuse. Facing me was a heavy door, lined with green baize, to which Holmes, who had relit his lantern, drew my attention, shining the light across its surface.

'Sound-proofed,' he said in a whisper. 'Interesting, do you not agree, Watson? Why should anyone wish to sound-proof a basement door in a furniture warehouse? Let us see where it leads.'

It was unlocked and yielded silently as Holmes put his hand against it.

Beyond lay a large room of such an extraordinary and unexpected appearance that I stood quite motionless for several moments, looking about me in utter astonishment. It was a large, vaulted chamber, well below street level and with no windows or even a grating through which natural light could penetrate, a feature which, together with the low arched ceiling, gave the place the claustrophobic atmosphere of a dungeon.

But here any comparison with a prison or an underground cell ended, for the room was furnished like an expensive West End club or the smoking-room of a gentleman's private residence. The stone floor was covered with sumptuous rugs and carpets, the walls with hangings, while upholstered sofas and leather armchairs were grouped round low tables, lavishly supplied with boxes of cigars and cigarettes.

Holmes's lantern picked out other details of the room, its light passing briefly over a carved sideboard loaded with glasses and bottles of wine and spirits, brass lamps with globes of engraved glass, waiting to be lit, and photographs of a salacious nature in which young women in a state of undress postured and smiled.

Among these luxurious furnishings, an ordinary roll-top desk which stood against the near wall seemed a prosaic item but nevertheless attracted Holmes's attention. Darting across to it, he pushed up its lid and began hurriedly to examine the contents of the pigeon-holes with which it was equipped, extracting several items.

I heard him give a chuckle of satisfaction.

'I think, Watson,' said he, 'that we have reached the heart of the labyrinth.'

But before he could explain what he meant or show me the papers he was holding in his hand, he glanced up towards the vaulted ceiling, his aquiline features alert with an expression of keen attention.

'Listen!' he exclaimed.

I strained my ears but could hear nothing.

'What is it, Holmes?' I asked.

'Footsteps,' he replied. 'Our caller is on his way downstairs. Come, Watson! It is time we found ourselves a hiding-place.'

This proved no difficulty. The hangings which covered the walls provided plenty of opportunity for concealment and we chose a corner near the door where the curtains, draped across the angle, afforded enough space for both of us, from which vantage point we could also keep the whole chamber under observation.

Here we waited in total darkness for several long minutes before a sudden draught of cold air as the baize-covered door was opened and the sound of voices alerted me to the arrival of not one but several unknown visitors.

A young man, his voice educated but slightly slurred as if its owner were the worse for drink, was exclaiming excitedly, 'I say, stop pushing, you chaps! Give a fellow time to light the lamps!'

The next moment, a match flared in the darkness, the lamps were lit and, through a gap in the curtains, I was able to see the newcomers. They were six young men, all in evening clothes and all in a state of mild inebriation, among whom, to my dismay, I recognized Teddy Venables, a silk scarf loose about his neck and his fair hair dishevelled. They were accompanied by four young women who, by their tawdry finery and heavily rouged faces, I took to be street-walkers of the commoner type.

Between them, the group was making so much noise, talking and laughing loudly as they poured drinks from the bottles on the sideboard or threw themselves down on the sofas to light cigars, that I thought it safe to whisper to Holmes that I had seen young Venables.

From the glance which Holmes gave me, I realized that this piece of information was not unexpected.

I was wondering how we should be able to make our eventual escape from the vault without being detected, when the nature of the activity in the room began to take on a considerably more immodest form. Not content with merely smoking and drinking, several of the young men had pulled their female companions down on to the sofas with them and had started to indulge in the type of behaviour which is normally conducted only in private behind closed doors. Heels were kicked up, revealing petticoats and ankles. Even a thigh was exposed.

I hardly dared look at Holmes but when I ventured a sideways glance, I saw his ascetic profile bore an expression of distaste. I was about to ask in a whisper what we should do in the circumstances – whether we should turn our backs on the scene or reveal our presence – when the decision was made for us in a quite unexpected and astonishing manner.

The green baize door was flung open and several police officers burst into the room, the lean, sallow-faced Inspector Lestrade of Scotland Yard at their head.

My own surprise was nothing compared with the shock and consternation shown by the young revellers. Faced by the presence of the law, they scrambled off the sofas, hastily adjusting their attire and, under Lestrade's orders, were soon lined up in a bedraggled formation against the far wall, some shamefaced, others, mainly the young women, brazenly defiant.

I heard Holmes murmur, a note of amusement in his voice, 'I never thought I should welcome Lestrade's intervention in a case with so much relief.'

With that, he swept aside the curtain and coolly stepped forward, much as an actor might walk to the front of a stage to receive the applause of his audience.

Lestrade spun about, his face expressing the same astonishment which only a few moments before I had experienced at his own sudden appearance.

'Mr Holmes!' he exclaimed. 'And Dr Watson, too! What in the name of deuce are you doing here?'

'I might ask the same of you, Lestrade,' Holmes observed drily. 'What investigation brings you to these particular premises at this hour of the night?'

Lestrade came forward to speak to us in a low, confidential tone.

'A forgery inquiry, Mr Holmes.'

Holmes raised a quizzical eyebrow.

'Forgery, my good Inspector? What on earth gave you that idea?'

'I have received reports of several young men seen entering this building late at night. As there have been a number of false banknotes circulating in the district, especially amongst the second-hand dealers in Cutlers' Row, I thought the felons had set up their printing press here in the basement.'

Holmes took a long glance about him, letting his gaze pass over the wall hangings and the sofas before finally coming to rest on the line of dishevelled revellers, especially the young women with their gaudy dresses and tumbled hair.

'I hardly think', he observed, 'that the young men intended to occupy themselves tonight with the printing of counterfeit banknotes. The making of money, however, is one of their concerns but in an entirely different manner to that which you suspected. If you care to examine the contents of that desk over there, Inspector, as well as the letters lying upstairs on the doormat, you will find enough evidence for charging them with obtaining money by deception.'

Under other circumstances, it might have been amusing to observe the alacrity with which Lestrade crossed the room to the desk and, throwing open its lid, started to ferret eagerly about among its contents, pausing only in his task to address my old friend when he saw we were about to leave.

'With your permission, I shall call on you later tonight, Mr Holmes; just to hear your opinion on the case, you understand.'

Holmes bowed in acknowledgement, making no comment until we had left the building, on this occasion by the more orthodox method of using the basement stairs, and had emerged into the street.

It was only then that he remarked, 'I fear I have set Lestrade back on his heels. You, too, Watson. Although we have found young Venables, I imagine it was not in quite the manner you had expected. I did warn you though that the affair in which he was involved was most probably unlawful. However, neither you nor your friend the Major have any reason to thank me for this night's work.'

'How did you reach the conclusion that it was a case of deception, Holmes?' I asked.

He held up a hand to detain me.

'No further questions, my dear fellow. This is neither the time nor the place. Once we have returned to Baker Street and are seated in comfort by our own fireside, I shall present the facts to you.'

It was doubtless a wise decision on his part. Nevertheless, I spent a miserable time while we changed back into our own clothes at Ikey Morrison's and took a cab to our lodgings, turning over in my mind how I was to face the Major, knowing that I was in part responsible for his son's arrest.

On our return to Baker Street, Holmes treated me with great solicitude. Although he could at times be selfish and inconsiderate, at others he was a most kind and generous friend, a quality of character I have remarked on elsewhere in the published chronicles.

It was so on this occasion. He seated me by the fire which he himself coaxed into a blaze before, pouring me a whisky and soda, he sat opposite me, his expression troubled.

'I think you should see these, Watson. I found them in the desk in Buckmaster's vault,' he said, handing me three visiting cards.

I looked at them disbelievingly. They were all similar in size to the one Venables had given me which he had found in his son's bureau drawer and all bore the same address of the A. M. S. Head Office in Titchbourne Street. Only the names were different. They were respectively those of a Canon James Micklewhite, Secretary of the Anglican Missionary Society; a

Captain Horace Landseer, a retired naval officer, Director of the Association of Merchant Seamen; and a Miss Florence Lovestanleigh, Lady Treasurer of the Actors' and Music-hall Artistes' Sanatorium.

'What does it all mean, Holmes?' I asked.

'I think this will explain it,' he replied, handing me a sheet of paper. 'It is a specimen letter, almost ready for posting, one of many I found in a compartment in the desk.'

The letter, which had been neatly produced on a typewriting machine, bore the same address as the cards – A. M. S. Head Office, Buckmaster Buildings, Titchbourne Street, London E. 1., and lacked only a recipient's name and a signature at the bottom to complete it.

It read:

As secretary of the Animals' Model Sanctuary, may I draw to your attention the work done by our organization to aid our four-footed friends?

I have particularly in mind the plight of aged cab-horses and costermongers' donkeys which, when they are too old to continue working, would, without our intervention, end their days miserably in a knacker's yard.

We have managed to rescue many of these pitiful dumb creatures, enabling them to live out the rest of their lives in peace and dignity at our sanctuary in the depths of rural Wiltshire, together with starving cats and dogs retrieved from the streets of all our major cities.

As an animal lover yourself, I am sure you can appreciate that much more needs to be done. However, A. M. S. depends entirely on the benevolence of its supporters in order to continue its good work.

May I therefore prevail on your generosity to send a contribution by postal order to the above address?

All donations are most gratefully received and you may rest assured that the money will be put to excellent use. I remain, Sir, Yours etc.

'You understand now?' Holmes inquired when I had finished reading the letter.

I burst out, 'Yes, Holmes; I do indeed! And a very despicable affair it is, too. God knows how Venables will take it when he discovers his son is involved in this kind of fraudulent activity!'

Aware of my distress, Holmes said quietly, 'I think, my dear Watson, that we should wait to hear what Lestrade has to say and we are in possession of all the facts before we speculate any further on young Venables' part in the affair.'

However, Lestrade, who arrived about an hour later and who joined us by the fire, could offer little comfort. Indeed, the information he had to tell us made matters worse, not better.

From the letters and papers found in the desk, together with the statements taken from the young men involved in the deception, the activities of the A. M. S. were more widespread than either Holmes or I had imagined. In addition to the bogus charities of which we were already aware, Lestrade added several more to the list, including the Agency for the Maintenance of the Sabbath, the Academy for Metaphysical Studies and the Alliance of Moon-worshippers and Satanists.

Lestrade had brought with him the A. M. S. ledgers, which showed that over a period of eighteen months, the length of time the fraudulent charities had been operating, the group had, discounting costs of postage and printing, amassed the considerable sum of £1,463. 15s. 8d.

The books also included long lists of the names and addresses of subscribers, indicating the amount each individual had donated, the sums ranging from a modest half-crown to five guinea contributions. Further moneys in the form of postal orders had been discovered inside the letters lying on the doormat in Buckmaster's vestibule.

'A very clever scheme,' Holmes remarked as Lestrade finished his account. 'Quite unlawful and reprehensible, of course, but one has to grant the young men a certain ingenuity of mind. They have even had the foresight to use the initials A. M. S. for each of the charitable organizations they claimed to represent, thereby saving themselves the cost of having separate letter-headings printed. One serves for all. I wonder what title we ourselves should give them? The Amateur Mendicant Society perhaps? It seems apt. They have turned the craft of the begging-letter, usually little more than a cottage industry, into a highly successful business venture.'

'That is only to be expected,' Lestrade replied heavily, in tones of deep disapproval. 'All the young gentlemen involved are well-educated and come from good family backgrounds. Indeed, some of the fathers are from the very professions which their sons claimed to represent in their charitable appeals. We've found the younger son of an archdeacon among them, as well as a naval officer and a retired major from the Indian Army.'

I groaned inwardly at this last remark of Lestrade's but kept silent as he continued, 'As I understand it, they are all black sheep of the family, short of money but disinclined to earn it honestly.'

'They will be charged?' Holmes inquired.

'Indeed so, Mr Holmes. We cannot allow even an archdeacon's son to deceive the public in this manner. It gives charity a bad name. My men are at this very moment informing the parents that the young men are being held in custody and of the charges which will be brought against them. What sentences are passed is for the courts to decide. One of them, the son of the Indian Army major I was telling you about, is likely to get off more lightly than the others. He only joined the conspiracy a few months ago and so wasn't one of its instigators.'

This was a small crumb of comfort and one which I fervently hoped would console Venables when he learnt of his son's arrest.

Lestrade, who had risen to his feet in preparation for leaving, added, as he buttoned up his overcoat, 'I forgot to mention that one of Buckmaster's employees was involved in the affair. The manager was paid a weekly fee for turning a blind eye to what was going on in the vault and to the fact that the young men had helped themselves to goods from Buckmaster's warehouse in order to furnish their secret club-room, although he swears he knew nothing about any conspiracy to defraud. I have no doubt, however, that he will be dismissed from his post.' Lestrade shook his head, his lean features sombre with disapprobation as he paused in the doorway to pass a final judgement. 'Greed, Mr Holmes. A terrible thing is greed.'

As the door closed behind him, Holmes turned to me.

'You will speak to Venables, Watson?'

'Yes; I shall call on him tomorrow.'

There is no need for me to describe my interview with the Major except to say it was a most painful occasion, made no easier by my old companion's pitiable attempt to see his son's disgrace in the best possible light.

'The law must take its own course, Watson,' he said as we shook hands before I left. 'At least I shall have the comfort of knowing where my son is, even though it may be behind bars. I can only trust that this will teach Teddy the lesson he so badly needs.'

Whether it did or not I have no way of telling. Soon after Teddy Venables' arrest, the Major moved away from the district, no doubt too ashamed to face his friends and neighbours. I never heard from him again and do not know what happened to him subsequently nor to his son after he had served his prison sentence.

In case Venables should still be alive, I have for his sake refrained from publishing an account of the case apart from making a passing reference to it in 'The Five Orange Pips', which I doubt my former army companion will ever read. He was not a man who found much pleasure in books and as neither his name nor his son's is mentioned in the relevant passage, no one is likely to connect them with the case of the Amateur Mendicant Society.

There are two short postscripts I wish to add to my account. The first concerns Inspector Lestrade who claimed all the credit for the uncovering of the fraudulent charities.

Whether it was for this reason that he failed to inquire why Holmes and I were concealed in the lower vault of Buckmaster's premises and how we had gained access to the building in the first place, or whether, in the flurry of official business after the arrests, the question slipped his mind, I do not know.

As for the forgery case which Lestrade was investigating when he burst so unexpectedly into Buckmaster's vault, this was later solved on information received from one of the gang in return for an undisclosed remuneration. The forgers had set up their printing-press in the cellar of the Britannia public house, in the very doorway of which one of Lestrade's own officers had been posted, disguised as a tramp, on the night the Inspector had raided Buckmaster's premises; the same man who, as Holmes had observed at the time, had failed to change his boots.

THE CASE OF THE REMARKABLE WORM

One of the most extraordinary cases in which my old friend, Sherlock Holmes, was involved and with which it was my privilege to be associated began with a dramatic abruptness one hot Friday evening in August, some time after my marriage to Miss Mary Morstan.

Having not seen Holmes for several weeks, I had called on him at my old lodgings in Baker Street to find him in a wry mood, inveighing with mock exasperation against the dearth of interesting stories in the newspapers.

'What has happened to all the criminals, Watson?' he complained in a half-serious, half-humorous fashion. 'Has the warm weather driven them all out of London to seek refuge at the seaside for the season? Not even the *Daily Telegraph* this morning could produce a single noteworthy case. It contained nothing but reports of regattas and garden parties. If this continues, I shall be forced to retire to the country and keep bees.'*

Hardly were the words out of his mouth than we heard through the open window the sound of wheels rapidly approaching and then drawing to a sudden halt outside, footsteps hurrying across the pavement and, seconds later, an agitated ringing at the front-door bell.

Holmes, who had been lounging back in his chair, sat up, instantly alert.

* Mr Sherlock Holmes did indeed take up bee-keeping after his retirement to Sussex. (Dr John F. Watson)

'A woman judging by the footsteps,' said he, 'and in considerable distress, too. I believe, my dear old friend, that we are about to receive a new client and that my bee-keeping will have to be postponed.'

At that, the door flew open and the woman in question rushed into the room.

It was a dramatic entrance, worthy of Grand Guignol or one of Verdi's masterpieces for she had about her a dramatic, not to say operatic, intensity. Young, beautiful, with her black hair tumbling loose and wearing a light cloak which even my unprofessional eye could detect had been hastily thrown over her shoulders, she confronted Holmes, who had scrambled to his feet, with this impassioned entreaty: 'Come at once! Is Isadora! 'E say, "Fetch Mr 'Olmes!"'

The message, spoken in a strong foreign accent, meant nothing to me but Holmes responded immediately. Seizing his hat and gesturing to me to accompany him, he ran after her down the stairs and out into the street where the four-wheeler in which she had arrived was still waiting.

There was only time, as the young woman was giving the driver an address in Kensington, for him to murmur to me, 'The man is Isadora Persano, a well-known, international journalist and an old acquaintance of mine.'

Once the cab had started off, Holmes was able to question her and it was possible to piece together some account of what had happened; no easy task because of her broken English and the hysterical and barely coherent manner in which she expressed herself.

It seemed that Isadora Persano had retired to his study earlier that evening to write an article. At some point during the evening, quite when it was not clear, a small parcel, addressed to Persano, had been delivered to the house and had been taken upstairs by Juan Alberdi, a Mexican manservant.

Some little while later, she, Persano's wife – although her hesitant manner in using the term suggested that their relationship had not been legalized – had heard Persano cry out and, on going up to the study, had found him, in her own words, 'very, very bad, Mr 'Olmes'.

'"Bad"?' Holmes inquired. 'You mean ill?'

'Bad in 'is 'ead. *Demente*. Crazy. He look at this box in 'is 'and. Inside is a little creature; small; like a snake. But is not a snake. I do not know the English. It live in the ground.'

'A *worm*?'

Holmes sounded quite incredulous.

'Yes, yes; a worm!' she cried, seizing eagerly on the word. 'A little worm. Isadora crazy when he looks at it.'

However, it appeared that Persano had managed to recover his sanity for a few moments, long enough to gasp out the one word 'Holmes!', an exclamation which she had perfectly understood as Persano had previously warned her that, should anything happen to him, she was without delay to contact Mr Sherlock Holmes, Persano's old friend the consulting detective, at 221B Baker Street.

Holmes was about to ask her why Persano had thought it necessary to give her these instructions when the cab drew up outside a tall house in a quiet Kensington side-street and Señora Persano leapt out and was running up the steps to the front door which was set wide open.

Holmes and I hastened after her, Holmes pausing only to fling some coins at the cab-driver.

Inside the house, I had a fleeting impression of a small, dark-faced man, presumably the Mexican manservant, cowering in a state of great terror at the back of the hall, before I followed Holmes and the Señora up three flights of stairs to a landing at the very top of the house where she unlocked a door and threw it open.

The scene which met my eyes almost defies description.

It was a study, lined with bookshelves and with a desk, on which was burning a single green-shaded lamp, placed at right angles to an open sash window which overlooked the back of the house.

A man was seated at the desk, crouched over and gazing down with great intensity at a small box which was lying in front of him. He was tall and well-built, with a deeply sunburnt face of a strong, hawklike cast, marked with a scar on his left cheek, and would have been handsome apart from the expression of mad frenzy which convulsed his features, setting his eyes rolling in his head and clenching his lips open in a terrifying grimace.

In the green light from the desk-lamp, he had the appearance of a tortured soul from a medieval illustration of the inferno.

Hardly had I time to absorb these details when, with a dreadful cry, the man jumped to his feet, overturning the chair as he did so and sweeping the papers off the desk with one wild lunge of his arm.

As they fluttered to the floor, he flung himself at the open window and, while we stood, horrified and transfixed in the doorway, disappeared from sight over the edge of the sill with another ghastly scream, as if all the demons of hell were at his heels.

There was a moment of absolute silence before the room erupted.

With a wild cry of her own, Señora Persano rushed to the window and would have hurled herself after him had not Holmes seized her by the waist and, spinning her round, slammed the sash down. The next moment he had bundled her out of the room on to the landing where he locked the door and pocketed the key before setting off down the stairs, I at his heels.

We raced through the house, past the cowering manservant in the hall and into a kitchen where a fat, red-faced cook and a thin, sharp-featured maidservant looked up from their tasks to gape at us, and from there through a door into the back garden where we found the body of Isadora Persano.

Despite my own experiences of violent death and appalling wounds in battle when I served in India as Assistant Surgeon during the second Afghan war, I hesitate even now in describing the scene.

Persano had fallen from the top storey on to the railings which surrounded the basement area with such force that two of the iron rods, tipped with spear-shaped spikes, had penetrated his chest to a depth of several inches.

Although I knew the task was hopeless, I felt for the carotid artery in his neck and, finding no pulse, I turned to Holmes.

'I am so sorry; there is nothing I can do. I am afraid he is dead.'

Rarely have I seen my old friend in such a state of shock. In the light streaming out of the open kitchen door, his features looked bleached, his lids drawn so far down over his deep-set eyes that they appeared hooded, like those of some gaunt, brooding, melancholy bird. But even in this first moment of horrified awareness of the tragedy, he was still in command of his reactions with that icy self-control which has led me at times to accuse him of deficiency in human sympathy.* I fear I may have maligned him. It was not always lack of emotion on his part but a deep-seated dislike of revealing to others those feelings which lay closest to his heart.

Within seconds, he had recovered sufficiently to take charge of the situation.

With the curt comment, 'We must send immediately for the police,' he strode back into the kitchen where, tearing a page from his notebook, he hastily scribbled a message which he handed to the servant girl with orders to deliver it immediately to Inspector Lestrade at Scotland Yard.

The girl having departed with the note and the money for the cab fare, Holmes turned to the red-faced cook.

'You speak English?' he demanded.

'That I do, surr,' the woman replied in a strong Irish accent.

'Then accompany Dr Watson upstairs and see what you can do to comfort your mistress.'

Indeed, we could hear even on ground level the young woman's hysterical sobbing echoing down from the top of the house.

Between us, the cook and I supported Señora Persano into her bedroom on the second floor where I administered smelling-salts and brandy. Once she had grown a little calmer, I left her in the care of the cook, who seemed a sensible enough woman, and returned upstairs to the study to join Holmes, who had passed us on the landing.

* Dr John H. Watson makes this accusation in the opening paragraph of 'The Adventure of the Greek Interpreter'. (Dr John F. Watson)

On entering, I found that he had lit the gas jets over the fireplace and it was possible to see more of the room.

It was a low chamber with sloping attic ceilings and a small hearth in which was set a basket grate, empty because it was summer of anything except some crumpled sheets of paper, covered with handwriting which I assumed was Persano's.

As I came in, Holmes, who was kneeling in front of this grate, carefully examining its contents, leaned forward with an exclamation of satisfaction and retrieved a square of coarse yellowish paper, quite different in colour and texture to the others.

'What do you make of this, Watson?' he inquired.

In my absence, he seemed to have recovered some of his usual control, apart from a certain grimness about the set of his mouth.

I said, 'Judging by the creases in it, it has been folded up to form a kind of packet. In fact, it reminds me of the old-fashioned apothecaries' method of wrapping up powders. Isn't that a small blob of wax still adhering to it where the edges had been sealed?'

'Correctly deduced, my dear fellow. The packet was indeed fastened with wax and then the seal was broken; fairly recently, too. The piece of paper was lying on top of the others in the grate but, while they were sprinkled with fine soot from the chimney, this was quite clean. However, you failed to remark that the paper is of a poor-quality, foreign make and that some small grains of a brownish powder are still adhering to the folds; too few, though, I fear, for successful analysis. We shall see what Lestrade has to say about it,' Holmes concluded, placing the square of paper in his pocket-book before conducting me across the room.

'And the desk, Watson? What deductions can you draw from this?'

It was a large desk but apart from the evidence which suggested that Persano had been working at it shortly before he plunged to his death, demonstrated by the open book – in Spanish, I noticed – and the scattered papers lying on the floor, I saw nothing.

Except, of course, for the worm.

I stooped down to peer at it gingerly.

It lay curled up in a matchbox and was a most curious creature. About the size of an ordinary earthworm, it was quite unlike any other I had ever seen before.

Along the length of its back ran a line of tiny, black spots which spread out over the head to form a V-shaped pattern, similar to the markings on a viper.

It stirred and I hurriedly backed away.

'What is it, Holmes?' I asked. 'Is it venomous? Was Persano bitten by it and this caused him to go mad?'

'It would certainly appear so,' Holmes replied. 'It would also seem that the small parcel which was delivered to the door earlier this evening contained the matchbox inside which was placed the worm. You no doubt noticed on the desk the piece of brown paper in which the package was wrapped with Isadora Persano's name and address written on it; not in an English hand, however. The writing has a foreign look about it.'

I could no longer contain my curiosity.

'Who is Isadora Persano and where did you meet him?'

'Persano *was*,' Holmes corrected me quietly, his eyes again hooded over with their lids, 'an internationally renowned journalist, who specialized in South American affairs. I met him several years ago under unusual circumstances in Paris where he was investigating the sale of forged Peruvian works of art for a newspaper article. Indeed, he claimed to have Inca blood in his veins. There was also a Spanish mother and a Quechua Indian grandfather. However, his antecedents are of little relevance to his death.

'A few weeks ago, I received a letter from him, informing me that he had recently returned from Mexico where he had been for the past six months, researching for a particular assignment, of what exact nature he did not specify. He suggested we should meet but unfortunately at the time I was engaged with the case at Longwater concerning the stolen diamond necklace.

'Once the investigation was completed, I had every intention of writing to him again to suggest a date for the proposed meeting. I fear I have left it too late.'

The last remark was spoken in a tone of deepest despondency.

'Did he mention in his letter that his life was threatened?'

'Not in so many words. He merely wrote that he had made many enemies while in Mexico but, as he was an expert duellist, both with sword and pistol, and was used to defending himself, I did not regard it as significant. He received that scar on his face during an attack by hostile Indians while on an earlier expedition to the Amazonian rain-forests. I very much regret that I failed to take his statement more seriously. He clearly considered himself in danger if he warned Señora Persano to contact me.'

To comfort him a little, I said, 'The Señora will surely be able to tell you who his enemies are.'

'Yes; indeed I must question her.'

'But not tonight, Holmes,' I urged. 'She is in no fit state to be cross-examined.'

Holmes acquiesced reluctantly.

'Very well, Watson. I am forced to bow to your professional judgement but at some point, and soon, she must be persuaded to tell us what she knows. And now, my dear fellow, before Lestrade arrives, take a final look at the desk and tell me if you have observed anything else which might be useful to the inquiry.'

I looked but could see nothing.

'No, Holmes. Only book and papers.'

'Well, well!' said he in a tone of mild surprise but he would not explain what, if anything, I had failed to notice and, turning about, he crossed to the shelves to examine the titles of the books, a task which occupied him until the arrival of Inspector Lestrade, who was accompanied by several other police officers.

Lestrade listened in silence to Holmes's account of what had happened from the time Señora Persano had arrived at Baker Street to Persano's leap from the window but he seemed less interested in Holmes's discovery of the piece of paper in the grate than in the matchbox containing the worm.

As I had done, he approached it cautiously, bending down to

peer at it and taking care, I noticed, to keep his hands clasped behind his back.

'Extraordinary!' he exclaimed. 'I have never seen anything like it before. A species of adder, would you say, Mr Holmes? It has the markings of one. I shall have to get this examined by an expert. But there is no doubt in my mind that it caused Mr Persano's sudden madness. It must have bitten him when he opened the box. Nasty-looking little thing, isn't it? It is going to need careful handling.'

Holmes said nothing during this monologue, merely standing by and watching as Lestrade sent one of his constables downstairs to ask the cook for a tin box with a well-fitting lid, a pair of thick leather gloves and some fire-tongs.

It was only after these articles had been produced and Lestrade, wearing the gloves, had picked up the matchbox with the tongs and deposited it very slowly and carefully inside the tin while an attendant subordinate clapped on the lid, that Holmes ventured a remark.

'Well done, Inspector!' he exclaimed.

Lestrade looked round, beaming with satisfaction. He had not apparently noticed the ironic tone in Holmes's voice nor the amused gleam in his eyes.

'And now that the little fellow's shut away,' he announced, 'I can make a start on the investigation.'

'You intend speaking to the servants?' Holmes inquired.

'Not for the moment, except for the girl who took in the parcel,' Lestrade replied with an offhand air. 'I shan't waste much time on the others. In my opinion, no one in the household is involved. We already have the villain who is responsible safely under lock and key.'

Laughing at his own joke, he rapped with his fingers on the lid of the tin.

'You have no objection if I question them?'

'Ask all you want, Mr Holmes. I shall be busy up here until the police surgeon arrives and I can arrange to have Mr Persano's body removed to the mortuary.'

However, as Holmes and I went to the door, Lestrade clearly had second thoughts for he suddenly asked, his sallow features sharp with suspicion, 'If any of them has anything useful to tell you, you will let me know, won't you, Mr Holmes? With your permission, I shall call at Baker Street tomorrow evening to discuss the developments in the case.'

'Of course, Inspector,' Holmes said graciously.

There was no sign of the Mexican manservant when we went downstairs to the hall, only the cook and the servant-girl whom we found in the kitchen, discussing with a horrified but excited animation the events of the evening, with the back door to the garden where Persano's body was still lying firmly closed and the blind drawn down over the window.

Holmes spoke first to the cook.

Once we had succeeded in comprehending her thick brogue, we learned little from her except for the fact that her name was Mrs O'Hara and that she did not live in but had been engaged as a cook-general on a daily basis from the time when Mr Persano had rented the house furnished two months earlier. She saw little of Mr Persano himself who spent most of the day upstairs in his study and rarely went out. The Señora, whom she referred to as Mrs Persano, was in charge of the household and gave the orders although how the two of them managed to communicate, the one with only a limited knowledge of English, the other with an almost impenetrable Irish accent, was a mystery in itself.

The servant-girl, Polly Atkins, was a quick, alert little Cockney. As she lived in, she was able to tell us a little more about the occupants of the house and Isadora Persano's daily routine. She confirmed the cook's statement that Persano rarely left the house and, in the short time he had lived there, had received no visitors and hardly any letters.

'Except for a small parcel which I understand was delivered this evening,' said Holmes. 'Who took it in?'

'I did, sir,' she replied promptly. 'It came about 'alf past seven, brought by a young lad.'

'Can you describe him?'

'Well, he was just an h'ordinary boy, sir. I didn't take no particular notice. 'E said the parcel was h'urgent and 'ad to be 'anded to Mr Persano straight away.'

'What did you do with it?'

'I give it to Juan to take upstairs. I'd 'ad strict h'orders not to disturb Mr Persano while he was writin' so, as me and Cook was busy in the kitchen, I reckoned Juan could do somethin' to earn 'is keep. 'E's Mr Persano's manservant; not that 'e does much except wait at table and clean the silver.'

'Where would I find this Juan?'

'In the boot-cupboard, under the stairs.'

'The boot-cupboard?'

''E allus 'ides in there when 'e's upset. But you won't get nothin' out of 'im,' she added, as Holmes made for the door. ''E's a proper 'eathen; don't speak a word of h'English.'

This proved only too true when, having located the boot-cupboard and found Juan closeted inside it, Holmes hauled him out into the light of the hall.

He was a small, dark-skinned youth with the broad and slightly flattened features of an Indian peasant and might have been any age from twelve to twenty for he had the old-young look I had observed before in the faces of London street-urchins who have grown wise beyond their years in the ways of the world.

He exuded fear. We could smell it on him – that feral odour which a terror-struck wild animal gives off when it is captured, and he clutched wildly at a gold crucifix about his neck as Holmes dragged him forward by the sleeve.

But we could get no response from him except for a dumb shaking of his head, even when Holmes tried him with a few words in Spanish.

Eventually, realizing the task was hopeless, Holmes released his grasp and the youth bolted up the stairs.

'Let him go,' Holmes said, as I prepared to start after him. 'We shall have to question him again tomorrow in Señora Persano's presence. She will be able to act as interpreter.' He seemed suddenly weary for he passed a hand over his eyes before continuing, 'There is nothing else we can do here for the time being. Let us find a cab and return to Baker Street.'

Outside in the street, we hailed a hansom and, as it drew up outside his door, Holmes said, 'Keep the cab, Watson. I should prefer you not to come in with me. I am in no mood for company and besides there is some research I must undertake which will engage all my attention. But should you be free tomorrow afternoon at two o'clock, my dear fellow, I shall be delighted to see you.'

As he climbed out of the cab, he added in a musing tone, half to himself, 'I wonder if Mrs Hudson has such a thing as a garden spade?'

Although I could understand his desire to be alone so soon after the death of his friend, I was nevertheless a little hurt by this dismissal and also intrigued by Holmes's parting remark. What possible use could he have for a garden spade?

It was a question which absorbed me on the homeward journey and one which I was convinced I had answered by applying Holmes's own deductive processes when, at two o'clock the following afternoon, I again presented myself at 221B Baker Street where I was admitted by Mrs Hudson.

'Were you able to supply Mr Holmes with a spade?' I asked, eager to put my theory to the test.

'Indeed I was, Dr Watson, although goodness knows what he wanted it for. He was out with a lantern turning over my flower-borders until gone midnight.'

Although I thought I could guess what lay behind Holmes's nocturnal activities, I was still not prepared for what he had to show me.

'I hear you were out last night digging for bait,' I remarked in a jocular fashion as I entered the sitting-room. 'Were you successful?'

'If by bait you mean the worm which was used to hook Persano,' said he, 'my efforts were rewarded. Come and look at this, Watson.'

Lying on the table was a saucer and in the saucer, stretched out at full length, was the remarkable worm which I had last seen curled up in the matchbox on Persano's desk, marked with the same line of fine black dots along its back and the chevron pattern on its head.

'Where on earth did you get it from, Holmes?' I asked,

assuming that he had acquired it from Lestrade by some nefarious means.

'Not *on* earth, Watson,' he corrected me with a smile. '*In* earth. It was one of several that I dug up last night from Mrs Hudson's back garden.'

'Several? I don't understand. Is there a sudden plague of these creatures? If so, should we not inform the police or someone in authority? They are venomous, are they not?'

Holmes burst out laughing and, although I was a little annoyed to be the source of his amusement, I was nevertheless gratified that he had recovered his good spirits after his low state of mind the previous evening.

'Take my word for it, my dear fellow, it is perfectly harmless!'

'But the markings . . .'

'Indian ink,' Holmes explained and, taking me by the arm, led me over to the table where he conducted his scientific experiments and where I saw several more dishes laid out in a row, each containing a worm with similar markings although on all of these the lines of dots were not nearly so distinct.

'My first attempts,' Holmes continued. 'I tried various substances as you can see from the bottles and jars: ordinary black ink, boot polish applied with the point of a pin – a singular failure, that particular one; the polish rubbed off too easily. Dye and paint were too liquid; so, too, was stove blacking. If you ever wish to draw a pattern on an earthworm, Watson, allow me to recommend Indian ink, applied with a fine-nibbed mapping-pen.'

'So Persano wasn't bitten by the worm?'

'No; although that was what we were meant to believe,' Holmes replied, his eyes once more assuming their sombre, brooding expression.

'Then how was he sent mad if it wasn't by some kind of poison?'

'That is what I propose asking Señora Persano this afternoon. I also intend to discover what was in the glass which had been placed on Isadora Persano's desk at some time yesterday evening.'

'What glass, Holmes? I saw no glass.'

'The object does not have to be present in order to convince one of its physical existence. It is not necessary for the bank manager to be confronted by the actual burglar for him to know his premises had been broken into. The blown safe is evidence enough. It was so in this case. Although the glass had been removed, it had left behind a ring which had marked the polished surface of the desk. As the stain was still damp, I deduced that the glass had been removed not long before our arrival and Isadora Persano's death. As the cook had no reason to go up to the study and the servant-girl was positively ordered not to do so, the only persons who could have taken the glass upstairs and then removed it were either Juan Alberdi or Señora Persano. I propose to find out which of the two it was. Come, Watson. The Señora should have recovered sufficiently to offer some explanation, if not the whole truth.'

Señora Persano had indeed recovered to the extent that she was no longer confined to bed but was lying on a sofa in the drawing-room, to which Polly Atkins, the little maid-of-all-work, conducted us.

It was one of the strangest rooms I have ever entered. Although it was furnished with the conventional items that are usually supplied with a rented house in the way of armchairs, occasional tables and whatnots, every surface was covered with an extraordinary collection of South American *objets d'art* which Persano must have brought back with him from his travels. There were woven rugs, painted pottery, carved figurines, all brightly coloured, and, weirdest of all, a whole wall filled with masks of gods and goddesses, saints and demons, some grotesquely grinning, others grimacing in pain or terror.

It was not a room in which one could feel at ease, especially as the blinds were drawn against the bright afternoon sunshine, and I was surprised that Señora Persano had chosen such a setting in which to convalesce although no doubt these bizarre objects were familiar to her.

She lay in the semi-darkness, covered with a silk shawl which was embroidered with exotic birds and flowers, looking very pale and languid, her black hair loose about her shoulders.

We approached the sofa and, drawing out two upright chairs,

sat down at her side, I taking care to place my own seat so that it had its back to the masks.

I still have my notes and from these, I have drawn up a summary of the conversation between Holmes and the Señora. It was conducted at times in Spanish, Holmes translating for my benefit, but largely in English, heavily fractured on the Señora's part and frequently interrupted by tears, sighs and impassioned lamentations in her own language.

However, little by little we were able to put together her story.

She had met Isadora Persano in Argentina the previous year when he had been travelling through South and Central America gathering material for a book he proposed writing on the sub-continent as well as for a series of newspaper articles, commissioned by the Washington *Gazette*.

They had fallen in love and, when he moved on to Chile, Brazil, Ecuador and finally to Mexico, she had accompanied him.

There was no mention of a marriage ceremony and I noticed that Holmes was careful not to query this point.

In Mexico, Persano had been engaged in collecting information about the *Porfiriato* under the dictator, General Díaz.*

Later Holmes was to explain to me the meaning of the *Porfiriato* and its political implications. After General Díaz had seized power in 1876, the country had been developed economically but at the cost of great human suffering and loss of personal freedom, particularly among the Indian peasants whose communal fields had been confiscated to enlarge the private estates of the Spanish-speaking landowners, encouraged in their actions by the General's policy of *pan o palo*, bread or the club.

It was this aspect of the General's dictatorship which particularly interested Persano, the Señora informed us. With his own Indian ancestry and his wide knowledge of the South American

* General Porfirio Díaz was created President of Mexico in 1876, after he led a rebellion against Benito Juarez. His dictatorship was finally overthrown in 1911. (Dr John F. Watson)

indigenous culture, he had sympathized strongly with the sufferings of the landless peasants.

It was for this reason that he had taken Juan Alberdi into his employment, having found the boy starving on the streets of Monterrey.

In the course of his researches, Persano had made many enemies, chief among them Carlos Vicente Gasca, a rich and powerful landowner who was notorious for his ill-treatment of the Indian peasants who worked his estates.

Persano had threatened to expose Gasca in his articles for the Washington newspaper. Gasca, in turn, had vowed to kill Persano.

There had been several attempts on Persano's life. He had been shot at twice while out riding. On another occasion, a man had broken into their hotel bedroom late one night and had attacked Persano with a knife. Persano had fought him off and the man had escaped.

After each failed attempt, Persano had received a piece of paper on which was drawn a skull, accompanied by a warning in Spanish that the attacks would continue. Persano was convinced that these had been sent by Gasca.

Realizing that the next attempt might be successful, Persano had decided to return to England, bringing with him the Señora and Juan Alberdi. He thought that he would be safe in London, where he would have the time and leisure to write his book and his newspaper articles without being under the threat of imminent death.

But Gasca must have followed him and found out where he was living because two weeks before, Persano had received through the post a sheet of paper bearing the skull and the warning.

It was then that Persano had told the Señora that if anything happened to him, she was to contact his old friend, Mr Sherlock Holmes, and had given her Holmes's address.

'Why did he not come to me himself?' Holmes exclaimed in some distress.

''E was too *orgulloso;* also *tenaz,*' Señora Persano explained, which Holmes translated for my benefit as 'proud' and 'stubborn'. ''E thought if 'e stay at 'ome and do 'is writing, there is no danger.'

She could give no detailed description of Gasca. Persano had been careful not to involve her in his political activities and she had seen the man only once, at a distance.

From her gestures, I gathered he was tall, *'alto'*, and broad-shouldered with dark hair, *'muy ondulado'* – very wavy. He also spoke good English – 'like a milord'.

As Holmes was to point out to me later, it made the task of tracking down Gasca extremely difficult. With a little disguise, such as a wig to cover his dark, wavy hair, he could easily pass himself off as an Englishman.

We then came to the events of the previous evening, painful both for Holmes and for Señora Persano, who frequently broke down in tears, but eventually, after much patient questioning on Holmes's part, a coherent account emerged.

Immediately after dinner, Persano had retired to his study, his habit on a Friday evening. During the week, his time was spent on his own book but Saturdays and Sundays were always set aside for writing the articles for the *Gazette*, which had to be posted on Monday.

Señora Persano knew nothing about the arrival of the parcel until later. The servant-girl had accepted it from the messenger and Juan had taken it upstairs. She herself had remained in the drawing-room, reading.

At about nine o'clock, she had heard Persano cry out and had gone upstairs to find him in the demented state she had described to us the previous day. When he had shouted out the name 'Holmes!', she had run out of the house and had immediately taken a cab to the address in Baker Street which Persano had given her.

And that was all she could tell us.

'I think not, Señora Persano,' Holmes said quietly. 'I believe you went upstairs to the study earlier in the evening to take Isadora a glass containing some kind of beverage in which you mixed a certain powder. I found the paper in which the powder had been wrapped in the grate. There was also a damp ring on the desk where a glass had stood. What was in that powder?'

Her response was immediate. Flinging herself back against the sofa cushions and covering her face with her hands, she burst into a flood of tears.

'Nothing!' she wept. 'I swear it!'

Holmes rose to his feet, his expression stern and unforgiving.

'In that case, Señora, you leave me no alternative. I shall be forced to place the facts before Inspector Lestrade.' When she said nothing, he continued, his voice rising, 'Do you not realize you risk being accused of causing Isadora's death? I do not believe you were responsible. But unless you tell me the truth, there is nothing I can do to save you.'

She sobbed helplessly for several minutes while Holmes and I sat by watching, he impassively, I deeply moved by her distress and also seriously concerned about the state of her health.

At last, drawing a deep, shuddering breath, she spoke.

'The powder is not 'armful. Is made from *guarana* seeds.* Is an old remedy, used by the Quaramis, to stop people from sleeping. Isadora buy in Brazil. 'E use it to keep 'im awake when 'e writes 'is stories for the newspaper. I give 'im in warm milk.'

'When?' Holmes demanded.

'Every Friday evening. Then 'e work all night.'

'And where do you keep the drug?'

'In there.'

She gestured towards a small bureau which stood against the far wall. Holmes stalked over to it and, jerking open the drawer, revealed a small pile of folded packets, made from the same coarse paper which he had retrieved from the study grate.

Unwrapping one, he showed me its contents – a brownish

* The seeds of *guarana* (Paullinia cupana), a shrub native to South America, contain 5% caffeine, three times more than that found in coffee. The seeds, after roasting and grinding, are mixed with a beverage and drunk as a strong stimulant to promote wakefulness. (Dr John F. Watson)

powder, similar in colour and texture to that which had been adhering to the folds of the packet found upstairs.

Behind us, Señora Persano was protesting, 'The one I give 'im Friday is one of those; is the same.'

His expression grim, Holmes refolded the paper square and put it away in his pocket-book, remarking to me in a low voice as he did so, 'I doubt that very much. The drawer is unlocked. Anyone in the household could have opened it and replaced the top packet with another. I propose questioning Juan Alberdi now, Watson, with the Señora acting as interpreter.'

It was at this point that I intervened, disastrously as it later transpired. Had I not done so, a life might have been spared.

'I cannot allow that, Holmes. Señora Persano is on the verge of a breakdown. As a medical man, I consider it most unwise to press her further. Come back tomorrow, if you wish, to interview the manservant. For the moment, however, I must insist that she is allowed to rest.'

Holmes acquiesced reluctantly and shortly afterwards we left, having made sure that Señora Persano was placed in the care of Mrs O'Hara.

As soon as we returned to Baker Street, Holmes went immediately to the bookcase and, pulling out volume 'D' in his encyclopedia of reference, opened it at a certain page and handed it to me silently.

I read:

> Drugs hallucinatory: derived from various plants and used world-wide in pagan religious ceremonies to alter consciousness and to induce mystical states of mind and strange sensations, e.g. the belief that the participant can fly. Viz. African tribes, Australian aborigines, Siberian *shamans* and many North and South American Indians. The Vikings may have used a species of mushroom to produce the 'berserk' state before going into battle. Many still widely used. Some smoked, some eaten or drunk, some absorbed into the bloodstream in the form of an ointment rubbed into the skin (see WITCHCRAFT).

One of the strongest hallucinatory substances is the Psilocybe Mushroom (Agaric family), species of which can be found in many parts of the New World. Known in Central America by the Chichimeca tribe as *teonanactl*, the Flesh of the Gods. Other Indian tribes who used it in their religious ceremonies were the Nahoas of Mexico and the Otomis of Puebla.

The mushroom produces coloured visions, alteration of time and space perceptions and a state of ecstasy bordering on frenzy, particularly in those unused to it.

The drug takes one to one and a half hours to become effective after ingestion.

It is prepared by drying the mushrooms, then reducing them to a powder which is added to a liquid before being drunk.

Holmes meanwhile had flung himself down in his armchair where he sat, his chin propped on his long fingers as he stared moodily into space.

When I had finished reading the passage, he said abruptly, 'You see the implications, Watson? Someone in the household was persuaded by Gasca to substitute for the packet of *guarana* seed powder which Persano took regularly every Friday evening as a stimulant another packet containing a hallucinatory drug made from the Psilocybe mushroom, which his system was unused to absorbing. All the symptoms were present in his apparent insanity – the 'berserk' state, the frenzied expression. Even his leap from the window can be attributed to the effects of the drug, which can induce in the person who takes it the belief that he can fly.'

'And you think that the culprit was Juan Alberdi, the manservant?'

'It is unlikely to be the other servants. How would they have access to such a drug? As for Señora Persano, she had nothing to gain and everything to lose by Persano's death. She is now left alone in a strange country with no protector.'

'But I do not see why Alberdi should have conspired with Gasca, Persano's sworn enemy. After all, Holmes, Persano had saved the young man from starvation. Alberdi had every reason to be grateful to him.'

'Not if the bribe Gasca offered were large enough. For some people, loyalty is like any other marketable commodity, to be bought and sold at the right price. Or Gasca may have threatened Alberdi in some way. It is also possible, of course, that Alberdi was persuaded that the drug he substituted was perfectly harmless. There is, however, no doubt in my mind that Alberdi was used as Gasca's tool. You should have allowed me to question him this afternoon.'

'Tomorrow will be soon enough, Holmes. In the meantime, Lestrade said he would call on you this evening. Why do you not speak to him and ask him to take Alberdi into custody for questioning? I am sure the Inspector could arrange to have a Spanish-speaking interpreter on hand when you interview the young man. That way, Señora Persano will not be placed under further stress.'

'You are probably right, my dear fellow,' Holmes agreed. 'But such arrangements must be made as soon as possible. Gasca must be somewhere in London, no doubt staying at an hotel. I am eager to run him to earth before he has the chance to leave the country. For you may be sure that, once he hears of Persano's death, he will not delay in making his escape.'

Lestrade arrived about an hour later, more eager to inform us of what he knew, or rather what he did not know, about the remarkable worm than to listen to Holmes.

'Extraordinary!' he exclaimed as soon as he set foot inside the room. 'I have looked up that creature in every book on snakes and reptiles I can lay my hands on and nowhere is it mentioned. It would appear to be unknown to science. Where do you think it came from, Mr Holmes? Some South American jungle or Mexican swamp?'

'I suggest you try a London park or garden.'

Lestrade stopped short, his mouth open in astonishment.

'You are not serious?'

'Indeed I am. Allow me to show you my own specimen, dug up from Mrs Hudson's flower-border only yesterday.' Holmes fetched the dish on which the earthworm was lying, adding as the Inspector backed away, 'There is no need to be alarmed, Lestrade. The creature is perfectly harmless. I myself painted on the markings with Indian ink.'

It was highly gratifying to see Lestrade's amazement and to hear him stammer, 'I don't understand. Why was the creature sent to Persano if it had nothing to do with his death?'

'It was a cunning ruse to throw us off the scent. The villain behind the plot intended that the police should waste time following up this false clue, thus giving him the opportunity to leave the country.'

Holmes then gave Lestrade a brief summary of what he had learned that afternoon from Señora Persano and his suspicions regarding Gasca, concluding with the words, 'You must put as many men as you can spare, Lestrade, on checking the hotels. It will not be an easy task, made more difficult by the fact that Gasca speaks good English and will no doubt be travelling on false papers. All that Señora Persano could tell us was that he is a tall, broad-shouldered man with dark, wavy hair, but that latter feature can be easily disguised. However, as he is rich and is used to having servants to wait on him, I suggest he will have at least one companion, possibly two. As for the boy who delivered the package containing the worm, take my advice and do not attempt to trace him. He is no doubt some urchin whom Gasca paid to run the errand and who will be impossible to identify from among the hundreds like him who roam the streets of our capital. In the meantime, we must return at once to Persano's house and take Alberdi into custody for questioning. It was he, I believe, who was bribed or coerced in some way by Gasca to substitute one packet of drugs for another.'

But we were too late. By the time we reached the house, Juan Alberdi had already fled. The only information we could learn of his departure was from a very embarrassed police constable whom Lestrade had left on duty at the front door and who told us that the manservant had gone out earlier that afternoon, carrying a letter in his hand as if on the way to post it, and had not yet returned.

Lestrade was furious but there was nothing he could do. He

had left no instructions that anyone should be prevented from leaving the premises.

'God knows where he could have gone to,' the Inspector said gloomily, turning to Holmes.

'Can't you guess, Lestrade? The young man was terrified of being accused of causing Persano's death. I suggest he has gone to seek out Gasca. Find one and you will find the other.'

'That is easier said than done, Mr Holmes,' Lestrade replied.

However, he did the best he could under the circumstances, issuing a description of Alberdi together with orders that, if found, he was to be arrested. He also instituted inquiries for Gasca and the missing manservant at all the London hotels.

There was nothing Holmes and I could do to assist this part of the investigation and we returned to Baker Street, where my old friend immediately retired to his bedroom and sought what solace he could find in playing the violin.

I was much concerned about his state of mind. However much my old friend might try to disguise his feelings, he was still deeply affected by Persano's death and blamed himself for not having contacted the man to suggest a meeting. He was convinced that had he done so, he might have learned of Gasca's threats and helped to save Persano's life.

I was afraid that, in his present mood, he might revert to the use of cocaine, a pernicious habit from which I was slowly managing to dissuade him.*

With this fear uppermost in my mind, I called several times at Baker Street over the next two weeks, anxious not only about Holmes's condition but also about the progress of the case.

Nearly a fortnight was to elapse before there was any fresh information and then, one afternoon towards the end of the month, when I had called yet again at my old lodgings and was sitting with Holmes, who was still in low spirits, in the upstairs room, there came a knock on the door and a constable entered with a note from Inspector Lestrade.

* There are several references in the published canon to Mr Sherlock Holmes's regrettable habit of injecting himself with a 7% solution of cocaine. He also on occasions used morphine. (Dr John F. Watson)

After perusing it, Holmes handed it to me. It read simply: Body found in garden of empty house, 14 Leverstock Avenue, Hampstead. Would be grateful if you could attend and give assistance.

We immediately took a cab and on our arrival were met by Lestrade who conducted us to what at first sight appeared to be a bundle of old clothes, lying under a bush. It had been found, he informed us, earlier that afternoon by the house-agent who had been showing some prospective tenants over the property.

The body was unquestionably that of Juan Alberdi although we identified it less by the features than by the clothing and the gold crucifix about its neck. The method of murder, however, was immediately apparent. A knife of curious workmanship protruded between the shoulder blades, the top of the handle in the form of a small, squat figure of a man with bulging eyeballs and hideously lolling tongue.

'Mexican,' Holmes said briefly. 'An Aztec design. I think we may safely assume that this murder is Gasca's handiwork. After Alberdi sought him out, Gasca had to kill him. He knew too much.'

Lestrade greeted our news with a sombre expression. 'At least we have a positive identification,' he said. 'There is precious little else to go on.'

It appeared that no one in the neighbouring houses had heard or seen anything suspicious during the previous weeks so there was no evidence as to when the body had been left in the garden, who had brought it there or where the murder had taken place.

As for the Inspector's inquiries at the hotels, these had been almost as unproductive. There had been several likely candidates who had moved out of their rooms at about the time of Persano's death: an elderly white-haired invalid with two male attendants, a French gentleman and his son, and two brothers, one tall and both dark-skinned, who had claimed to be Italian.

A watch on all the ports had also yielded nothing. As Lestrade had no detailed descriptions and Gasca and his accomplice or accomplices were, as Holmes had pointed out, doubtless travelling with false papers, he had very little information. It was possible that Gasca was already on the high seas, having embarked at Liverpool or some other port.

Holmes remained in low spirits for several weeks after Persano's death and the discovery of Alberdi's body. Indeed, it was not until the arrival one morning, at his lodgings, of a client who heralded his involvement in the curious adventure of the Ramsgate recluse and his encounter with the extraordinary Lady Studberry that he recovered his former ebullience.

As for the case of the remarkable worm, he counted it as one of his failures. Not only had he lost a friend but he had been unable, despite his great deductive powers, to bring Gasca to justice, although he never gave up hope.

As he remarked to me, 'One day, Watson, I hope to see Gasca standing in an English court of law, charged with the double murder of Isadora Persano and Juan Alberdi.'

In the meantime, he has refused to allow me to publish an account of the inquiry. Nothing I can say has been able to dissuade him from this resolve and I have had to be content with writing out my own narrative of the case, making only a passing reference to it in the chronicles of those adventures of Sherlock Holmes which my old friend has permitted me to place before the public.*

* Dr John H. Watson refers to the case in 'The Problem of Thor Bridge'. (Dr John F. Watson)

THE CASE OF THE EXALTED CLIENT

Although the account of the following adventure cannot be published either in Holmes's lifetime or mine and may, indeed, never see the light of day, I have nevertheless decided to commit it to paper and to deposit it among my other unpublished records rather than allow it to pass into oblivion, in the hope that in the far distant future some editor of the exploits of my old friend, the great consulting detective, might see fit to print it.

As far as the present situation is concerned, Holmes is quite adamant; the case must not be made public. It is his unshakeable resolve that the confidences of certain persons of exalted rank who have sought his services in private must be preserved at all costs and must not be referred to, even in passing.* I have given Holmes my word on this. Therefore no mention of the inquiry will be found anywhere in the published chronicles.

I must confess, however, that my decision to make my own record of the case is due in part measure to the role I played in it, as well as to the unusual circumstances which surrounded it.

The adventure began at the time after my marriage when, my wife having gone to Sussex to nurse her elderly aunt, I had moved back temporarily to my old lodgings at 221B Baker Street which, in my bachelor days, I had shared with Holmes.

* Dr John H. Watson refers to Mr Sherlock Holmes's refusal to allow the publication of cases involving 'the secrets of private families' in 'exalted quarters' in the opening paragraph of 'The Problem of Thor Bridge'. (Dr John F. Watson)

It was one of those foggy mornings in late November when it was almost impossible to see across the street to the houses opposite, while the passing cabs and pedestrians loomed suddenly into sight before vanishing once again into the thick, ochre-coloured mist like so many spectres.

The weather had an adverse effect on Holmes's spirits. He was in a sombre mood, sent his breakfast away almost untouched and retired to the sofa, where he lay smoking and staring up silently at the ceiling.

Even the arrival of the morning's post failed to rouse him.

'You open it, Watson,' he told me. 'It is bound to be nothing but bills. It is too much to expect such a wretched day to produce anything of interest.'

The first two were indeed bills, one from his tailor and one from his bookseller, which I propped up on the mantelpiece until he should find the strength of mind to deal with them. But the third was a different matter altogether.

'It is from a Mrs Mary Woods, requesting an interview,' I said, opening the envelope and glancing at the sheet of paper it contained.

'What does she require of me? To find her lost pet dog?' Holmes inquired in a bored manner.

'There is no mention of any dog. On the contrary, the lady writes that the matter is of extreme urgency and delicacy.'

I saw a spark of interest show in Holmes's deep-set eyes but he merely said with the same indifferent air, 'Be a good fellow and read it out loud to me. I really cannot summon up the energy to bestir myself.'

Having cleared my throat, I did as he requested.

'"Dear Mr Holmes, I understand you are a gentleman in whom one may place one's trust. I have a matter of extreme urgency and delicacy which I should be most grateful to discuss with you in complete confidence. I therefore request an interview with you at three o'clock on Tuesday afternoon." Why, that's today, Holmes!' I broke off to exclaim. 'The letter is signed Mary Woods, Mrs. There is, by the way, no address although it carries yesterday's date.'

'And what other deductions have you made about the letter?' Holmes inquired.

'Well,' I began, hesitating a little for, knowing Holmes's own detective skills, I have never felt confident about putting forward my own opinions. 'The paper the letter is written on is of an excellent quality; most expensive, I should say, and possibly hand-made. It is strange, therefore, that there is no engraved address at the top of the sheet. More remarkable still, the envelope does not match the writing-paper. It is white and of a much inferior quality.'

'What do you deduce from that?'

'That Mrs Woods may have run out of matching envelopes?'

'Hum!' Holmes exclaimed in a sceptical tone. 'But pray go on, Watson. What can you tell me about the lady's handwriting?'

'The style is distinctive, educated and well formed on the whole although there is an irregularity in some places which suggests the writer was under considerable emotional strain. This is particularly evident in the signature.'

Without speaking, Holmes held out a languid hand and I passed the letter to him to read, eagerly waiting to hear how far my own deductions were correct. I was gratified to see that, after only a few seconds' perusal, he sat up, suddenly alert, his aquiline features assuming an expression of keen attention.

'You are quite right about the quality of the paper,' he remarked. 'It is indeed hand-made and is sold exclusively by Threadwell and Barnet, the Bond Street stationers. I have spent several years studying different types of paper, both their manufacture and their chemical and organic components, with the idea of writing a monograph on the subject. As for the absence of an address at the top, that is easily accounted for. Our correspondent has been careful to use a plain continuation sheet which carries no engraved heading. You are also correct, my dear fellow, in discerning that the handwriting shows signs of stress although you failed to notice that it is a young woman's. Take my word for it. I have also made a study of handwriting styles and how they relate to the correspondent's age. But you were wrong on two particular points.'

'Was I, Holmes?' I asked, a little crestfallen. 'What were they?'

'Firstly, the envelope. It is highly unlikely that a young lady who can afford such expensive writing-paper should be forced to use an inferior envelope merely because, as you suggested, she has run out of supplies of any others. It is much more probable that she has chosen the white envelope deliberately because those which matched the paper bore some distinguishing mark such as a family crest or a coat of arms. As for the signature, while it indeed bears signs of stress, it demonstrates something much more interesting – an attempt to cover up her real identity. If you look more closely at it, Watson, you will see that the "y" on the end of "Mary" is almost closed and resembles a letter "g". I believe that our correspondent, no doubt under emotional strain as you rightly observed, began to write her correct name which is Margaret and then, realizing her mistake, left that part of her signature incomplete, hoping it would be read as "Mary".'

'So she is really Mrs Margaret Woods?'

'I doubt that very much. If we accept that her Christian name is false, I think we may safely assume that her surname is also part of a *nom de plume*. Now from past experience, I have noticed that those who wish to hide their identity under an alias, whether for innocent or guilty purposes, usually choose one which approximates to their real name. It is more easily remembered and saves the embarrassment of hesitation when one is unexpectedly asked to use it or respond to it. Remember Harry Johnson, the notorious confidence-trickster? His aliases were Sir Henry St John-Smythe, Lieutenant-Colonel Jonathan Harrison and Jan Henrikson, the South African diamond millionaire. But to return to our correspondent who signs herself as Mrs Mary Woods. *Woods*, Watson! Mark that fact. Mark also the other deductions I have drawn from the letter, including her real Christian name, Margaret, the expensive quality of the paper, the handwriting style, the lack of address at the top of the letter and the use of the plain white envelope. Taken all together, I think we may safely assume that our prospective client is a young, wealthy and titled lady whose correct name, address and coat of arms would immediately identify her.'

Seeing by my puzzled expression that I had not yet grasped the significance of his remarks, he leaned forward and, taking down from the bookcase volume 'W' in his encyclopedia of reference, he turned to a page before silently handing the book to me.

The entry read:

Welbourne, Duchess of; Margaret Elizabeth Helena, formerly Lady Margaret Desbois, only daughter of Sir Hugo Desbois of Parkwood, Surrey. Presented at Court in 1885. Married in 1887 to George Henry Lancelot, seventh Duke. Well-known society beauty and hostess; also patroness of many charities including: The League for the Reclamation of Fallen Women, the Orphans' Benevolent Society and the Association for the Improved Education of the Labouring Poor. Addresses: Carlton House Terrace, London; Heywood Hall, Norfolk; Drumlochlie Castle, Scotland.

'Good Lord, Holmes!'

'Exactly,' said he. 'You now see, I assume, the significance of the surname "Woods"?'

'Yes, of course. But why should the Duchess of Welbourne wish to consult you under conditions of such secrecy?'

'Is not that obvious, my dear fellow? The matter of extreme urgency and delicacy to which she refers in her letter can only involve some indiscreet action on her part. If it were merely the theft of her jewels, she would not describe it in those terms. I strongly suspect that she has been indulging in some romantic liaison and is now being blackmailed.'

'How can you be so sure?'

'If the affair were still undiscovered, she would hardly need to confide in me. In my experience, ladies of her rank and distinction do not usually consult private detective agents unless there is a threat of scandal. Besides, consider the lady's situation. She is young and beautiful . . .'

'Yes, indeed, she is!' I agreed warmly. 'I saw the pictures of her in the illustrated papers at the time of her marriage to the Duke.'

I did not add, being a little sensitive about Holmes's reaction, that I had cut out one particular illustration of the wedding which I had kept in my desk for several weeks. In it, the Duke and Duchess were seen emerging from St Margaret's, Westminster, she with her bridal veil thrown back, revealing the delicate beauty of her features and her large, brilliant eyes, the richness of her dark hair enhanced by the Welbourne diamond tiara. In comparison with her radiant youth, the Duke seemed taciturn in appearance with a proud, austere profile.

'And married', Holmes continued, ignoring my interruption, 'to a man much older than herself who is more interested in his country estates than accompanying his young wife to those social functions which her charitable activities as well as her position in society oblige her to attend. However, we shall know if my deductions are correct when the lady in question arrives this afternoon at three o'clock. If she is indeed who I think she is, she will not come in her own coach which is emblazoned with the ducal coat of arms but in an ordinary cab, her features hidden under a thick veil. But no covering can entirely disguise her appearance. The Duchess is distinguished by her height and her grace of carriage. She has also, I understand, a remarkably beautiful voice which is low and musical. But we shall see, Watson. We shall see.'

It was with considerable impatience that I waited for three o'clock, eager to discover if Holmes had been right in his predictions and whether his prospective client answered his description and was indeed the Duchess of Welbourne.

Holmes himself seemed unmoved by any such emotions and spent the intervening hours smoking and lounging on the sofa.

Shortly before the appointed time, I rose from my chair by the fire, where I had been reading in a desultory fashion, and took up a position by the window which overlooked the street. As I arranged the curtains to make sure they concealed me from view, I was somewhat disconcerted to hear Holmes give a sardonic chuckle behind me although, as the clock struck three and the sound of wheels was heard approaching through the fog, his own curiosity finally overcame him and he joined me at my vantage point in time to witness the arrival of a four-wheeler which drew up outside the house.

'You see, Watson,' he remarked with evident satisfaction as the door of the cab opened and a tall, graceful figure alighted, dressed in a long black cloak, her face and shoulders covered by a thick veil.

Moments later, we heard light footsteps mounting the stairs and Holmes, crossing to the door, ushered in his client. I, meanwhile, had hastily resumed my place by the hearth where I remained standing, in readiness to be introduced and in some trepidation at meeting so exalted a person.

'Mrs Woods?' Holmes inquired. 'Pray come in and be seated.'

She accepted the invitation without speaking, merely giving a small bow of acknowledgement before taking her seat in the armchair which Holmes had indicated, at the same time glancing in my direction as if to inquire into my presence in the room.

'This is Dr Watson, my colleague,' Holmes informed her. 'I can assure you, *madame,*' pronouncing the word with a French inflection, 'that he is totally trustworthy and that whatever you choose to say in his hearing, as well as mine, will be treated in the utmost confidence.'

Another slight inclination of her head indicated that she accepted Holmes's explanation and, as he and I seated ourselves in preparation for the interview, I took the opportunity to glance at her surreptitiously.

Despite the thick cloak and veil, neither of which she made any attempt to remove and which effectively hid her form and features, it was still possible to discern by the graceful manner in which she sat, her slender back held very erect, the head poised at an elegant angle, that the Duchess of Welbourne was both young and beautiful.

Remembering the picture of her in the illustrated paper, I fancied, as I took my seat, that I caught a gleam of that rich dark hair and a faint outline of those exquisite features under the heavy veil but I fear my imagination may have been too eager to supply these details.

She remained silent, as if reluctant to open the interview, and, after a few moments, Holmes addressed her directly, his manner grave and courteous.

'You mentioned in your letter, *madame*, that the matter on which you wished to consult me was one of great urgency and delicacy. May I suggest that it might concern an *affaire de coeur* which you are anxious should remain secret?'

She was too well-bred to show any overt emotional response although I noticed that her black-gloved hands stirred momentarily in her lap.

'You are quite correct, Mr Holmes, although I cannot possibly imagine how you came to such a conclusion,' she replied.

If I had any lingering doubts about her real identity, they were entirely banished when I heard her speak. Her voice, as Holmes had predicted, was low and musical, perfectly controlled like a well-modulated instrument and yet with a faint suggestion of *vibrato* on the lower notes which hinted at the emotional stress from which she was suffering.

'Although,' she continued, 'I should explain that the relationship was indiscreet; nothing more. However, as I am a married woman and my husband prizes his own and his family honour most highly, any breath of scandal could have the most dire consequences. I dread to think of my husband's reactions should any word of my imprudence reach his ears.'

At this point, the tremulous note in her voice became more pronounced and Holmes and I waited in silence until, with a proud lift of her veiled head, she indicated that she had regained her composure and could continue the interview.

'About six months ago, I had reason to attend a charity concert alone – that is, apart from my companion who usually accompanies me on such occasions. My husband's business affairs frequently take him out of town for long periods and, besides, he does not much enjoy social functions. At the concert, I was introduced to a young man, unmarried and of good family connections. In the course of our conversation during the interval, we discovered we had many interests in common, among them music and literature. He had in his possession, he told me, an 1863 first edition of the poems of

Verlaine and when I expressed a desire to see it, he promised to send it to me. The volume duly arrived with an accompanying letter and on returning the book I, in turn, wrote him a short letter of thanks. A little later, he wrote to me again, enclosing a donation to a charity with which I am connected and to which I replied, expressing my gratitude.

'You may imagine for yourself what subsequently occurred. The correspondence continued and grew more warm and intimate although it never transgressed the boundaries of friendship and we never met privately, only in public at certain social occasions attended by mutual friends and acquaintances. Innocent though these meetings were, they had the effect of deepening our regard for one another and I fear this warmth of feeling was expressed in our correspondence. However, Mr Holmes, in the wrong hands, those letters could be misinterpreted as evidence of an adulterous affair and could be used by my husband, if he ever learned of their existence, as grounds for a legal separation or even a petition for divorce, should he be so minded.'

'And you have been threatened with exposure of the letters?' Holmes asked. 'By whom?'

'That is the baffling part of it, Mr Holmes. I neither know the identity of the person who has written to me, threatening to reveal the correspondence, nor how my letters could have come into that person's possession. Apart from the first two exchanges of correspondence which were dictated to my secretary and transcribed by her on to the typewriting machine, and neither of which contained any expression open to misinterpretation, all other letters have been written by me in private in my own handwriting and no one, not even my secretary, can know that we have continued the correspondence.'

'Could they have been intercepted between the time you wrote them and they were posted?'

'That is not possible, Mr Holmes. I wrote the letters in the evening alone in my study, after my secretary had left the house. She does not live in but comes daily to deal mostly with the correspondence arising out of the charitable work with which I am associated. As soon as the letters were completed, I took them upstairs to my bedroom where they were locked away in a bureau to which only I have the key. They were never left lying about. The following day they were posted.'

'By whom?'

'By my companion.'

'Could she have had access to them?'

'No, Mr Holmes. Although most of the post is left in the hall for a manservant to handle, as I have a great deal of correspondence to attend to regarding the charities, some of which is urgent, I quite often arrange for my letters to be dealt with separately in order to catch an earlier collection. This is always done when I am taking an afternoon drive or visiting an acquaintance. The carriage is stopped at a convenient post-box, my companion then alights and places the letters inside it. I was most careful when the correspondence contained a letter to the gentleman to make sure that it was placed in the centre of the bundle and that I watched from the carriage to see that none of the letters was inadvertently dropped or held back; not that I have any reason to mistrust my companion. She is my former governess and a highly respectable person.'

'Who has access to your study?'

'Only my secretary and the housemaids.'

'And to your bedroom where the bureau is kept?'

'Again the housemaids. Also my companion. But none of them has a key to the bureau. The lock is a strong one and has never shown signs of having been forced.'

I thought Holmes put the next point with extreme delicacy.

'Is it possible that the gentleman could be involved – indirectly, of course; I imply nothing more – perhaps by being careless in leaving your letters lying about where a servant or casual visitor might have access to them?'

Even so, despite Holmes's discretion, the lady for the first time showed a strong response. Clearly angered, she lifted her chin below her veil and I swear I saw the glitter of her dark eyes.

'That is entirely out of the question, Mr Holmes! He is a gentleman of honour, utterly trustworthy and anxious to preserve his good name as well as mine. Any scandal would be as damaging to him as to me. It would not only destroy his standing in society but his regi . . .'

She broke off at this point, aware that her warmth of feeling might have betrayed her into revealing too much about the gentleman's identity. Then, recovering her self-control, she resumed her account.

'Since I received the letters threatening exposure, I have spoken to him and he has assured me that as soon as he had received and read my letters, they were locked up in his writing-box, to which only he has a key. The box has not been tampered with. I was as scrupulous with his, making sure that they were read in private and were immediately placed inside my bureau. In addition, both of us were most careful to mark our letters 'Private' so that they would not be opened by anyone except ourselves although it would appear that only my letters to him have been intercepted. However that has been achieved, I can assure you that there was no opportunity for an inquisitive servant to gain access to them. I need hardly add that, since I have received the first threatening letter, I have ceased all contact with the gentleman and all correspondence between us has been destroyed, together with the blackmailer's.'

'That is a great pity,' Holmes remarked. 'The blackmail letters might have contained many useful clues as to the writer's identity.'

'I did not dare keep them in case they, too, fell into the wrong hands,' the lady replied. 'Besides,' and here the slender shoulders made an involuntary movement suggesting a shudder of revulsion, 'I felt too contaminated by them to wish to preserve them. However, I can describe the letters to you. There were three in all, and I received them at intervals over the past few weeks. They were written in capitals in a hand I did not recognize on cheap paper, demanding that certain sums of money be sent to a Mr P. Smith, care of the Coventry Hotel, Newton Street in Bayswater. If I failed to do so, the writer would inform my husband of my relationship and exchange of correspondence with the gentleman.'

'Could the handwriting have been disguised?'

'That is possible. The capital letters were awkwardly formed as if written with the left hand although the style of the contents was fluent. The postmarks were always WC1.'

'Were there any spelling mistakes?'

The lady seemed surprised at the question.

'No, Mr Holmes. In fact, I should say that the letters displayed a good level of education.'

'And how were the threats carried out? Did the blackmailer, for example, enclose a copy of your letters? That is often the case in these situations.'

'Not in this instance. The writer merely quoted certain words and phrases I had used in my correspondence with the gentleman, placing them between inverted commas to show that they were direct references.'

'Indeed!' Holmes remarked, as if he found this significant. However, he made no further comment, merely continuing with his questioning. 'What sums of money were demanded?'

'The first was for twenty guineas, the second for fifty. I complied with the instructions and sent the money to the address I had been given. The third demand, which I received yesterday and which prompted me to write to you, requesting your assistance, was not for money this time but for a pair of pearl earrings. I do not know what to do, Mr Holmes! The earrings are not only extremely valuable but they are a family heirloom and, should I part with them, my husband is almost certain to notice their absence. He is due to return from the country next week for an important social function at which I shall be expected to wear them. How am I to explain what has happened to them and what am I to do in the future to protect myself against these demands and the continuing threat of exposure?'

At this appeal, spoken from the heart, Holmes rose from his chair and paced up and down the room silently for a few moments, deep in thought. All the while, the lady's veiled face was turned towards him, waiting with evident anxiety for his reply.

Then, as abruptly as he had risen, Holmes resumed his seat and, leaning forward, began to address her with great earnestness.

'The case has many extraordinary features, *madame,* but I believe it can be solved if you trust me and carry out my instructions without question. First, send the earrings as you have been instructed. No! No!' he insisted as she began to protest. 'It is essential that you do so otherwise the blackmailer will be forewarned and may be forced into taking more extreme action. See that they are posted off today without fail. I can guarantee that the earrings will be returned to you before your husband's arrival next week.

'Secondly, make sure that you are absent from home on Thursday afternoon between the hours of two and four. Can you arrange that?'

'Certainly, I can. But I do not see . . .'

'Without question!' Holmes reminded her.

She acquiesced with a gesture of one black-gloved hand.

'Excellent! Then, *madame,* if you care to return here on Friday afternoon at the same hour, I believe I shall have good news for you.'

'Can you guarantee the return of the earrings, Holmes?' I asked when he returned to the room after having escorted the lady downstairs to her waiting cab. 'Isn't that promising rather too much so early in the case?'

'I think not,' he replied.

'But that surely implies that you already know the identity of the blackmailer?'

'I am almost certain although I shall be quite positive of that by tomorrow.'

'I do not see how,' I persisted, a little exasperated by his self-assurance. There were times when I found Holmes over-confident of his own abilities.

'From the evidence, my dear fellow.'

'What evidence? You have not even examined the blackmail letters. I cannot possibly see what evidence you are referring to.'

'Then allow me to recapitulate the facts for your benefit. The Duchess of Welbourne, alias Mrs Woods, enters into an indiscreet correspondence with a gentleman. The letters are written by her in private in her own handwriting, posted under her supervision and kept locked up by him in a box which shows no sign of having been tampered with. There would appear to be no means by which her letters could have been intercepted. And yet an anonymous blackmailer has managed to gain access to her correspondence and to threaten our client with exposure, quoting certain words and phrases from the lady's letters. Note that particular fact, Watson. "Certain words and phrases". It is not without relevance to the inquiry.

'As to the blackmailer, we can deduce certain irrefutable evidence concerning his or her identity. Much of it is, I admit, negative but it has always been one of my most firmly held maxims that, in the process of deduction, negative evidence can be as useful as the positive sort. Given that tenet, what do we know that the blackmailer is *not* which can be advantageous to the inquiry?'

'I really cannot say, Holmes,' I replied, surprised by this novel approach to the investigation.

'Oh, come, my dear Watson! Is it not obvious? The person who is threatening our client is not an expert although, when I first read her letter and deduced she was being blackmailed, I assumed that some professsional extortionist was behind it who makes his living from preying on wealthy victims. But, having heard the lady's account, I am now convinced that this is not so in her case. The sums of money involved are too small. The man I have in mind* would expect to milk his clients of several thousand pounds, not a few guineas. And he would certainly not demand jewellery as part of his payment. Jewels are too difficult to dispose of. It would involve a receiver of stolen property, which would lead to complications and the introduction into the transaction of a third party who might betray him or resort to blackmail himself. No; the man I was thinking of deals strictly in cash and keeps his business entirely in his own hands.

* Mr Sherlock Holmes is doubtless referring to Charles Augustus Milverton, 'the king of all blackmailers', whose death at the hands of one of his high-born victims is chronicled in 'The Adventure of Charles Augustus Milverton'. (Dr John F. Watson)

'Then there is the question of the earrings themselves. Knowing as we do the real identity of Mrs Woods, I assume that the family heirlooms to which she referred are the Welbourne pearls, a pair of perfectly-matched, pear-shaped drops, quite flawless and of a rare *rosé* colour, famous for their translucency and orient, as the surface lustre is known in the jewellery trade. What possible reason would a professional blackmailer have for acquiring them? They are too well-known for any receiver to dare to handle them and they cannot be broken up. Had the blackmailer demanded the Welbourne diamonds, which could have been sold on as separate stones, I might have been persuaded that the extortionist knew exactly what he or she was doing. And that raises the whole question of the motive behind the threats. However, there is not time to discuss that particular aspect of the case for the present. Fetch your hat and coat, Watson. We are going out.'

'Where to?' I asked.

'To the Coventry Hotel in Newton Street,' he replied. 'I wish to test out a theory.'

It would have been quicker to walk to Newton Street. The journey by hansom through the fog was painfully slow, the cabby not daring to urge the horse into anything faster than a walk and, at some of the busier crossroads, we came to a complete standstill while the driver listened for approaching vehicles before venturing forward.

Holmes fretted at the delay but there was nothing he could do to hasten the journey and it was almost an hour before we alighted outside the Coventry Hotel.

It was a small establishment, intended for the use of clients of modest means who could not afford more luxurious accommodation. The foyer was shabbily furnished and the only person on duty was an elderly clerk behind the reception desk who seemed to be slightly deaf, for he leaned forward to catch Holmes's request.

'I have come to collect some correspondence which has been forwarded to me here. The name is Sanderson.'

'Sanderson?' repeated the man, cupping a hand round one

ear. 'There ain't bin nothin' delivered 'ere for anyone of that name.'

'You must be mistaken, my man. I can quite clearly see some packets in the pigeon-hole marked "S" behind you,' Holmes insisted, pointing to a rack on the wall for the storage of residents' post. 'Would you kindly check that neither of those is for me?'

The clerk removed the packets and placed them on the counter, announcing as he did so, 'There you are! They're addressed to a Mr P. Smith, not Sanderson.'

'I am so sorry,' Holmes apologized and, handing over a shilling, he took me by the arm and drew me away from the counter, commenting loudly as he did so on the unreliability of the postal service.

Once outside the hotel, however, he gave a gratified chuckle.

'Just as I thought, Watson! The money has not been collected; another piece of negative evidence to add to what we already know about the identity of the blackmailer. I am now in possession of nearly all the data I need. All that remains is to collect the final facts which will lead to the unmasking. I believe you will be returning home tomorrow? I remember your telling me that you expected Mrs Watson to arrive at Victoria on the ten-fifteen train on Wednesday.'

'Yes, Holmes. I was proposing to leave tomorrow morning immediately after breakfast.'

'A pity. But no doubt Mrs Watson could spare you for a couple of hours after luncheon on Thursday afternoon?'

'I am sure she would be agreeable.'

'She is a woman of commendable tolerance,' Holmes remarked. 'Then, if you are quite certain she will not object, be good enough to call in at Baker Street promptly at two o'clock. I believe you will find the events that will take place later that afternoon of particular interest.'

He would say nothing more on the subject either on the journey home or during the rest of the evening and, as soon as dinner had been served and cleared away by Mrs Hudson, he retired to his room, on purpose, I suspected, to avoid my questioning, and spent the rest of the intervening hours until bedtime playing the violin, leaving me alone by the fire to ponder over the case.

I confess I could make little of it. The negative evidence which, according to Holmes, pointed to the identity of the blackmailer, remained an enigma. Nor could I see the reason behind the threats of exposure. If monetary gain was not the motive, what possible purpose was served by it?

Holmes was as disinclined to discuss the case the following morning over breakfast and, apart from a brief remark that he was pleased to see that the fog had lifted, he turned his attention to reading the newspapers, making no reference to the case in hand except obliquely when I was about to depart.

'You have not forgotten, my dear fellow, our arrangements for Thursday afternoon? I can expect you no later than two o'clock?'

'I shall be here on the hour,' I assured him.

Despite my pleasure at my wife's return and the resumption of our domestic life together, I have to admit that it was with considerable impatience that I looked forward to the following afternoon, eager to discover what would be the events to which my old friend had referred and wondering if they involved the unmasking of the blackmailer.

Promptly at two o'clock, as arranged, I again presented myself at 221B Baker Street and, having been admitted by the page-boy, made my way upstairs.

Although the fog had cleared, the weather was still overcast and, in the gloomy light of that November afternoon, the sitting-room was mostly in shadow, apart from the red glow thrown out by the fire which was blazing cheerfully in the grate.

There was no sign of Holmes, the only occupant of the room being an elderly clergyman seated beside the hearth.

I was annoyed at my old friend's absence. I had hurried over my luncheon in order to be exactly on time to find that not only had he gone out and had not yet returned but there was another client waiting to see him whose business would clearly delay us still further.

'Good afternoon,' I said a little sharply, addressing the elderly clergyman and allowing my impatience to show.

"Good afternoon,' said he, rising to his feet and peering at me myopically.

He was a tall old gentleman, dressed in clerical attire, with thinning white hair and whiskers and very bowed about the shoulders. His age, I estimated, was in the late seventies.

'You, too, are waiting, I see, for Mr Holmes to return,' I continued more pleasantly, a little ashamed, in the face of his obvious age and infirmity, of my earlier impatience.

'Indeed not. I was waiting for your arrival, Watson,' he replied unexpectedly. As he spoke, he threw back his shoulders and in that instant changed, apart from the outward trappings of his disguise, into the figure of my old friend and companion.

'Good Lord! Holmes!' I exclaimed. 'This is most extraordinary! I could have sworn that I had never set eyes on you before.'

'Then my disguise is obviously successful. But come, Watson,' he urged. 'Time is short. You have to change and then we have an appointment to keep at Carlton House Terrace for three o'clock.'

'What on earth are you talking about?' I demanded, bewildered by this turn of events. 'What appointment? I remember you specifically asked Her Grace, the Duchess, to be absent from home on Thursday afternoon between two and four. And why should I have to change? Into what, my dear fellow?'

'Into the Reverend James Applewhite. I have the necessary ecclesiastical garb here,' Holmes replied, reaching behind the armchair and retrieving a large brown-paper parcel. 'Clerical collar. Black coat and trousers. Black silk stock. While you are making your transformation, I shall give you a full explanation.'

This he did through the half-open door of the bedroom where I scrambled out of my own outer clothing and replaced it with the clergyman's attire.

'You and I, Watson, are highly-respected members of the Committee for the Relief of Anglican Clergymen's Orphans and Widows, a most worthy cause, I assure you. In my capacity as Canon Cornelius Blythe-Wilson, chairman of the committee, I have written to a certain titled lady, well known for her benevolence, requesting an interview for three o'clock this afternoon in order to explain our aims and to prevail on her generosity for a donation to our funds. As you pointed out, Her Grace will unfortunately not be at home. However, I have every hope that she has left instructions that we are to be admitted into the house.'

At this point, having put on my black clerical coat and examined myself critically in the cheval glass, I emerged from the bedroom, well pleased with what I had seen, and was further gratified by Holmes's response.

'I say, my dear fellow! What a conversion! Had you not chosen medicine, I am sure you would have made an admirable vicar although with low church leanings, I suspect, rather than high Anglican aspirations. However, you make a most convincing-looking member of the clergy; apart, that is, from the broad smile. May I suggest a more serious expression? Ah, that is much better! Do try to remember that philanthropy is a very grave subject, not to be treated with levity. Here is your card, by the way. Pray do not lose it.'

He handed me a small pasteboard oblong which I glanced at quickly before stowing it away safely in an inner pocket. It read:

THE REVEREND JAMES APPLEWHITE M.A. (Oxon.)

Secretary

(Committee for the Relief of Anglican Clergymen's Orphans & Widows)

'I had my card and yours printed, together with a sheet of the Committee's headed writing-paper, by a jobbing printer in Clerkenwell, Gill by name,' Holmes explained. 'I also spent part of yesterday afternoon undertaking a little research at the offices of the *Morning Gazette*, a most excellent journal which covers in great detail all important society functions and which also keeps a library of back editions. I am quite sure I have established the identity of the "certain gentleman" whose interest in music and poetry caught the attention of our exalted client. You will no doubt recall, Watson, that "Mrs Woods" told us they first met at a charity concert six months ago? That, I believe, was a recital of chamber music given by Lady Veyse-Chomleigh on May 6th, tickets five guineas each by private subscription only, the proceeds to be donated to the Society for the Promulgation of Bible Studies in Fiji.

'According to the *Morning Gazette,* among the distinguished audience were the Duchess of Welbourne and Lord Paxton, heir to the Marquis of Salthurst and an officer in the Buff and Royals, who had recently returned from India, where his regiment had been serving, in order to take up a post as equerry to Her Majesty. You can therefore appreciate, I am sure, Watson, that any scandal concerning him and a married lady with whom he was conducting an imprudent correspondence would have serious repercussions in royal circles.'

The sound of hoofs clattering to a halt was heard at the street door and Holmes broke off to remark, 'I believe our cab has arrived. I ordered a four-wheeler for half past two in preference to a hansom, which I thought an unsuitable conveyance for two respectable clergymen; far too lightweight and frivolous. And speaking of frivolity, Watson, please remember the expression!'

With that final warning, he preceded me down the stairs, assuming the uncertain gait of an elderly gentleman, while I followed behind him still aghast at the implications of what he had just told me.

A scandal which could involve not only a duchess but an equerry to the Queen!

I could only trust, as I took my seat beside him in the cab and Holmes instructed the driver in a quavering voice, 'Carlton House Terrace, my man!' that the expedition on which we were embarking would be successful in revealing the identity of the blackmailer.

These thoughts occupied my mind until our arrival at Carlton House Terrace where we alighted and where Holmes ordered the cabby to wait.

My concern was temporarily forgotten, however, in my admiration for Nash's magnificent building with its lofty façade and Corinthian columns and, as we mounted the steps to the Duchess of Welbourne's residence, I felt more than a little awed by its splendour.

On presenting our cards, we were admitted by a liveried

footman, who had evidently been told to expect us, into a large entrance hall, hung with family portraits, and from there were conducted up a wide staircase.

Once we had reached the upper gallery, we were shown into a room on the first floor, probably intended, judging by the elegance of its fittings, to serve originally as a small withdrawing-room or a lady's boudoir but transformed into a well-furnished but practical study. Glass-fronted cabinets containing books and files lined the walls while a rosewood desk with ormolu fittings was placed directly in front of the window which overlooked St James's Park.

Just inside the door and standing at right-angles to it was another plainer and more serviceable desk, equipped with a typewriting machine and other office impedimenta in the way of racks for stationery and receptacles for stamps and india-rubber bands.

A lady, who was seated at this desk engaged in addressing envelopes, rose to her feet as the footman announced us.

In appearance she was as plain and as serviceable-looking as the desk itself, dressed from throat to toes in plain brown holland, its drabness unrelieved by any frill or ornament apart from a pair of gold pince-nez hanging on a chain round her neck, her mouse-coloured hair dragged back into a severe bun.

'I am Miss Gordon, the Duchess of Welbourne's private secretary,' she said, holding out a chilly hand for us to shake. 'Her Grace very much regrets that she is unable to receive you personally. She has another engagement elsewhere. However, she has instructed me to express her interest in your charitable organization and to pass on to you this donation to assist you in your work.'

At the end of this homily, uttered without a glimmer of benevolence, she picked up an envelope which was lying on her desk and passed it to Holmes who bowed and immediately launched in a reedy old man's voice into a speech of his own, a little rambling and repetitive, expressing his gratitude not only on behalf of the committee he represented but of the widows and orphans of deceased Anglican clergymen whose burdens would be considerably lightened by Her Grace's generosity.

At the same time, as if trying to keep Miss Gordon in focus through short-sighted eyes, he took several tottering steps forward at which Miss Gordon promptly retreated, keeping her distance from this elderly, garrulous cleric, until, by the time Holmes had finished speaking, they had advanced into the centre of the room.

Here he paused, blinked all round him and having remarked inconsequentially on the view from the window – 'How delightful it must be for Her Grace to sit here and look out at God's creation!' – he retreated once more towards the door where I was waiting for him, taking care to look suitably grave although I was highly diverted by Holmes's performance.

We left shortly afterwards, climbing back into the four-wheeler, Holmes instructing the cabby to drive us to the Coventry Hotel.

Once inside the cab, he broke out into a fit of silent laughter and it was several moments before he had sufficiently recovered his composure to inquire, 'Well, Watson, what did you think of our interview with Miss Gordon?'

'You were capital, Holmes. You played the part to perfection.'

'I thought you put on a very good performance yourself, my dear fellow.'

'Did I? But I cannot see,' I continued, expressing a doubt which had occurred to me while we had been in the Duchess's study, 'what possible use that little charade of ours can be to the investigation.'

Although I would not have dreamed of admitting it to Holmes, I was disappointed at the outcome of the interview. I had secretly hoped for a dramatic scene of confrontation in which Holmes, throwing off his disguise, would point an accusing finger at the culprit, the police would be sent for and the blackmailer would be marched off in handcuffs.

But nothing of the sort had happened.

I could not even be certain that Holmes had found the final piece of evidence which he had assured me would lead to the positive identification of the criminal. Was it Miss Gordon? If so, what had he discovered that proved her guilt? Or was it the footman? Or the housemaid we had passed in the upstairs corridor?

Holmes, meanwhile, seemingly unperturbed by such questions, was getting out his pocket-book.

'Allow me to give you this,' he said, handing me the envelope containing the Duchess's donation. 'It would appear to contain two guineas which I am sure the inestimable Mrs Watson will be able to give to some worthy cause. May I also ask you to take charge of this for the time being?'

As he spoke, he began removing his clerical neckband which he passed to me, substituting for it a starched collar and a grey silk cravat which he took from his coat pocket. A gold watch and chain looped across his waistcoat front and a pair of steel-rimmed spectacles perched on his nose completed the transformation. In a few seconds, he had thrown off his role of an elderly cleric and had assumed that of a retired clerk or shopkeeper, dressed in old-fashioned black attire.

'Mr P. Smith, dealer in antiquarian curios, semi-retired and resident in Brighton. As I can only get up to town from time to time, I occasionally ask my clients to forward any items for appraisal to a convenient hotel. It saves the trouble of carrying them up to London on the train. Here is my card,' he explained, producing it from his waistcoat pocket. 'I asked Gill to run it off for me yesterday when he printed the other items. And now,' he continued, as the four-wheeler approached the Coventry Hotel, 'I shall only be a few moments, Watson, collecting my curios. Wait for me here. We shall take the same cab back to Baker Street.'

He was as good as his word. Within minutes, he had returned, carrying not two but three packets, the third a little larger than the others.

'The Welbourne pearls,' he said in a low voice, turning it over in his hands as soon as he had given directions to the driver and the cab had started off. 'Are you not curious to see them, Watson? I know I am. Although the packet is sealed with wax, I am sure I could open it without arousing the owner's suspicions.'

'Now look here, Holmes – !' I began.

I was not only about to protest at this suggestion, eager though I was to see the famous Welbourne heirlooms, but also to demand a full explanation. It seemed beyond doubt that Holmes had reached a conclusion regarding the identity of the blackmailer, for he clearly intended to return the earrings the following afternoon to his client.

But Holmes forestalled me. Placing a finger against his lips to advise silence, he indicated the cab-driver's back and, seeing the wisdom of his warning, I was forced to contain my impatience.

Even when we were installed in the privacy of his rooms in Baker Street, Holmes was still not prepared to offer an account.

Without waiting to remove his disguise, he carried the package over to his desk, selected a small scalpel from among his scientific instruments and, with one dexterous movement, sliced through the wax seal. Unfolding the brown paper, he revealed a small jeweller's box with the ducal coat of arms stamped in gold on the lid. Inside, nestling in a cocoon of quilted satin lay the Welbourne pearl earrings.

At the sight of them, my curiosity overcame me and I pressed forward to look over Holmes's shoulder at the jewels.

They were exquisite; two perfectly-formed, lustrous drops of a delicate rose-pink colour and glowing with such a deep nacreous sheen that they seemed as if they must contain in the hidden heart of them some soft, living radiance of their own.

'Impressed as I am by their beauty,' Holmes remarked, 'as a student of chemistry, I can only wonder that a concretion, largely composed of the common inorganic compound calcium carbonate which has been produced by a sea-water mollusc in order to isolate an irritant inadvertently introduced into its shell, should be considered such a valuable rarity. And now,' he added, more briskly, snapping shut the lid of the box, 'we have more practical matters to attend to. You, Watson, must change out of your clerical disguise. It might tax Mrs Watson's tolerance too far if you returned home dressed as you are. I, meanwhile, have a letter to write which must catch this afternoon's post.'

Even before I had retired to the bedroom to change, he had seated himself at his desk and had commenced writing. By the time I returned, the letter was finished and Holmes was in the act of handing it to Billy, the page-boy, with instructions to run to the nearest post-box in order to catch the five o'clock collection.

The boy in buttons having departed, Holmes turned his chair about to face me.

'I know what you are waiting for, my old friend, and your patience shall now be rewarded. I propose to reveal to you the identity of the blackmailer and to give you a complete account of how I reached my conclusion.'

'About time, too, Holmes,' I remarked, taking a seat by the fire and giving him my full attention.

'It was quite evident from the interview with our client that someone among her own staff had gained access to her letters,' Holmes began. 'Note that fact, Watson. *Her* letters; not his. That is crucial to the investigation. The question was – who? There seemed to be several possible candidates but I was able to eliminate all but one on the basis of negative evidence, the importance of which I stressed at the beginning of this inquiry.

'Firstly, it could have been one of the housemaids whose duties took them into both the study and Her Grace's bedroom where she kept her letters before they were posted. But that seemed unlikely. The letters were securely locked in the bureau and besides, the blackmailer was evidently educated, could spell correctly and could express him or herself with ease. Most ordinary servants have no more than an elementary education.

'Then there was the footman who, under normal circumstances, would have been responsible for collecting any correspondence and seeing that it was posted. Again, he had to be eliminated. The lady's letters had not been handed to the footman but had been placed in a post-box by her companion and former governess.

'What of the lady-companion then? She had accompanied Her Grace to the concert and no doubt to other social functions and could have witnessed our client in conversation with the gentleman, from which she could have deduced that a relationship was forming. She was also asked to post the letters to him and could have read his name and address on the envelopes. But did she have the opportunity? Our client insisted that she placed these letters inside a bundle of other correspondence and her companion had no time to examine the separate items. Besides, like the housemaids, she had no access to the bureau.

'This left the secretary, Miss Gordon . . .'

'Now, wait a moment, Holmes!' I protested. 'She, too, can surely be eliminated on the basis of negative evidence? She had no access to the bureau either and I cannot see how she knew that the correspondence had continued.'

Holmes leaned back in his chair, his expression indulgent.

'Go on, Watson. Pray explain your theory.'

'Well,' I began a little hesitantly, struggling to put my argument into a cogent form. 'The Duchess of Welbourne specifically stated that, apart from the first two letters which Miss Gordon produced on the typewriting machine and which were merely formal, all subsequent correspondence with the gentleman was conducted in private, after Miss Gordon had left the house, and was written in Her Grace's own hand. The letters were then locked up in the bureau in the bedroom and were subsequently posted by the companion under the Duchess's supervision. As far as Miss Gordon was concerned, all contact with the gentleman had ceased after the exchange of those first two letters.'

'A valid objection on the basis of negative evidence and well argued, my dear fellow. My congratulations! But you have failed to take one important factor into account.'

'And what is that, Holmes?'

'The fact that the gentleman's letters were delivered to the house and would have been handled by Miss Gordon in the course of her normal duties. As they were marked "Private", she would not, of course, have opened them but she would have recognized the handwriting from her previous acquaintance with the first two letters. By that means, she was perfectly well aware that the correspondence had continued.'

'Oh, yes, I see,' I said, considerably dashed by this simple explanation. 'But how could Miss Gordon have known about the contents?'

'She had no knowledge of the contents of the gentleman's letters. Remember, Watson, I stressed that point from the beginning. I also stressed that the blackmailer was cognizant of *certain words and phrases* only from our client's correspondence. That, too, is vital. Can you offer an explanation for this fact?'

'I am afraid not, Holmes,' I confessed. 'It is quite beyond me.'

'Then permit me to do so. You may have noticed that, during our interview this afternoon with Miss Gordon, I took care to advance into the room, well beyond the doorway where her desk was placed. This was done with a purpose. I wished to examine the contents of the Duchess of Welbourne's desk, which was placed by the window and where she had sat in private to write her letters to the gentleman. What I saw laid out on its surface was most revealing. Apart from a solid silver desk-set of rare workmanship and a tray of stationery of the same quality as that on which she wrote her letter to me, there was a large leather-backed blotting-pad of the type which contains several sheets, the topmost of which can be easily removed once it has been used and which it would be Miss Gordon's duty to replace each morning before Her Grace arrived. All Miss Gordon had to do was to hold up an ordinary looking-glass in front of the discarded sheet and any words or phrases which had been written the evening before and had been absorbed into the blotter because the ink on them was still wet, could be easily read.'

'By Jove, Holmes! The answer is so obvious that I cannot for the life of me think why it didn't occur to me.'

'I believe I have remarked to you before that the most puzzling of mysteries usually has the simplest explanation. For that reason, it is often overlooked.'

'But I still fail to understand the motive. As you yourself pointed out, it cannot have been pecuniary. The sums asked for were too small and, besides, she made no attempt to collect the money. And why demand the earrings? She could not hope to make any money by selling them. They were too easily recognizable as part of the Welbourne family jewels.'

'Miss Gordon may have started off her blackmailing career with the intention of making money out of it but, when the time came, it is my belief that she was too frightened to go to the hotel to collect it. However, money was not her primary consideration. I think her main motivation arose out of malicious jealousy. That is why she demanded the earrings. They would be missed by the Duke when he returned to town and our client would have had an extremely difficult time explaining what had happened to them, a distress which Miss Gordon would have the pleasure of witnessing. The Germans have a word for it – *Schadenfreude,* which translated means "pleasure in the misfortune of others".

'Servants always know about such family tensions, however exalted the household and however careful the attempts may be to keep such disagreements concealed. And that, I believe, was the real reason behind the blackmail. Miss Gordon is a poor, unattractive spinster; our client a popular society hostess, famous for her beauty and philanthropy and married to a rich and powerful husband. We should perhaps pity the Miss Gordons of this world rather than condemn them. No doubt Miss Gordon considers that Fate has dealt her a very poor hand, as she would describe it. I prefer to regard it as the accident of birth. Perhaps, in all charity, we should consider her action as a protest against the prevailing social inequalities.'

'But what are you going to do about her, Holmes? Despite what you say, she has broken the law. You can hardly allow her to continue in the Duchess's employ.'

'The letter I wrote was to Miss Gordon. She will receive it tomorrow morning by the first delivery. In it, I have laid out the case against her and advised her to retire immediately from her post otherwise I shall be forced to name her as the blackmailer. I have left it to her own good sense to supply an excuse for her resignation. I do not believe that she will ever try blackmail again. She is not by nature a criminal. One has to have some faith in the goodness of mankind, or at least, most members of it, or one would become a mere misanthrope. For the same reasons, I shall leave the decision as to her ultimate future in the hands of our client. It will be interesting to see tomorrow afternoon when the Duchess of Welbourne again calls here exactly what she proposes to do about the sudden departure of her secretary. You will be present, will you not, Watson? I cannot imagine that you would want to miss the opportunity of witnessing the return of the Welbourne pearls and the final act of our little drama?'

'No, indeed not, Holmes,' I said warmly.

The appointment was for three o'clock and I returned to Baker Street in good time, well before the arrival of the Duchess.

As on the first occasion our client, heavily cloaked and veiled, arrived in a four-wheeler and was shown upstairs to where Holmes and I were waiting and where the packages were laid out in readiness on the desk, the one containing the pearls so skilfully rewrapped and sealed by Holmes that it was impossible to tell that it had ever been opened.

Holmes handed the three packets to her with a small bow, assuring her as he did so that there would be no further attempts at blackmail.

'You have my word for that, *madame*.'

'I do not know how to express my thanks, Mr Holmes,' the lady replied. 'I shall leave here with a happy heart. We did not, by the way, discuss your fees.'

'Your happiness is sufficient reward,' Holmes told her with a touch of Gallic gallantry.

'You are most kind. I shall make sure that the money you have returned to me is donated to some worthwhile charity. Would you agree that the Society for Distressed Gentlewomen might be suitable? Or would you recommend the Committee for the Relief of Anglican Clergymen's Orphans and Widows?'

The last question took Holmes completely aback and, unusually for him, he was at a loss for words.

'Perhaps the Society for Distressed Gentlewomen might be more worthy,' the lady continued, holding out a black-gloved hand to each of us in turn. 'And speaking of gentlewomen, Mr Holmes, you may be interested to know that my secretary, Miss Gordon, gave in her notice this morning. It appears she received a letter informing her that her mother has suddenly been taken ill. Consequently, she has had to leave my service in order to take care of her. I have arranged for a yearly annuity to be paid to Miss Gordon so that she will not be in any financial hardship and will not therefore be forced to seek a secretarial post elsewhere. On that understanding, I have not given her a reference.'

'A most generous decision,' Holmes murmured as he escorted her to the door. 'And, if I may be allowed to say so, also a wise one under the circumstances.'

A few minutes later, we heard her cab drive away.

There was, however, a small denouement to the case, or drama, as Holmes had described it. To expand on his metaphor, it was in the nature of a curtain-call in which he received the well-deserved acclaim for his undoubted skills.

A few days after the Duchess of Welbourne's final visit, my professional duties took me into the Baker Street area and I called in on my old friend to find him in the act of opening a small parcel which had not long been delivered by the afternoon post.

When the wrapping was removed, a solid silver cigar box was revealed, engraved with his initials on the lid and with a short inscription on the inside.

It read simply:

'To Mr Sherlock Holmes, Famous Consulting Detective, From a Grateful Client, Mary Woods.'

THE CASE OF THE NOTORIOUS CANARY-TRAINER

In 'The Adventure of Black Peter' I referred in passing to the other cases which engaged Holmes's attention in the year '95,* among them that of Wilson, the notorious canary-trainer whose arrest 'removed a plague-spot from the East End of London'.

In the same account, I also remarked on my old friend's capriciousness in refusing to help the powerful and wealthy where a problem failed to engage his sympathies, preferring to devote his time and effort to the affairs of some more humble client whose case appealed to his imagination and challenged his ingenuity.

Although these two references may appear to be unconnected except in the most general way, there is, in fact, a direct link between them which will be apparent only to those who were involved in the investigation.

As for the case itself, Holmes and I have spent many hours discussing the merits and demerits of publishing a full account of the facts.

On the one hand, it would bring to public attention a most unsavoury aspect of life in the great metropolis of London – and no doubt other cities, too – as well as serving as an awful

* These cases occurred after Mr Sherlock Holmes's apparent death at the hands of Professor Moriarty at the Reichenbach Falls in May 1891 and his return three years later in the spring of 1894. In the meantime, although the exact date is uncertain, Mrs Watson, *née* Mary Morstan, had died. *Vide* 'The Final Problem' and 'The Adventure of the Empty House'. (Dr John F. Watson)

warning to the young and gullible on whom such abominable creatures as Wilson and his accomplices have preyed.

On the other, we are most anxious not to offend the sensibilities of our readers, most particularly the fair sex and those gentlemen of a refined and sheltered upbringing to whom such revelations would be an all too shocking exposure of some of the worst aspects of our society.

After much earnest debate, Holmes and I have concluded that the present-day moral climate is not yet ready for the publication of the truth. However, I have my old friend's permission to make a record of the case which I shall preserve among my papers in the hope that, at some future date, a more robust readership will be prepared to accept in print the full and unexpurgated account of the case of Wilson, the notorious canary-trainer.

The adventure began prosaically enough one evening in January of '95 with the arrival at Holmes's rooms at 221B Baker Street of Mrs Annie Hare. I use the word 'prosaically' quite deliberately for there was nothing about either Mrs Hare herself or her story which suggested that the case she laid before us was anything more than a commonplace affair concerning a missing daughter, a misfortune which had, no doubt, happened to many other mothers in Mrs Hare's position.

In appearance, Mrs Hare herself was unremarkable. She was a small, slight woman, with worn features, shabbily dressed in black and with nothing more than an old red shawl over her shoulders, an inadequate covering for such a bleak winter's evening. Even as Mrs Hudson showed her into the sitting-room, Holmes and I, seated on either side of a blazing fire, could hear the wind rattling the window-frame and flinging handfuls of hard raindrops, like scatterings of gravel, against the panes.

I shall summarize her story as she was too much intimidated by Holmes's reputation and too inarticulate to relate it in a consecutive and coherent form. Indeed, it took much patient questioning on my friend's part to elicit all the facts of the case, which amounted to this.

She was the widow of a hansom-cab driver who, succumbing

to pneumonia, one of the hazards for anyone following that particular profession, had died several years before, leaving her with a daughter to support, which Mrs Hare had done by taking in washing and acting as charwoman to those of her neighbours in Bow, in the East End of London, who could afford the pitifully small charge she asked for her services.

But – and she was most anxious to stress this point – she had always kept herself decent and had brought up her daughter in a respectable manner. Indeed, the words 'decent' and 'respectable' figured largely in her account.

The daughter, whose name was Rosie – and in speaking of her Mrs Hare's eyes lit up and her haggard features took on an animation which suggested that she herself when young must have possessed a beauty of her own – was a pretty, intelligent girl who, in her mother's words, had been 'good at her schoolwork' and whose ambition it was to rise above her situation and to find employment either as a shop-assistant in a West End store or as a maidservant to a good family, aspirations which the mother had encouraged.

At this point in Mrs Hare's narrative, I saw Holmes's aquiline features soften with an expression of keen compassion, a response I shared. For what chance had a young woman from such a background and with, no doubt, a limited education of fulfilling such a dream?

Indeed, as Mrs Hare's account continued, it became apparent that both the young woman's and her mother's hopes had received an early set-back. On leaving school at the age of thirteen, Rosie had been able to obtain no better employment for herself that that of a trimmer in a wholesale milliner's in Wapping where she worked long hours in a basement room for the princely sum of five shillings and sixpence a week.

And then, the year before, when Rosie was fifteen, her fortune had suddenly changed.

An advertisement had appeared in the local newspaper, the *Bow and Wapping Gazette*, appealing for young women to apply for well-paid domestic posts in good-class households.

'Do you have the advertisement with you, Mrs Hare?' Holmes inquired.

She had and, taking a worn purse from her skirt pocket, handed a piece of paper to Holmes who, having read it and raised a quizzical eyebrow at its contents, passed it to me.

It had been carefully cut from the newspaper and read as follows:

> The Hon. Mrs Augustus Clyde-Bannister, Proprietress of the Exclusive Bellevue Domestic Agency, hereby invites Girls and Young Women between the ages of fourteen and eighteen to present themselves for a Private and Personal Interview at the Temperance Rooms, Patten Street, Bow on Friday afternoon next, May 4th, between the hours of two and six, for a few Select Vacancies for Parlourmaids, Nursery-maids and Ladies' Companions in the very best households.
>
> * No Experience Needed
> * Training Given Free
> * Wages of £50 a year Guaranteed
> * Positively no Deductions
> * Applicants must be of a Personable Appearance
>
> and of a Sober and Willing Disposition.

'May I keep this?' Holmes asked when I had returned the cutting to him, and, on receiving Mrs Hare's consent, he continued, 'I take it your daughter attended the interview?'

'She did, sir,' Mrs Hare replied. 'She asked for the afternoon off work, even though it meant losin' part of 'er wages, and went along to the address given in the paper. And Lor', sir! She said there was dozens of girls waitin'. It were gone four o'clock afore she was seen.'

'By the Honourable Mrs Clyde-Bannister, I assume. Did your daughter describe her to you?'

'She said she was a large lady, very well-spoken and dressed like a duchess in black silk. And diamond rings! Rosie said she'd never seen the like of them.'

As Mrs Hare continued, I noticed that Holmes's features, while not losing their expression of compassion, had grown sharper and more attentive as if the story itself, rather than the pitiable circumstances which surrounded it, had caught his interest.

To sum up the rest of Mrs Hare's account, it seemed that Rosie was only one of two successful applicants, the other being a young apprentice dressmaker named Mary Sullivan. The week following the interview, both young women were taken to live at the Hon. Mrs Clyde-Bannister's West End house, number 14 Cadogan Crescent, where for the next month they were to be trained in the duties of parlourmaids.

The training having been successfully completed, the two young women were then placed in households, Rosie Hare with the Duckham family in Streatham, Mary Sullivan somewhere in Hampstead although Mrs Hare did not know the exact address.

At first, Mrs Hare had received regular weekly letters from her daughter while she was living at Cadogan Crescent and with the Duckhams in Streatham, saying how happy she was and expressing her gratitude both to the Hon. Mrs Clyde-Bannister and to the Duckhams for their kindness.

When Holmes asked her if she had brought the letters with her, Mrs Hare produced a small packet from under her shawl, carefully wrapped up in brown paper, which Holmes said he would examine at his leisure and return to her at a later date.

And then the letters from her daughter had stopped coming.

'When was this?' Holmes asked.

'Five months ago, sir, in September last year,' Mrs Hare replied.

She went on to explain that she had waited for several weeks and then, thinking that her daughter might have been taken ill, had asked a neighbour to write on her behalf to Rosie at the Duckhams' address.

'You see, Mr 'Olmes,' she said, twisting one corner of her shawl nervously between her fingers, 'I never was much of a scholar, not like Rosie. I can't read nor write. This neighbour of mine, Mrs 'Arris, always read Rosie's letters to me. That's one of the reasons why I never went to the 'ouse when the letter I'd sent to Rosie was returned, marked "Gone Away" or somethin' like that on the envelope. I can't read the street names to find my way there and I couldn't ask Mrs 'Arris to come with me. She's got the five little ones to look after.'

'But you found your way here,' Holmes pointed out.

'Oh, that was different, Mr 'Olmes. Afore I married my Albert, I used to work as a charlady at an 'ouse in the next street, so I knows my way 'ere on foot. And anyway, I didn't like to turn up at the Duckhams' in case I got Rosie into trouble. She said that at the interview Mrs Clyde-Bannister asked perticular if she 'ad any family, 'cos she'd 'ad bother in the past with girls gettin' 'ome-sick. So Rosie said, no, she 'adn't. She was a n'orphan. That's why I've come to you, sir. I've 'eard you're a famous detective; but you're not like the regular police. I couldn't go to them. Even if they was interested in finding my Rosie, which I doubt, I wouldn't want them causin' trouble in case they lost Rosie 'er place. But you're different, sir. I wondered if you'd ask around, quiet-like, and find out what's 'appened and where the Duckhams 'ave moved to. I couldn't come afore this 'cos I 'ad to save up the money. I've got it now, though,' she added timidly. Fumbling again in her shabby purse, she took out some coins which she laid on the table. 'I don't know what your charges is but there's fifteen shillin's there.'

'Keep the money,' Holmes said, pressing it back into her hand.

'You mean you won't look for my Rosie?' Mrs Hare asked on the brink of tears.

'I mean, Mrs Hare, that I charge only by results and, in the case of an interesting investigation such as yours, there are no fees whatsoever. I shall certainly make inquiries about your daughter. I gather all the addresses I shall need, including yours, will be found in the letters? Then all I shall require from you at the moment is a description of your daughter.'

'Well, sir, she's a bit taller than me and she's got dark 'air and eyes. And, like I said, she's as pretty as a picture.'

'Any distinguishing features?' When Mrs Hare appeared not to understand, Holmes rephrased the question. 'Any scars or marks by which I might recognize her?'

'Oh, I see, sir. Yes; she 'as a mole on 'er neck just below 'er right ear; only a small one; more like a beauty spot.'

'Thank you, Mrs Hare,' Holmes said. 'That is all I shall need for the time being. I shall call on you in Bow when I have any news. And now, madam, I am going to order a cab for you. No, no!' He held up a hand as she began to protest. 'You cannot possibly walk all the way home in this weather. As for the fare, I shall see that the driver is paid. You can settle with me at some other time.'

'Oh, Mr 'Olmes, I don't know 'ow to thank you!' Mrs Hare cried.

Holmes looked deeply embarrassed.

'Please, no thanks,' he murmured, rising to his feet.

'And no comment from you either, Watson,' he added when, having escorted Mrs Hare downstairs and seen her into a hansom, he returned to the room.

'I was only going to remark,' I said mildly, knowing Holmes's dislike of having attention drawn to his generosity, 'that if Mrs Hare had been taught to read and write she could have pursued her own inquiries.'

'We can only hope that, with the introduction of the Board schools,* education will become so widespread that in fifty years' time, illiteracy will be a thing of the past. But I doubt whether, even if Mrs Hare had been sent to the most exclusive academy for young ladies, she could have undertaken an inquiry of this nature. The case has too many complexities.'

'Has it, Holmes? It sounded straightforward enough to me. A young woman betters herself and then chooses to have nothing more to do with her mother. We shall no doubt find her living happily with the Duckhams wherever it is they have moved to.'

'I trust you are correct, Watson. For my part, I fear the case is not so simple. But we shall see. For the moment, I shall content myself with reading Rosie Hare's letters to her mother and seeing if I can find any useful information in them.'

* Mr Sherlock Holmes comments on the Board schools in 'The Adventure of the Naval Treaty', referring to them as 'Beacons of the future!'. (Dr John F. Watson)

He settled himself at his desk, occasionally passing a letter to me. But I have to confess I soon grew bored with reading them. Despite Mrs Hare's insistence that her daughter had been 'good at her school-work', they were ill-written, misspelt accounts of the trivial events in Rosie's life and I soon transferred my attention to the evening newspaper.

After a quarter of an hour's silence, Holmes put the letters away and asked, 'Can you be free tomorrow, Watson, or will your professional duties keep you busy?'

'No. My practice has been remarkably quiet for the past week or so. I have no urgent cases.'

'Then be good enough to return here* at ten o'clock when we shall take a cab and visit Cadogan Crescent where the Honourable Mrs Clyde-Bannister has her establishment as well as the house in Streatham where the Duckhams used to reside.'

'Are you also proposing to call in at the Temperance Rooms in Bow?'

'I see no point in going there at this stage in the inquiry. It is nearly nine months since the Honourable Mrs Clyde-Bannister rented them and I fear the trail may well have gone cold.'

On my return to Baker Street the following morning, Holmes ordered a hansom and we set off first of all for number 14 Cadogan Crescent, an imposing residence just off the Square, where Holmes alighted and rang the bell. After a short conversation with the parlourmaid who opened the door, Holmes returned to the cab to announce that the house was no longer occupied by the Honourable Mrs Clyde-Bannister. The present residents had taken over the lease in June of the previous year and knew nothing about any earlier tenants.

* There is some uncertainty about the exact year when Dr John H. Watson sold his Kensington practice and returned to 221B Baker Street to share lodgings again with Mr Sherlock Holmes. Some scholars place the move in 1895. However, in 'The Adventure of the Veiled Lodger', which is internally dated as occurring 'early in 1896', a year after 'The Case of the Notorious Canary-trainer' took place, Dr John H. Watson writes of receiving 'a hurried note from Holmes' requesting his attendance at Baker Street, suggesting that he had not then moved back to his old address. (Dr John F. Watson)

From there, we drove to Maplehurst Avenue, Streatham, where we hoped to have better luck.

Maplehurst Avenue was a pleasant, tree-lined road of modern detached houses, standing in quite large grounds, number 26 being situated about half-way down. But from the neglected state of the garden and the absence of smoke from the chimneys, the place appeared to be empty, an impression confirmed by the 'To Let' board nailed to the front gate post.

The house-agents were Palfrey and Dickinson, with an address in Streatham High Road to which, on Holmes's instructions, the cab-driver took us.

On this occasion I accompanied him into the office, where Holmes spoke to Mr Palfrey, explaining the reason for his visit. Mr Palfrey, however, could tell us very little about his erstwhile tenants, the Duckhams. They had rented the house furnished the previous summer for three months, the rent being paid in advance by Mr Duckham, whom Mr Palfrey described as being 'tall and well-dressed but not really what he would call a gentleman'.

'A little too flash, if you know what I mean,' Mr Palfrey added.

As for Mrs Duckham, Mr Palfrey had seen neither her nor any domestic staff who might have been employed in the house.

The Duckhams had moved out at the beginning of September, their three-month lease having expired. They had left no forwarding address. Only one letter had arrived after their departure, which Mr Palfrey had opened and had returned to an address in Bow, marking the envelope 'No Longer in Residence'.

And that was all he could tell us about the Duckhams, apart from the canary cage.

'Canary cage?' Holmes inquired.

'Mr Duckham asked if he could have a shelf put up in the conservatory. Evidently he had a large cage of canaries which he wanted to raise off the floor because of the draughts. I agreed and recommended a jobbing carpenter. As far as I am aware, the shelf is still there. And that is really all I know about them,' Mr Palfrey concluded.

Holmes was in a pensive mood on the return journey and I knew better than to break the silence although I could not understand why the case should require such deep contemplation on his part.

It seemed ordinary enough to me.

At Baker Street, I kept the cab to go on to my consulting rooms, realizing that Holmes would probably prefer to be alone with his thoughts.

As we parted, he remarked, 'I shall be in touch with you, Watson, as soon as there are any developments in the case.'

But I heard nothing from him and I did not, in fact, see Holmes again for another three weeks. There was a sudden outbreak of bronchial infections due to the cold weather and my time was taken up with visiting patients.

It was a Friday evening in February before I had the leisure to call in again at Baker Street to find Inspector Lestrade of Scotland Yard already there, seated by the sitting-room fire, while Holmes was pacing up and down in a state of considerable excitement.

'My dear fellow!' he exclaimed as I entered. 'How fortunate you have come! The Inspector has just been telling me of an extraordinary case. Pray repeat the details of it, Lestrade, for Watson's benefit.'

'I don't know about it being extraordinary,' Lestrade said, turning his lean, sallow face in my direction. 'God knows we get enough suicide victims fished out of the Thames, especially at this time of the year. They're usually poor, homeless devils, beggars and such-like, who can't face another winter's night sleeping on the streets. But this one is different. She was found floating in the river near Wapping about two hours ago by a bargeman; a young woman, well-dressed and nourished; pretty, too, if you disallow for the effects of drowning. The fact is, Dr Watson, and it's the reason I've called on Mr Holmes, it's the second case like it in the past six months . . .'

'Holmes, you don't think – ?' I began eagerly, interrupting Lestrade's account.

I had been about to ask if he thought either of the young women could be Rosie Hare. But Holmes frowned and gave a little shake of his head to indicate that I was to say nothing on the subject.

Lestrade was watching us, his sharp, little eyes bright with curiosity.

'Yes, Dr Watson?' he asked. 'You were saying?'

'My old friend was merely going to remark,' Holmes put in easily, his expression perfectly bland, 'that I might find the case useful for the statistical tables I am compiling on suicide victims – their ages, social backgrounds and so on. But pray continue, Lestrade. You were speaking of the similarity of this case to another six months ago.'

'So I was. Well, Dr Watson, both victims were young women who, judging by their appearances, didn't seem the type to chuck themselves into the river. And both had been struck on the temple before they drowned. Now, I'm not saying it's murder. They could have injured themselves as they fell. But it's too much of a coincidence for my liking. There's another odd thing as well about that first suicide. No one reported a young woman of her description as missing and no one came forward to claim the body. That's why I have called on Mr Holmes this evening. As they say, two heads are better than one.'

'Or three in this instance,' Holmes remarked. 'What do you say, Watson? Lestrade tells me the body has been taken to Wharf Street police station. I was about to accompany him there. Would you care to join us? As a medical man, you may very well be able to help the inquiry by examining the corpse and giving us your professional opinion.'

'Of course, Holmes,' I said. 'Although the police surgeon has no doubt made his own examination, there may be some further details I can add to his report.'

We left the house shortly afterwards and, as Lestrade hurried ahead to hail a passing cab, Holmes took the opportunity to say to me in a low voice, 'Say nothing to Lestrade about Rosie Hare.'

I could not understand his reticence over the case but I

complied with his request and kept silent on the journey to Wharf Street, merely listening as Lestrade described a series of burglaries at large country houses in which valuable art treasures had been stolen.

'I am surprised,' Lestrade remarked at one point, 'that none of the victims has asked for your help, Mr Holmes, for I don't mind admitting that neither the local constabularies nor us at the Yard have been able to discover who is behind these felonies.'

On our arrival at Wharf Street police station, we were conducted by the duty sergeant into a small back-room which had been turned into a temporary mortuary and where the body, covered with a rough blanket, was lying on a trestle table.

Lestrade declined to come with us, having made his own examination earlier, and Holmes and I entered the room alone.

As I removed the blanket, I immediately saw the bruise to which Lestrade had referred. It was a large contusion and, in my opinion, would have caused unconsciousness but whether the injury was the result of a deliberate blow or an accident there was no way of telling.

Apart from this bruise, the face was unmarked, except for the obvious signs of drowning, never a pleasant sight. But, as Lestrade had pointed out, beneath the discoloration and the bloating of the features, it was still possible to discern that, when alive, the young woman, who could have been no more than fifteen or sixteen, had been remarkably attractive. The hair was long and dark, the form slim and shapely while the clothes she was wearing, a red silk dress and a fur-trimmed cloak, were fashionable and of a good quality.

From the degree of rigor mortis, I estimated that she had been dead for about twenty-four hours.

Holmes, meanwhile, was making his own examination, lifting each flaccid hand in turn and then moving the head a little to the left to expose the neck, revealing as he did so a small black mole just below the right ear.

'Good Lord, Holmes!' I exclaimed. 'Mrs Hare said her daughter had a mole in just that position!'

'Exactly,' Holmes said grimly. 'I fear, Watson, that we have found Rosie Hare but too late to save her. As Mrs Hare will have to be sent for to identify her, I shall have to tell Lestrade a little about our inquiries. But leave that to me. I shall say nothing at this stage about the Duckhams nor the Honourable Mrs Clyde-Bannister. Nor about my suspicions regarding the case.'

'What suspicions, Holmes?'

'Look at her hands, my dear fellow. Her mother last received a letter from her six months ago when she was engaged as a parlourmaid in the Duckhams' house in Streatham. The question is, what has she been doing since that time? Not housework, that is certain. The hands are soft and white, the nails unblemished. Even if she had undertaken only the lightest of household duties, she could not have kept them in so perfect a condition. They are a lady's hands; not a servant's.'

'Then what do you think she has been doing?'

'I have my own theory which I shall explain to you when there is more time. At this moment, we must find Lestrade. But leave the explaining to me, there's a good fellow.'

We ran Lestrade to earth in the duty-room, warming the backs of his legs before a huge coal fire.

He listened sombrely to Holmes's explanation, which was a brief summary of the interview with Mrs Hare, and then, having dispatched a constable in a cab to fetch Mrs Hare from her address in Bow, he turned back to remark, 'If I may say so, Mr Holmes, Mrs Hare doesn't seem a likely client for someone with your reputation. I thought it was only the well-to-do and the famous who came looking for your services.'

He clearly suspected Holmes of holding back information although my old friend merely replied with a shrug, 'I accept any client, Lestrade, rich or poor, as the mood takes me. I just happened to have time on my hands when Mrs Hare called at Baker Street. Unfortunately, my inquiries about her daughter had reached an impasse until this evening when you arrived to inform us of the suicide. I shall, of course, be willing to assist you in your own investigation, should you so wish, but at the moment I know no more about the facts of the case than you do.'

Strictly speaking, this was true. As Holmes had pointed out, he had only suspicions which it seemed he was unprepared to confide even to me.

I prefer not to dwell on the arrival of Mrs Hare and the distressing scene which followed her identification of the body as that of her daughter. It is painful to recall and all of us, Lestrade included, were in a subdued mood when she departed, accompanied by a police constable who had orders to see that she was placed in the care of a woman neighbour.

To my surprise, when Holmes and I left, I assumed to return to his lodgings, Holmes instructed the cab-driver to take us to the Burlington Hotel, Piccadilly, not to Baker Street, although he refused to explain the purpose behind this unexpected visit.

When the cab halted outside the hotel, Holmes alighted, telling me to wait as he would be only a few minutes.

From inside the hansom, I watched him go up the steps but, instead of entering, he remained on the portico, deep in conversation with the uniformed doorman. Then, having given the man a coin, Holmes climbed back into the cab.

'What was all that about, Holmes?' I asked, as the cab started off again, this time for Baker Street.

'I was merely confirming my suspicions,' said he, 'and opening up a new avenue of inquiry which we shall explore together, my dear Watson. Be good enough to call at Baker Street at nine p.m. tomorrow, wearing evening dress.'

'Evening dress?' I exclaimed, quite taken aback by this request.

'Yes; evening dress, Watson; white tie, tails, silk hat. I assume you have the necessary attire?'

'Of course I do. I was merely questioning the need for it. Where are we going? To the theatre? Or to dine somewhere in the West End?'

But all Holmes would say in reply was, 'Wait and see, Watson,' before adroitly changing the subject by remarking, 'By the way, speaking of the theatre, I hear there is a very good play on at the moment at the Adelphi.'

Nor would he discuss his plans when we arrived back at

Baker Street and, when I left that evening to return home, I was no wiser than I had been before.

It was in a state of considerable curiosity that I returned to Holmes's lodgings the following evening at nine o'clock, dressed, as he had stipulated, in evening wear, to find him similarly attired, his silk hat and silver-knobbed cane lying ready on the table.

'Excellent apart from the final touch,' he said, placing a gardenia in my buttonhole. 'You now look the perfect man-about-town, ready for a little diversion in what I believe the French call a *maison de tolérance*. Or in good, plain English, Watson, a brothel.'

'Now look here, Holmes!' I protested. 'I am a respectable widower* and doctor. I cannot possibly accompany you to one of those places. Supposing I were recognized?'

'I thought you might object so this morning I took the precaution of purchasing two simple but effective pieces of disguise – a pair of side-whiskers for you, my dear old friend, and a rather splendid waxed moustache for myself. The gum arabic is on the table. The looking glass is above the mantelshelf. As we glue our facial adornments into place, I shall explain why our inquiries will take us to a certain West End bordello. You remember I remarked on Rosie Hare's hands and posed the question of what she had been doing in the six months since she last wrote to her mother? There seemed to me to be only one profession open to a girl of Rosie's background which enabled her to lead a life of leisure. Her clothes, which were fashionable and expensive, also bore out that impression.'

He broke off at this point to help me fix my side-whiskers into place and to examine both our reflections in the glass with a critical eye before continuing, 'You will also recall that I spoke to the doorman at the Burlington Hotel?'

'Of course I do. As a matter of fact, I was rather surprised at your doing so. What could he possibly know that could be of use in our inquiries?'

'A great deal, Watson. If you want to discover anything about

* See footnote to page 132. (Dr John F. Watson)

West End night life, ask a hotel doorkeeper. He is acquainted with the names of all the bordellos and quite used to directing male guests to the best establishments. On the basis of what I have already told you, I asked him to recommend a good-class brothel in the area where the girls are young and pretty. He named ten.'

'Ten? Good Lord!'

'Quite, Watson. And that does not take into account the hotels and accommodation houses which let rooms by the hour for the use of the many scores of prostitutes one can see walking about the streets of the West End. Among those he named was one in Montrose Street, just off the Haymarket, run by a couple called the Wilsons. It is called the "Canary Club".' He paused for a moment and then said, 'I can see by your expression that you have not made the connection.'

'No, Holmes; I am afraid I haven't.'

'Remember Palfrey, the house agent? He informed us that Mr Duckham asked for permission to put up a shelf in the house in Streatham to support a large cage of canaries.'

'Oh, yes, of course! I see the significance of it now. But you are surely not suggesting . . .!'

I broke off, horrified by the implications.

'Indeed I am, my dear fellow. Allow me to refresh your memory on the advertisement which Mrs Hare showed us. I have it here. It reads: "Girls and young women between the ages of fourteen and eighteen" – mark that, Watson! – are asked to present themselves for selection as parlourmaids et cetera in the "best households" with "no experience needed". And this was intended to be read, remember, by young women from the East End, apprentice dressmakers and milliners' assistants in the back-street sweat-shops. No wonder they flocked to the Temperance Rooms in Bow to be interviewed by the Honourable Mrs Clyde-Bannister, especially when they saw the wages which were offered. Fifty pounds a year! Even an experienced butler would count himself lucky to earn that amount. Consider also the fact that not only the Honourable Mrs Clyde-Bannister but also the Duckhams are no longer to be found at their former addresses and that all of them moved away in the summer or early autumn of last year, which was the time that Mrs Hare last heard from her daughter. All of this convinces me that the whole affair from start to finish, from the interview at the Temperance Rooms in Bow to Rosie Hare's employment with the Duckhams, was a conspiracy to lure gullible young women and girls like her into what I believe is termed the "flesh trade".'

'But that is absolutely appalling, Holmes! Something must be done about it!'

'My sentiments entirely. That is why you and I, Watson, are going to visit the "Canary Club" tonight in the guise of two gentlemen out in the West End, looking for a little "fun". So, please, my dear fellow, when we arrive there, do look as if you are enjoying yourself.'

Having never set foot in such an establishment in my life, I was not at all sure what to expect when the hansom deposited us outside number 45 Montrose Street.

From the outside, it seemed innocuous enough. It was one of those tall, elegant town houses with several steps leading up to a pillared porch. Only a discreet brass plate engraved with the words 'The Canary Club. Members Only' and a man in livery on duty at the front door marked it out as anything other than a select private residence.

Once inside the entrance hall, however, I soon realized that the place lived up to its name and reputation.

The first object to meet the visitor's gaze as he entered was a large gilded cage, shaped like a Chinese pagoda, which contained about two dozen small, bright yellow canaries which hopped from perch to perch or fluttered against the wires, their sweet, chirruping song filling the air.

The foyer itself was lavishly and elaborately furnished but with that flamboyant and over-decorated taste of the *nouveaux riches*. Huge chandeliers hung from the ceiling, their lights glittering on the crystal prisms and reflected back from the gilt-framed mirrors which lined the walls.

At the far end, a pair of double doors had been flung open to reveal a drawing-room or *salon*, decorated in red and gold, with elegant chairs and tables, at which couples were sitting, placed against the walls while in the centre of the room men strolled about or stood talking to young women who were dressed in evening gowns of quite alarming *décolletage*.

Holmes had already instructed me in the cab on what I was to expect and how I was to behave. I was to leave most of the talking to him and I was to show no surprise or shock at anything I might see or hear. I was also to remember that Holmes would address me as 'Bunny', a sobriquet which, he explained with a smile, suited me on account of the side-whiskers.

As the cab had turned out of the Haymarket, he had added, 'Once we are there, I shall ask specifically for a red-haired girl.'

'Why is that, Holmes?'

'If you had read Rosie Hare's letters, Watson, you would not need to ask. You may recall that a girl called Mary Sullivan was the only other successful candidate at the interview and accompanied Rosie Hare to the Honourable Mrs Clyde-Bannister's house in Cadogan Crescent for training as a parlourmaid. In her letters, Rosie described Mary Sullivan, with whom she appeared to have struck up a friendship, as very pretty with beautiful red hair. She is, I gathered, of Irish extraction. If my theory is correct, then I believe we shall find that she is one of the young ladies on offer at the "Canary Club".'

At this point, the cab had drawn up outside the establishment and, once we had entered, my attention was taken up by other matters. These included not only the appearance of the place but the presence of two more male attendants who came forward as soon as we stepped inside the door, one in livery who took our coats and silk hats, the other a tall, broad-shouldered man, whose impeccable evening clothes contrasted oddly with his brutal, prize-fighter's face and who relieved us of five guineas each as membership fees.

I tried to appear as cool as Holmes as I parted with this outrageous sum, for Holmes seemed perfectly at ease as he stood with his hands in his pockets and a cigar in his mouth, surveying his surroundings with a swaggering air.

We had hardly turned away from paying this bruiser when a large, heavy-bosomed woman of middle age, dressed in extravagantly ruffled black silk, came towards us, holding out her hand; her smile, however, barely disguising the hard glitter in her eyes.

'I am Mrs Wilson,' she announced. 'I believe you gentlemen are new members. Who recommended you?'

'The doorman at the Burlington,' Holmes drawled nonchalantly. 'He said the girls here were very choice.'

'The best in London. Have you gentlemen any preferences?'

Holmes turned to me.

'What d'you fancy, Bunny, old chap? I think I am in the mood for a little red-head.'

'Céline is free at the moment,' Mrs Wilson remarked, waving a hand towards the drawing-room.

Holmes nodded to her and strolled off towards the double doors, the cigar still in his mouth, although, once we were out of earshot of Mrs Wilson, he removed it for long enough to murmur to me, 'We have just met the madam of the place, alias, I believe, the Honourable Mrs Clyde-Bannister.'

There was no time for me to reply. Holmes had entered the room and was approaching one of the tables at which was sitting a very pretty red-haired young woman, wearing a green silk evening gown which left all of her arms and most of her bosom bare.

'Céline?' Holmes inquired, drawing out a chair. 'May we join you?'

In the moments before she was aware of our presence, I had been able to observe her. She had been staring straight in front of her, her face quite empty of any emotion as if there were nothing behind the pretty mask of her features except a void.

That expression still haunts my memory. The girl could not have been much more than sixteen.

A second later, the vacant look had vanished and she was smiling up at us coquettishly and rearranging the folds of her skirt to reveal a shapely ankle.

'Of course you can join me, darlin',' she said, addressing Holmes. 'Would your gentleman friend like another young lady to sit with us? There's Mimi or Georgette, depending on whether he prefers a blonde or a brunette.' Her voice had a carefully refined overtone but beneath this it was still possible to discern a less cultivated Cockney-Irish accent.

'Later, perhaps,' Holmes told her. 'At the moment, my friend, Bunny, and I are more interested in the arrangements of the establishment.'

'You're new here, aren't you, darlin'? I thought you were. Well, the arrangements, as you call them, are these. Usually the gentlemen walk about for a while, seeing which young ladies they fancy. Then, when they think they've made their choice, they take the young lady in question to sit down at a table and settle the details. That's always done over a bottle of bubbly. It's one of the house-rules. If you sit down, you have to buy champagne. Once you've made up your mind, you go over there to settle up with Mr Wilson.'

She nodded across the room to where a man was sitting, like a king on a throne, on a large gilt and red velvet chair which was placed on a silk-draped dais. He was a huge man in evening dress, monstrously fat, his starched shirt-front glittering with diamond studs. Lolling back in his chair, he was surveying the promenade of men and women and those couples seated at the tables with a proprietorial air, his round, white face, like a full moon, glistening with sweat, and quite motionless apart from his eyes which were constantly roving to and fro.

'When you've paid Mr Wilson your dues,' Céline continued, 'he'll give you the number of a room that's vacant and then you're free to take the young lady upstairs.' She raised her fan and fluttered it in front of her face with mock modesty. 'I think I can leave the rest to your imagination, gentlemen.'

As she was speaking, a waiter had crossed the room to our table carrying a silver salver on which were placed three glasses and a champagne bottle in an ice-bucket.

'How much?' Holmes inquired.

'A guinea, sir.'

A guinea!

It said much for Holmes's perfect self-control that not even his smile wavered as he paid over the money together with a florin tip.

When the man had gone, Holmes filled the glasses and then, passing one to the young woman, remarked in a casual manner, 'Céline. That's a pretty name but I rather doubt it is your real one.'

She looked across at him, the glass half-way to her lips, not sure how to respond.

'Perhaps you're right,' she began.

'Not perhaps. I am quite positive. In fact, I know who you are and how you came to be here,' Holmes continued, leaning forward and speaking now with great earnestness. 'You are Mary Sullivan, a former apprentice dressmaker, and you attended an interview at the Temperance Rooms in Bow last May with the Honourable Mrs Clyde-Bannister – Mrs Wilson, to give her her real name. With you at the interview was another young woman, Rosie Hare. You and Rosie were the only two successful candidates. After a period of training at Mrs Clyde-Bannister's house in Cadogan Crescent, Rosie was sent to a household in Streatham to serve as a parlourmaid while you were dispatched to a family in Hampstead. I believe I can guess what happened while you were there but I should like my suspicions confirmed. You were compromised in some manner. Am I not correct? And the price you had to pay was your agreement to work at the "Canary Club".'

'Compromised!' Mary Sullivan said bitterly, the Cockney-Irish accent becoming more pronounced. 'That's one way of putting it! I don't know who you are or what your game is but you look like the sort a girl could trust. Yes, we went to Cadogan Crescent where we was supposed to have been trained as parlourmaids but it was mostly about how to speak proper and make ourselves look nice. There was a bit about waiting at table and serving wine but not much. Then we was sent off to these different addresses as parlourmaids. I never knew where Rosie went so I couldn't write to her.

'My place was all right – to begin with. The lady and gentleman of the house, Mr and Mrs Mallinson, was kind and the duties wasn't hard. They had a cook and a woman came in daily to do the housework. Then one evening before dinner, there was such a set-to! Mrs Mallinson said she'd left a bracelet on her dressing-table and now it was missing. She accused me of stealing it, which I denied 'cos I hadn't so much as set eyes on it. Then Mr Mallinson said, "In that case, you won't mind if we look in your room, will you?" And I said, "You look all you like. You won't find it."'

'But they did,' Holmes said softly. The remark was more in the nature of a statement than a question.

'Course they did! It was where they must have put it – in the top drawer under my chemises. Then Mr Mallinson said he'd have to send for the police. Well, naturally, I was ever so upset and I cried and Mrs Mallinson said, "Now Arthur," – that was Mr Mallinson's name – "we don't want to get the girl into trouble, do we? You go and fetch Mr Wilson and ask him what we can do for the best." So Mr Mallinson went off in a cab and came back with Mr Wilson.

'I'd seen Mr Wilson before. He'd called several times at the house and been ever so kind to me, treated me like a real gentleman and gave me half a crown. Anyway, when Mr Wilson arrived, he talked to me and explained how serious it was to get caught stealing and how I could be sent to prison but I wasn't to cry any more 'cos he knew of a way out. I couldn't go on working for the Mallinsons but he owned a very select gentlemen's club in the West End and he was looking for an attractive young lady like me to serve drinks to his clients. If I agreed to work there, he'd persuade the Mallinsons not to charge me with stealing. So I said I would although if I knew then what I know now I'd have sooner gone to prison.'

'And the select gentlemen's club was, of course, this place?' Holmes said quietly.

'That's right, darlin'. I came here and finished up as one of Mr Wilson's little canaries, trained to sing for the customers and hop about prettily on my perch.'

'Do they ever open the cage door and let you out?'

Mary Sullivan laughed.

'Oh, we get taken out for an airing from time to time, carefully chaperoned by Mrs Gough in case we try to fly away.'

'Mrs Gough?'

'She's in charge upstairs and a right tartar she is, too. It's her husband on the door who acts as chucker-out in case any of the gentlemen turns awkward. He used to be a prize-fighter. You don't want to get on the wrong side of him.'

'Have any of the little birds managed to escape?'

'Not that I know of. Most of them don't want to anyway. They enjoy being in their cage. It's warm and they're well fed. They don't much care as long as they're given champagne and pretty clothes to wear.'

'And what about the ones who do care? What happens to them?'

'They get sent on.'

I saw Holmes's expression sharpen.

'"Sent on"? Where to?'

'Nobody's supposed to know but the maids upstairs, them that cleans the rooms and helps us dress, warns us sometimes, "You watch out! If you don't mind your p's and q's you'll finish up on the train from Victoria with the Goughs." That's what happened to Rosie.'

'Did it?' Holmes asked with an offhand air. 'When was this?'

'A couple of nights ago. She arrived here in September, about a week after I did and with exactly the same story as me. *She'd* been accused of stealing and Mr Wilson had offered *her* a job in his gentlemen's club. Marguerite, they called her. But she was always crying and not singing as nicely for the clients as she was supposed to. Then Mr Wilson caught her trying to get one of the gentlemen to post a letter to her mother. We're not supposed to have any family who cares about us. I know my old ma was glad to see the back of me. The Honourable Mrs Clyde-Bannister, Mrs Wilson to you, dear, made a special point of that at the interview. "Any close relatives or friends?" she said. "I only ask because sometimes my girls are sent abroad with the families they'll work for and I don't like to think I'm causing distress at home." The bloody old hypocrite! Anyway, as I was saying, Rosie tried to pass on a letter and Mrs Gough locked her in one of the upstairs rooms. Then, a couple of nights ago, a four-wheeler came to the house and the next day Rosie had gone. And so had the Goughs. "She's been sent on," was all Mr Wilson would tell us. But all of us girls knew where.

Can't you guess, darlin'? No? Gay Paree. Where else? It seems French gentlemen like little English canaries.'

'Good Lord!' I exclaimed involuntarily, quite forgetting the warning Holmes had given me in the cab.

But my horrified exclamation was covered up by Mary Sullivan's own cry of, 'Oh, my Gawd, Mr Wilson's coming over! Now I'll be for it! He don't like us girls wasting time chatting to the clients when we should be getting down to business.'

Wilson was indeed making his way across the room to our table, moving with surprising agility and silence for a man of his vast bulk.

'Anything the matter, gentlemen?' he inquired, smiling unctuously but fixing both Holmes and me with a hard stare from pale blue eyes which were almost hidden in the folds of fat round his cheeks.

'No; why should there be?' Holmes drawled carelessly, lounging back in his chair. 'We are simply enjoying a pleasant little chin-wag, old fellow.' Turning to me, he went on, ignoring Wilson, 'What d'you say, Bunny? Shall we take a stroll and see what other little birds are on offer before making up our minds?'

With a wink at me, he got up and walked away, leaving me to follow after him which I did with some haste, eager to escape from the unspeakable Wilson.

Once we were well clear of the man and had joined the other promenaders in the centre of the room, I grasped him by the arm and said in a low voice, 'How are we going to get out of this dreadful place without arousing Wilson's suspicions even further?'

'Leave it to me, my dear fellow,' Holmes replied. 'I have already thought of a way. After a couple more turns up and down the room in which we shall ogle the *jeunes filles* as if we had every intention of making an offer for two of them, you will suddenly be taken faint and will have to be escorted off the premises. Do you think you can manage that?'

'With no trouble at all,' I assured him fervently.

Indeed, when the time came, there was hardly any need for me to feign a sudden indisposition. The heat in the room combined with the champagne, the odour of cigars and the heavy perfume with which the young women were liberally doused caused me to feel quite light-headed and, with Holmes's arm in mine, I staggered into the entrance hall, my old friend announcing loudly as he collected our coats and silk hats, 'Too much bubbly, that's your trouble, Bunny old chap!'

I felt better as soon as we reached the fresh air of the street where Holmes left me in the care of the liveried doorman, remarking to him as he went back inside the house, 'Damned stupid of me! I've left my cane behind.'

He was back within minutes, the cane under his arm although he waited until we had started walking back towards the Haymarket before explaining to me in a low voice, 'Just as I thought. When I went back into the place, Mary Sullivan was being escorted upstairs by Mrs Wilson. I have a strong suspicion that the young lady is about to be "sent on".'

I stopped in my tracks.

'But that's quite dreadful, Holmes! I fear we are to blame. We must return at once and prevent it!'

'My dear old friend, you will achieve nothing by charging in there like a knight on a white horse, waving a sword. Evil monsters like the Wilsons have to be snared before they can be slain. We must have proof and for that we have to wait for them to make the first move which will be later tonight; at half past midnight to be precise.'

'How can you be so sure?'

'You will recall that Mary Sullivan spoke of the Victoria train and how Rosie Hare was, as she thought, "sent on" to catch it two nights ago? Well, there is a boat train which leaves Victoria at one fifteen to connect with the night-ferry from Dover to Calais. I believe a four-wheeler will be sent for at half past twelve to collect Mary Sullivan and her escort, the Goughs, to catch that train. Observe, Watson, that the nearest cab-stand is over there on the corner from where one has a clear view down Montrose Street. I want you to stay here and keep a watch on both the cab-stand and the "Canary Club". Should anyone come out of the house and approach any of the drivers, it is your responsibility to prevent the cab from setting off.'

'But how?'

'I leave that entirely to your discretion, my dear Watson. I, meanwhile, shall take a hansom to Scotland Yard to alert Lestrade.' Holmes glanced at his pocket-watch. 'I have an hour and a half to persuade our friend the Inspector that action must be taken; not long as Lestrade is not a man who is normally quick-thinking but I hope time enough.' The next moment he had crossed to the cab-stand and had leapt into a hansom, leaving me standing alone on the pavement.

Rarely have I spent a more uncomfortable hour and a half with the exception of the time I served in India and was wounded at the battle of Maiwand in '80 during the Afghan War.

A bitter wind blew down Montrose Street, bringing with it small crumbs of frozen snow which swirled and eddied across the pavements.

Although at the far end of the road I could see the bright lights of the Haymarket, there were few passers-by apart from the occasional late reveller looking for a cab and the street-walkers who continued plying their trade. I was accosted more than a dozen times.

To keep warm, I walked up and down stamping my feet, seeking shelter from time to time in a doorway where I anxiously consulted my own pocket-watch.

At twenty minutes past twelve when I had given up hope, a four-wheeler, followed closely by two more, drew up beside me and my old friend jumped out, accompanied by Lestrade and two police officers, eight more emerging from the other cabs, all in plain clothes.

'Thank God, Holmes!' I cried. 'I thought you would not get here in time!'

'Then we are not too late?' he asked. 'We had to wait for warrants to be drawn up.'

Lestrade said defensively, 'It all has to be done by the book, Mr Holmes. The "Canary Club" is a private gentlemen's establishment. We can't just force our way in without the proper authorization. But murder and White Slave trafficking! That's a serious matter!' He turned away to address the ten officers who had accompanied him and Holmes. 'Now I want you men to walk along easy-like, as if you're out strolling in the West End, enjoying yourselves. And none of you is to make a move until I give the word. Have you got that?'

The men murmured in assent and the group split up, Holmes and I walking with Lestrade along Montrose Street, the plain-clothes officers spreading out singly or in pairs on either side of the road.

It was only when we had drawn level with the entrance to the 'Canary Club' that Lestrade gave the order.

With a shout of 'Right, men!', he charged up the steps, knocking aside the liveried porter, and flung himself against the door.

What happened next occurred so quickly that I have only a blurred impression of the events.

I remember bursting into the entrance hall on Lestrade's heels with Holmes a few paces in front of me, the other men bundling in behind us. I also recall Gough coming for us like a maddened bull and three officers wrestling him to the floor. The rest is a confusion of women screaming, men shouting, glass breaking.

And then Holmes broke free of the mêlée and, calling to me to follow, ran towards the staircase, taking the steps two at a time.

On the landing, we were faced by many doors, some closed, some open, the occupants of the rooms having come out in a state of considerable *déshabillé* to see what the noise was about. Ignoring them, Holmes sprinted down the corridor, trying the handles of the doors which were still closed until he came to one which was locked.

'Watson!' he shouted. 'Help me by putting your shoulder to this!'

I did as he ordered and, under our combined weight, the door crashed inwards and we were precipitated into the room.

It was a bedroom, containing a great quantity of mirror-glass and silk draperies but what immediately caught my attention was the figure of Mary Sullivan lying asleep on the bed, guarded by a gaunt, hard-faced woman, dressed in black – Mrs Gough, I assumed – who had been seated on a chair but who ran from the room as Holmes and and I burst into it.

'Let her go!' Holmes ordered. 'Lestrade's men can deal with her.' He bent down over Mary Sullivan's recumbent form to sniff at her lips and then turned to me, his expression grim. 'She's been chloroformed, Watson. Help me carry her out into the fresh air.'

Wrapping her in the quilt from the bed, Holmes and I between us supported her downstairs and out into the street where I hailed a passing four-wheeler in which we conveyed her to Charing Cross Hospital.

Having seen her safely placed in the hands of the medical staff at Charing Cross, we returned by cab to Prince's Street police station where Lestrade had arranged for the Wilsons and their accomplices to be taken for questioning.

We found Lestrade in the middle of interviewing Wilson, who was seated on a chair, his starched shirt-front burst open and his face the colour of grey blubber.

The Inspector greeted us as we entered.

'Come in, gentlemen. We have rounded up all the occupants of the "Canary Club" including this fine, fat bird who's been singing his heart out,' Lestrade said with a smile of satisfaction. 'It seems they set up these interviews for young women in various parts of the East End, not just in Bow but all over the place. He's also given us the names and addresses of the couples who rented the houses where the young women were supposed to have gone into service. I've sent some of my men to arrest them. He was just telling me about Rosie Hare when you arrived. Go on, Wilson. Tell us what happened to her and the other girl who was found dead in the Thames six months ago. What was her name?'

'Lizzie Hamilton. And I had nothing to do with either of them!' Wilson protested, his fat cheeks trembling with terror. 'It was the Goughs! They were supposed to take them to another establishment in Paris. Lizzie Hamilton was the first. She'd been chloroformed to keep her quiet but she came to in the cab on the way to Victoria station and started struggling and screaming. Gough was worried the cab-driver would hear her so he hit her on the head. It was Mrs Gough who suggested they dump her in the Thames. They couldn't be sure she wouldn't kick up another rumpus on the boat or on the train to Paris. So they told the driver the girl had been taken ill and, instead of going to Victoria, he was to drive them to Wapping where they said her mother lived and to put them down in a quiet street near the river. Once the cab had gone, they carried her along an alley to the bank and threw her in. The same happened with Rosie Hare. After Lizzie's death, I told them it wasn't to occur again. But they wouldn't listen – '

He broke off, blubbing like a child.

Holmes and I left soon afterwards, neither of us caring to wait for Wilson and the others to be charged and both of us eager to return to the sanctuary of Holmes's rooms in Baker Street.

Lestrade, of course, took all the credit for the successful raid on the 'Canary Club' and the arrest of Wilson and his accomplices.

Holmes was quite resigned to it, having grown used to the Inspector's habit of stealing the limelight.

As for the Wilsons and the Goughs, they paid their dues to society, the Goughs with the ultimate punishment for the deaths of Rosie Hare and Lizzie Hamilton. The Wilsons both received long gaol sentences for their part in the conspiracy and for being accessories to murder; the others, varying terms of imprisonment.

I wish I could state that the successful conclusion of the case put an end to the monstrous trade in young female flesh but I fear this is not so. On my rare visits to the West End, I occasionally recognize among the street-walkers the faces of young women whom I last saw taking part in the promenade up and down the *salon* of the 'Canary Club'.

There was, however, one small ray of hope and happiness in this whole sad and sordid affair. When Mary Sullivan was discharged from hospital, she called on Holmes to thank him and to ask for Mrs Hare's address. The last we heard of them, Mary had found employment in an East End dressmaker's, a decent place run by a kindly couple, and she had moved in with Mrs Hare as a surrogate daughter.

Holmes summed it up very aptly, I thought, by quoting indirectly from Shakespeare's *Merchant of Venice*: 'Just one small good deed, Watson, shining like a candle in a very naughty world.'

THE CASE OF THE ITINERANT YEGGMAN

Another case which engaged Holmes's attention in the busy year of '95 occurred in June, several months after the arrest of Wilson and his accomplices which brought the 'Canary Club' conspiracy to a successful conclusion.

I was apprised of this new investigation by the arrival at my consulting-rooms of a telegram from my old friend which read: 'COME TWO-THIRTY THIS AFTERNOON BAKER STREET STOP INTERESTING CASE PENDING.'

I was quite used by this time to these peremptory summonses and, having arranged for a colleague to take over my professional duties that afternoon, I caught a cab to my former lodgings where I found Holmes in a state of some excitement.

'My dear Watson,' he said as I entered, 'I am delighted you were able to come. A most fascinating investigation has been placed my way this very morning. You remember Lestrade referred to a series of burglaries which had taken place at country houses and in which valuable art treasures had been stolen?* Well, read this!'

He thrust a letter into my hand. It bore the previous day's date, the address: 'Whitestone Manor, Little Walden, Suffolk', and read:

Dear Mr Holmes,

Two days ago my house was broken into and several rare

* Inspector Lestrade refers to the burglaries in 'The Case of the Notorious Canary-trainer'. (Dr John F. Watson)

family heirlooms were stolen. The local constabulary have undertaken an investigation but have so far discovered no clues whatsoever. Consequently, I have no faith in their competence.

Having heard of your great ability to succeed where the official police have failed, I should be most grateful if you would make inquiries on my behalf. I propose calling on you at three o'clock on Tuesday afternoon to discuss the case with you.

I am, sir, yours sincerely,
Edgar Maxwell-Browne (Bart.)

Hardly had I finished reading it than, with the curt command, 'Now look at this!', Holmes snatched the letter away and substituted for it one of his cuttings books in which it was his habit to paste those newspaper articles which had caught his interest.

There were five such items, dating back over the past two years and all were concerned with burglaries at country mansions. But I had very little opportunity to peruse them in detail for Holmes insisted on leaning eagerly over my shoulder to comment out loud on their contents.

'You see, Watson, all of them follow a pattern or *modus operandi*. The burglaries always take place in the summer months at country houses situated not too far from London. I have looked up the places on a large-scale map and without exception they are located three miles or less from a mainline station; within walking distance, in other words. In every case, the burglary has been carried out with great skill and cunning for no one in any of the households was aware at the time of the felonies, while in two instances a dog, which was supposed to guard the property, had been put to sleep by means of a piece of drugged meat.

'Another curious feature of all these burglaries is the discrimination of the villain or villains involved. Only certain choice items of rare historical or artistic interest have been taken while other objects of considerable value such as plate and jewellery have been left untouched. In short, Watson, I am convinced that we are dealing here with a very clever professional thief, based in London, who travels down by train to commit the burglaries, having first chosen his site with extreme care.'

'And the police say they have no clues,' I remarked, pointing to Sir Edgar's letter.

'Pshaw!' Holmes exclaimed scornfully. 'They are simply not looking in the right places. I have been following these cases for months, hoping that one of the victims might ask for my services. And now my chance has come! For believe me, my dear fellow, there is a very cunning and subtle mind at work here. It will afford me the greatest pleasure to pit my wits against his!'

He was positively rubbing his hands together with delight at the prospect and could hardly contain his impatience, pacing up and down the room until the bell rang to announce the arrival of his new client.

Sir Edgar Maxwell-Browne was a bluff, middle-aged, red-faced man who came straight to the point.

No sooner had he entered the room and introduced himself than he announced, 'I do not propose wasting your time or mine, Mr Holmes. The facts of the case are these. The burglary took place either late on Friday night or in the early hours of Saturday morning. No one in the household heard anything, including myself, although that may not be altogether surprising as the servants sleep in the east wing, quite separate from the part of the house where the crime was committed, while my own room is also some distance away. It occurred in the drawing-room in the old west wing, where a circular piece of glass was cut out of one of the window-panes, the catch was released and the casement was then opened. It was from this room that the objects were stolen.'

'I take it that all the items were extremely rare and of great artistic or historic value?' Holmes inquired.

Sir Edgar sat up, astonished at my old friend's deductive skills.

'I don't know how you came to that conclusion, Mr Holmes, but you are perfectly correct. All the objects were irreplaceable family heirlooms, including a miniature by Nicholas Hilliard of an ancestor of mine, a prayer-book with a pearl-embroidered cover which had belonged to Mary Queen of Scots and a gold chalice said to have been used in Catherine of Aragon's private chapel. They were not only priceless; they were unique! The most baffling part about it is that there was no attempt to make off with the silver in the dining-room or other valuable pieces in the drawing-room or elsewhere in the house.'

'I assume from your description that all the stolen objects were small and easily portable?'

'You are correct again, Mr Holmes! They would have fitted into a carpet-bag or a small portmanteau. I ought to add that none of the heirlooms taken were displayed openly. They were all secured inside two cabinets which were fitted with strong locks. As the glass had not been smashed, I can only assume that the locks were picked.'

'Ah!' Holmes exclaimed, his eyes very bright under their dark, heavy brows.

'Now to get down to business,' Sir Edgar continued briskly. 'If you are willing to take on the case, I am prepared to pay whatever fees you charge. I should, of course, prefer that my property were returned but, failing that, I shall be satisfied if whoever is responsible is apprehended and placed behind bars. I am a great believer in the old adage that an Englishman's home is his castle. No householder can sleep easy in his bed while these villains are at large.'

'*These* villains, Sir Edgar? You sound quite positive. Have you any evidence that more than one man is involved?'

'Indeed I have. There are two to be precise. Did I not mention the port? No? Well, before they left, they had the infernal cheek to help themselves to a glass each of my '67; cool as you please. The empty glasses were found in the dining-room.'

'Have they been touched?' Holmes asked quickly.

'No; as soon as the burglary was discovered, I gave orders that the drawing-room and the dining-room were to be locked and that nothing should be removed or handled until the police arrived. Inspector Biffen, who is in charge of the so-called investigation, showed no interest in examining the glasses and therefore the dining-room has remained closed off. He and his men seemed more concerned with trampling over the gardens, looking for evidence. They have done irreparable damage to a bed of very fine gloxinias. It was one of the reasons I decided to write to you, Mr Holmes, and ask you to take up the case before Biffen and his subordinates ruin any more of my borders. To add insult to injury, the Inspector has admitted that he has found no clues, not even a footprint, and has no idea who is behind this outrage. Indeed, yesterday he spoke of calling in Scotland Yard which will mean more men in boots tramping about!'

Sir Edgar's bright blue eyes positively blazed at the idea.

Holmes said soothingly, 'I shall be delighted to take the case, Sir Edgar. I assume you have no objections to my colleague, Dr Watson, accompanying me? Then let me assure you that, as far as the doctor and myself are concerned, your flower gardens will be sacrosanct.'

'That is settled then,' Sir Edgar remarked, slapping his knees. 'Now, I have looked up the timetable and the 10.15 from Liverpool Street station to Ipswich stops at Great Walden. If that train is convenient to you, I shall send my carriage to meet it. It is only a two mile drive from the station to my house at Little Walden. You will stay for luncheon, of course? Excellent! Then I shall inform Biffen that you will arrive tomorrow morning.'

Sir Edgar had risen to his feet as if about to depart when Holmes held up a hand to detain him.

'Two final points before you leave, Sir Edgar. Firstly, will you make sure that no one, not even Inspector Biffen, enters the dining-room and handles the two port glasses?' On receiving Sir Edgar's assurance, Holmes continued, 'My last inquiry is this – have any strangers visited the house recently?'

Sir Edgar seemed less positive about this last query.

'Not to my knowledge,' he said after a moment's pause. 'But I shall certainly make inquiries of the servants.'

After he had shaken hands and left, Holmes turned to me with a triumphant expression.

'You see what I mean about *modus operandi*, Watson? This case follows a similar pattern to the others. The house is approximately two miles from a mainline station; no one heard anything; the burglary was carried out extremely skilfully and only a few choice items were taken. We can now add to our knowledge the fact that two men are involved, both of whom are exceptionally skilled. I am looking forward to this investigation with the greatest of pleasure.'

'Why did you ask Sir Edgar about strangers visiting the house?'

'Is that not obvious, Watson? The thieves entered by the drawing-room window, the very room where the family heirlooms were kept, and made off with only the most valuable of them. Does that not suggest to you that they knew exactly where to find them and what their value was before committing the burglary? And now, my dear fellow, before you leave, if you would be good enough to hand me down that volume marked "Country Houses", I shall begin work on the case. I may expect you tomorrow morning, may I not, say at nine o'clock, in good time to catch the 10.15 from Liverpool Street station?'

Having been so imperatively summoned, I was a little piqued at being dismissed in a similar fashion but Holmes, quite unaware of my annoyance, had already seated himself at his desk, a large-scale map of South East England spread out in front of him, together with the volume on country houses, and was engaged in making notes.

I let myself quietly out of the room.

He was in the same ebullient mood when I returned the following morning.

A cab had been ordered and, as the hansom rattled off for Liverpool Street station, he explained to me the results of his previous day's researches.

'I have written over two dozen letters, Watson; five to the owners of those houses where the earlier thefts occurred and a score or more to others whose properties seemed likely targets for future burglaries. It is surprising how many country houses fulfil the necessary criteria I remarked on yesterday.'

'You are quite sure there will be other attempts?' I asked.

'Oh, quite positive! These burglaries are part of a series which take place, as I pointed out to you, during the summer months. It is now June. I think we can safely count on at least one more before the season is out. I shall be better informed where exactly it will take place when I receive answers to my letters.'

We caught the train at Liverpool Street station and, after a journey of about an hour, alighted at Great Walden, a prosperous market town, where we found Sir Edgar's coachman waiting with the carriage.

Before we set off, Holmes inquired of the man, 'Which is the best inn in the town?'

'The George, sir,' the coachman replied without any hesitation.

Holmes sat back with evident satisfaction but said nothing to explain the reason for this inquiry, merely looking about him with great attention as the carriage drove away.

Whitestone Manor was a large, rambling house of several architectural styles, one wing being Tudor, another Carolean, while a fine Palladian façade had been built in front of the main Georgian structure. It was here, on the steps of the pillared portico, that Sir Edgar met us and conducted us inside the house.

'Now, Mr Holmes,' he said, with his usual forthrightness, 'where do you wish to begin your investigation?'

To my surprise, Holmes replied, 'In the dining-room, Sir Edgar. I should like to examine the two port glasses.'

The dining-room was situated in the Tudor wing and was a low, panelled room, furnished with the heavy oak pieces of the period on which was displayed a quantity of silver plate which the thieves had left behind.

The glasses in question stood on the end of a long refectory table, the dregs of dried port still evident at the botton of them. Without touching them, Holmes bent forward and scrutinized each glass carefully through the powerful magnifying glass which he took from the small leather grip he had brought with him, before turning to Sir Edgar. 'If I might have a cardboard box and some cotton wadding, I should like, with your permission, to take these back with me to London for further examination.'

'Of course,' Sir Edgar replied, pulling on a bell rope to summon a servant, 'although I fail to see what possible use they could be to the inquiry. However, I am in your hands, Mr Holmes.'

A servant having arrived and been duly sent off again to return with those articles which my old friend had requested, Holmes lifted each glass carefully by the stem and laid them side by side in the box on top of some of the wadding. More wadding was placed over them, the lid was replaced and tied on with string and finally the box was placed inside the grip.

Both Sir Edgar and I watched this operation with considerable interest, Sir Edgar baffled by it; I, who knew something of Holmes's methods, not entirely surprised at his interest in these objects.

'And now,' Holmes announced, having fastened up the grip, 'I should like to examine the room where the burglary took place.'

It was while we were walking along the passageway towards the drawing-room that Sir Edgar suddenly remarked, 'The port glasses have reminded me, Mr Holmes. Yesterday you asked if any strangers had been to the house. At the time, I could think of nobody. But seeing the glasses again, I have just remembered that there was a visitor although it was so long ago, I doubt if he has anything to do with the burglary. I offered him a glass of port after luncheon and he remarked on the excellence of its quality.'

Holmes lifted his head, his expression alert and keen-eyed, like a gun-dog scenting game.

'How long ago was this visit, Sir Edgar?'

'Let me see. It must have been last November. He was an American professor who wrote asking to look over the place. He said he was an expert on Tudor architecture.'

It was Holmes's habit to become very tense and still when he had reached a significant stage in an investigation, as if all his attention were concentrated on this one point although, under the apparently calm exterior, one could feel the energy vibrating like a finely-tuned engine.

I was aware of that hidden power when in a quiet voice he inquired, 'Do you happen to have the letter?'

'It may still be among my papers. If you wish, I can look for it while you examine the drawing-room,' Sir Edgar replied, throwing open a door.

While Sir Edgar departed to search for the correspondence, Holmes and I stepped inside the room. It was a large chamber, beamed and panelled like the dining-room, and with three long windows overlooking the garden. Even from the doorway, it was possible to see the circular hole which had been cut in one of the panes immediately above a window-catch, large enough to admit a man's hand.

Holmes strode across the room to examine both the hole and the window-ledge.

'Neatly made, Watson, with a diamond-tipped glass-cutter; the sign of an expert. Observe also the marks on the sill where our villains climbed in and out. No footprints in the flower-bed below the window,' he continued, opening the casement and leaning his head out, 'apart from some heavy trampling in the surrounding area which I assume is the work of Inspector Biffen and his subordinates. But aha! What have we here? Kindly pass me the tweezers, there's a good fellow.'

I did as he requested, eagerly stepping forward to observe the object which he had retrieved.

'It is just a small piece of fluff,' I remarked.

'Fluff? Nonsense, Watson! If you examine it with the aid of the lens, you will see that it consists of fibres torn from a piece of brown felt. They were caught on a splinter of wood on the lower frame of the window. You can also observe, can you not, the earth which has been trodden into them? No wonder our villains were so silent and left no shoe-prints. They were careful to encase their feet in felt slippers. It is all so highly professional that it is a privilege to observe their methods. And now,' he concluded, depositing the fibres in an envelope which he placed inside his pocket-book, 'let us examine the cabinets from which the art treasures were taken.'

The cabinets stood in the chimney alcoves on either side of a large stone fireplace. Both were glass-fronted and the doors, which had been fitted with strong, brass locks, had been left ajar. Inside, gaps between the objects displayed on the shelves showed where the missing items had once stood.

It was while Holmes was kneeling on the floor, examining the key escutcheons, that Sir Edgar entered the room, a sheet of paper in his hand.

'I have found the letter,' he announced, handing it to Holmes who, having read it, passed it to me. It was written on paper which bore the printed heading, 'The University of Chicago, Department of History', and the date October 6th of the previous year.

It read:

> Dear Sir Edgar,
>
> I am engaged in writing a monograph on Tudor country houses and their interior design and should count it a great privilege if I may have your permission to visit Whitestone Manor which I understand has a superb Elizabethan wing with original panelling.
>
> I shall be in London between November 1st and the 20th, staying at the Desborough Hotel, Strand, and should be most grateful if your reply could be addressed to me there.

It was signed 'Jonas T. Vanderbilt, Professor of History'.

'You wrote to him and arranged a visit?' Holmes inquired of Sir Edgar.

'Indeed I did. I sent a letter to his London hotel, suggesting he should come on November 10th by the same 10.15 train that you caught. But you are surely not implying that he was behind the burglary? He seemed most respectable. Why, I even sent the carriage to meet him at the station!'

'What was his appearance?'

'He was a tall, elderly, white-haired gentleman; a little stooped in the shoulders; spoke, of course, with an American accent and was highly knowledgeable about Tudor architecture.'

'He was shown over the house?'

'Not all of it but, yes, I conducted him round the main rooms, including this one, the dining-room where we had luncheon, and some of the bedrooms. He was most grateful for the opportunity and wrote me a charming letter of thanks.'

Sir Edgar broke off at this point as the butler entered to announce that Inspector Biffen had arrived and was waiting in the hall. Having conducted us there, Sir Edgar introduced us to the man before excusing himself on the grounds of some matter of urgent estate business which had to be completed before luncheon.

Biffen, who was accompanied by a police constable, was a lean, narrow-eyed and thin-lipped man who clearly resented Holmes's presence and mine for he shook hands stiffly, remarking in a sneering manner, 'Sir Edgar has every right to call in whom he pleases, Mr Holmes. But for all your reputation, you will not have any success with this case. The clues are too few. In fact, I have this very morning sent a telegram to Scotland Yard, requesting assistance. I am expecting a reply at any moment. Not that we have been exactly idle. Only half an hour ago, my men, continuing the search of the gardens under my express orders, have discovered the place where the villains entered the grounds. I doubt if you would have found it.'

'Probably not, Inspector,' Holmes agreed suavely. 'I should like, however, to be shown where it is.'

With bad grace, Biffen conceded and we followed him across a large sweep of lawn, surrounded by carefully tended herbaceous borders, to a shrubbery at the far side of which he halted in front of a high brick wall.

'That's where they got in, Mr Holmes,' Biffen announced with an unpleasantly triumphant air. 'You can see where the ivy has been disturbed on the top of the coping.'

'But how', Holmes inquired, 'did they manage to scale the wall? It is all of fifteen feet high.'

Biffen's smug smile immediately faded, to be replaced by a much more chastened expression. It was quite clear that the question had not occurred to him. The mystery, however, was soon solved, at least to Holmes's satisfaction.

The constable was despatched to fetch a ladder and, when he returned with it, Holmes leaned it against the brickwork and, mounting the rungs, carefully parted the strands of ivy before examining the stone coping with the aid of his powerful pocket lens.

'Most satisfactory!' he remarked, descending and dusting off his hands. 'As I had expected, Watson, it is yet another example of the high degree of efficiency with which this pair of thieves operates. But come! We must return to the house and complete our examination of the scene of the crime.'

Deliberately ignoring Biffen, he set off through the shrubbery although, once we were out of earshot of the Inspector, he remarked to me in a low voice, 'Judging by the two parallel marks in the coping, our villains used a rope ladder fitted with hooks. By such means, it would be a matter of a few minutes for them to enter and leave the grounds. I wonder if Biffen will come to the same conclusion? I admit I could not resist the temptation to goad him a little by withholding the information. He is such an insufferable fellow.'

He turned to look back and, following his glance, I saw Biffen hastily scrambling up the ladder, shouting to the constable who remained below to hold it steady. At the sight, Holmes gave a chuckle of sardonic amusement.

On our return to Whitestone Manor, Holmes resumed his minute scrutiny of the cabinet locks, finally laying down his lens with the remark, 'Whoever picked these was an expert, Watson. Apart from a few tiny scratches, the brass escutcheons are barely marked.'

At this juncture, luncheon was announced and we joined Sir Edgar in the dining-room where our host informed us that only minutes earlier Inspector Biffen had received an answer to his telegram, brought from Great Walden by a constable on a bicycle, its message being that a Scotland Yard detective would be arriving on the two minutes past three train from London.

'Did Biffen happen to mention the name of this Inspector?' Holmes inquired with an offhand air.

'A Letrade or Lestrade,' Sir Edgar replied.

Holmes exchanged a glance with me.

'In that case, Sir Edgar,' he said in his blandest manner, 'I think it better that Dr Watson and I should leave before he arrives. We should not wish to cramp the style of the official police. Besides, we have completed our investigation here for the time being. No doubt you will be sending the carriage to meet this Scotland Yard detective at the station? Then, to save a double journey, Dr Watson and I shall take the opportunity of travelling in it to Great Walden.'

'But the next train to London does not leave until twelve minutes past four!' Sir Edgar protested. 'You will have a wait of nearly an hour.'

'The time will not be wasted,' Holmes assured him. 'There are several inquiries I wish to make in Great Walden before returning to town.'

'What inquiries, Holmes?' I asked when, the carriage having arrived, we had taken leave of Sir Edgar and seated ourselves inside it.

'At the George inn, my good Watson.'

'Oh, yes! I remember now you asked the coachman when we first arrived which was the best hostelry in the town and he recommended the George. At the time, I wondered why you should be interested.'

'Is it not obvious, Watson? We have already deduced that it is more than likely that our villains travelled down by train from London. As it is also highly probable that they would not have arrived on a late train which would have few passengers, thus making their presence conspicuous, we may further deduce that they would have chosen one which arrived in the late afternoon or early evening. Now even burglars have to eat, so I have assumed that they would have dined somewhere in Great Walden. Hence the inquiries I propose to make at the George.'

'Wait a moment, Holmes,' I put in, perceiving a flaw in his chain of reasoning. 'Why are you so convinced they dined at the George and not at some other hostelry in the town?'

'Because, my dear fellow, it is the best, as the coachman indicated, and Vanderbilt, as we have learned from Sir Edgar's evidence, has a taste for the good things of life. No man who can appreciate a glass of '67 port is likely to dine anywhere except at the finest inn a town can boast of.'

The George, where on Holmes's instructions the carriage

deposited us before continuing its journey to the railway station to meet Inspector Lestrade's train, was a large, well-appointed inn, probably dating back to the days of the stage-coach, if not earlier.

Inside the hostelry, Holmes sought out the head-waiter, inquiring of him, after a half-crown had exchanged hands, about any gentlemen who had dined there on the Friday evening, the night before the burglary at Whitestone Manor.

'There were two of them,' Holmes concluded, 'one of whom was carrying quite a large bag, such as a portmanteau.'

Yes, the head-waiter did indeed remember two gentlemen dining together that evening, one a tall, well-built man with a brown beard and eyeglasses. His companion who was much shorter, with a pale face and a dark moustache, had been in charge of a carpet-bag.

They had arrived at about quarter to eight and had left shortly after ten o'clock, the taller of the two, who had paid the bill and had done all the talking, announcing that they intended to catch the ten twenty train to Ipswich.

'Although I doubt if that was their destination,' Holmes remarked as we set off on foot for the railway station.

Here, further inquiries of the porter established the fact that the down train from Liverpool Street station arrived at Great Walden at seven thirty-five on a weekday evening, although the porter had not remarked on any individual passengers, there being too many arrivals.

'And what is the first train to London on a Saturday morning?' Holmes asked.

'The twelve minutes past five,' the porter replied.

After further questioning on Holmes's part, we learned that only a few individuals had travelled on that train the previous Saturday, among whom had been two men, one a tall, clean-shaven, grey-haired gentleman, the other much shorter, dressed like a working-man in a cap and corduroy trousers and carrying a carpet-bag which the porter had assumed contained the tools of his trade. But, the porter added, they were not together and had stood at opposite ends of the platform as they waited for the London train.

At this point, our own train arrived and Holmes and I climbed into a first class carriage where my old friend threw himself down on the seat with a chuckle of satisfaction.

'A most satisfactory day's work, Watson! We have uncovered a great deal of useful and pertinent information and shall still be back in time for dinner.'

'Yes, I suppose it has been successful,' I replied.

'"Suppose", my dear fellow? There is no "suppose" about it! We are now in possession of a large number of facts, particularly those concerning Professor Jonas T. Vanderbilt, which no doubt is an alias but which will serve as his name until such time as we discover his real one. Not only is he a master of disguise but he is a man who plans these burglaries in meticulous detail. He has even gone to the trouble to have some writing-paper printed with the University of Chicago's letter-heading. You noticed, I assume, how he changed his appearance from the elderly, white-haired professor who visited Sir Edgar last November to the gentleman with the brown beard who dined at the George, and again to the grey-haired, clean-shaven passenger who caught the early train to London? Three separate disguises designed, of course, to throw the police off the scent! He and his accomplice were also careful not to make the return journey together but appeared to be travelling separately. But height is less easily concealed and Vanderbilt is invariably described as being a tall man. He is almost certainly the brains behind these burglaries. His companion, who is much shorter, is probably what is referred to among the criminal fraternity as a yeggman.'*

'A yeggman?'

'Have you not heard the name before? It is a slang term of uncertain etymology which means an itinerant burglar or safe-breaker who travels from "drum" to "drum" committing the actual felony. A "drum", by the way, Watson, in case that word is also unfamiliar to you, is a house or building, in this case the premises selected for the robbery.'

* According to the *Oxford English Dictionary*, 'Yegg' is said to be the name of a certain American burglar or safe-breaker. (Dr John F. Watson)

'Yes, I am aware of that, Holmes,' I put in.

'We also know', Holmes continued, ignoring my interpolation, 'what equipment the yeggman brought with him. Apart from the usual cracksman's tools of a glass-cutter and a set of "bettys" – picklocks to you, Watson – it included a rope ladder. It was for this reason I inquired at the George about a man carrying a large bag. Even rolled up, a rope ladder is quite bulky. The bag must also have contained the various wigs and moustaches, as well as the changes of clothing, with which they altered their appearances.

'As for their movements on the night of the burglary, we can establish these in such detail that it is almost as if we are treading on their heels! They travelled down from London on the 7.35 train, dined at the George and then probably made their way to Whitestone Manor across the fields by a footpath. I noticed a sign for such a path on the drive from the station. Having gained entry to the grounds of the manor, they waited until all the lights of the house were extinguished before, donning their felt slippers, they effected their entrance through the drawing-room window and quietly helped themselves to those art treasures which Vanderbilt had already selected on his previous visit to the house last November.

'On the same occasion, Vanderbilt was shown over the upper floor so he would have know exactly which bedrooms were occupied by Sir Edgar and the servants. He would also have had the opportunity to ascertain whether or not a guard dog was kept on the premises. Once the burglary was successfully completed, they then changed their appearances and walked back across the fields to Great Walden station in time to catch the 5.12 train to London. There is no doubt about any of that. The question is – was a third man involved?'

'A third man, Holmes? But there can't have been. There were only two glasses.'

'I do not mean at the actual burglary, Watson. I am speaking of an agent of Vanderbilt and his yeggman who was responsible for the disposal of the art treasures once they were stolen. Alternatively, there may have been no middleman and Vanderbilt sold the objects directly to a collector with whom he had already struck up a deal.'

'You are surely not implying that the items were stolen to order?'

'It is not entirely impossible. You will recall the theft some time ago of the Fragonard from the Walpole collection which was purloined on the specific directions of Monsieur Henri de la Bertauche, the *escargot* millionaire, to add to his own collection of that artist's work. We may be dealing with a similar situation here. Of course, if that is the case, the heirlooms can never be placed on public display but will have to remain for the private delectation only of whoever arranged their thefts. We may discover the truth when we apprehend Vanderbilt and his accomplice.'

'You sound very sure they will be arrested.'

'I have every confidence, Watson.'

To tease him a little, I remarked, 'Now that Inspector Lestrade has been called in on the case, you may find our old friend from Scotland Yard will beat you to the finishing post, Holmes. After all, if the evidence is there for you to uncover, there is nothing to prevent Lestrade from coming to the same conclusions.'

'But he will fail to make the right connections, Watson. Take my word on that. I have studied Lestrade's methods and I know exactly how his mind works. He may indeed uncover some of the facts of the Whitestone Manor burglary but he will not look further afield to the other similar thefts which have occurred over the past two years. It is one of the greatest weaknesses of our police force as it is at present organized. It is too fragmented. Each county constabulary is isolated within its own boundaries. They are like gamekeepers, concerned only with what happens inside their own little estates while the criminals, such as Vanderbilt and his yeggman, who recognize no such bounds, move freely between them. One would think the railways had not been invented! What is needed is some central intelligence agency to which each police force would send details of all major crimes that occur in their area. I know if I were ever appointed head of Scotland Yard – which Heaven forbid! – I should make the establishment of such a bureau my first priority.

'It is because I have collected up all the relevant data that I am confident of bringing Vanderbilt and his accomplice to justice. Indeed, Watson, if you care to call in at Baker Street on Friday afternoon, I shall lay those facts before you. You can arrange to be free at half past two, can you not, my dear fellow? I shall be most disappointed if you deny me that pleasure.'

It was difficult to refuse Holmes at any time, more particularly when he was in such a sprightly and good-humoured mood and, as he had requested, I returned to Baker Street at the appointed time to be met in the hall by a harassed-looking Mrs Hudson who, on my inquiring if anything were the matter, burst out with uncharacteristic agitation for one usually so calm, 'It's Mr Holmes, Dr Watson! He's been up and down to the kitchen for the past two days asking for baking-powder and rabbits' feet and goodness knows what else besides. And saucers! I have hardly a clean one left in the house. And that isn't all. He's asked the maid, the page-boy, even the postman, to pick up those little glass slides he puts into his microscope. He says it is part of a scientific experiment but it makes it very difficult for me to carry out my work.'

I thought I could guess what lay behind the experiment although I admit some of the ingredients puzzled me and, on entering the sitting-room, I inquired, 'What's all this I hear about baking-powder and rabbits' feet, Holmes?'

Holmes, who was stooping his long, thin frame over his scientific bench, looked round at my query.

'Rabbit's *foot*, my dear Watson,' he corrected me. 'Singular, not plural. I fear Mrs Hudson has been confiding in you. An excellent woman in many ways but, like all her sex, she prefers the routine of daily life to an exploration of the esoteric. And not just baking-powder either. Come over here and see what I have been doing.'

The bench was strewn with a motley collection of objects. In addition to the microscope slides laid end to end, there was a small regiment of saucers containing different substances amongst which I recognized soot, cigar ash, powdered charcoal and flour. The rabbit's foot was also in evidence together with a selection of brushes which included Holmes's own badger-hair shaving-brush. In pride of place in the centre of the bench stood the two port glasses from Whitestone Manor.

'First of all, examine the glasses through the lens,' Holmes continued, handing me that object. 'You will observe that three fingermarks are clearly discernible on their surfaces, on one the imprint of a thumb and a little finger, on the other a second thumb impression. Do not trouble with the other marks. They are too blurred to be of any use.'

'Yes, I can indeed see them!' I exclaimed, surprised to discover how clearly the prints, which had been dusted over with a white powder, stood out against the glass. It was possible to discern the patterns of each individual mark.

When I commented on this, Holmes replied, 'Precisely, Watson! That is the whole point of the experiment. Now, if you care to look at this sheet of paper, you will see that I have made exact drawings of those prints, marking in the patterns of loops, whorls and ridges. You will observe that the two thumb marks are quite different, one possessing a double loop while on the other, which has only one, the lines are much farther apart. Now if you compare those with these other thumb impressions on the microscope slides, belonging respectively to Mrs Hudson, the postman and the boy in buttons, you will also observe that they also have their own distinctive patterns. In other words, Watson, the chances of one person's finger patterns matching another's is so small that the figures are hardly worth taking into account.

'Now I do not know if you are aware that in October of last year, a committee under the chairmanship of Mr Troup of the Home Office issued a report following their inquiries into the best method of identifying habitual criminals – whether the Bertillon anthropometric system was to be preferred over the alternative suggestion of recording the felons' finger marks.'

'I thought you were a keen supporter of the Bertillon method, Holmes.'

'Indeed I was, my dear Watson. At the time, it was the only means by which the habitual criminal could be identified. But first one had to catch one's felon before one could photograph him and take all the necessary detailed measurements of his physiognomy. However, I am now an enthusiast of the alternative system – that of finger impressions. I have been closely following the pioneer work done in this field, undertaken in Britain by Sir Francis Galton, the eminent anthropologist and eugenist, and by the Argentinian, Juan Vecutich, both of whom have done sterling service in devising methods by which the individual finger patterns can be identified and recorded. In fact, I understand the Central Police Department of La Plata, Argentina, introduced a finger pattern system four years ago and have therefore stolen a march on our own Scotland Yard. But it will come, Watson! It will come!*

'However, we can comfort ourselves with the thought that it was two fellow countrymen of ours, Dr Henry Faulds and Sir William Herschel, who first suggested the value of finger marks for purposes of identification and who published articles on the subject in the magazine *Nature* as long ago as 1880. Indeed, Sir William can rightly be called the father of the finger pattern method for it was he who initially introduced the system into the prisons when he was administrator of the Hooghly district of Bengal.

'But, useful though the method is for identifying felons once they are in custody,' Holmes continued, his voice growing vibrant with excitement, 'as far as I am concerned, the beauty of it is its application at the scene of a crime *before* the villain is apprehended. Think of it, Watson! A burglary, say, or a murder is committed. The perpetrator leaves the marks of his fingers on some object. These impressions are then matched to records held at Scotland Yard of known felons, by which means his identity is immediately established. Or, should he not have a criminal record, they can be kept on file until such time as he is arrested. Either way, the villain is linked as indisputably to his crime as if he had had his photograph taken at the moment of committing it! It adds a new interpretation to the old saying "to be caught red-handed".'

* Mr Sherlock Holmes was correct in his prophecy. In July 1901, a Fingerprint Bureau was established at New Scotland Yard by Sir Edward Henry. (Dr John F. Watson)

'Yes, I see that, Holmes. But what are all these saucers and brushes for?'

'Oh, those!' Holmes said carelessly. 'I have been experimenting with various substances to dust over latent finger marks in order to make them more visible to the naked eye. Powdered chalk is the best, I find, applied with a fine camel-hair brush, using only the tip of it with quick, curving strokes. I am considering writing a monograph on the subject. And speaking of writing, Watson, I have received a number of replies to those letters I wrote the other day. To save you the trouble of reading through the whole collection, I shall summarize the information for your benefit.

'Firstly, the houses that were burgled over the past two years. All five owners have replied and without exception, each one of them received a visit from a man five to six months before the actual felonies were committed. Let me go briefly over them in turn. In one case, it was our old friend Professor Vanderbilt but on this occasion he was in his forties, dark-haired and came from the University of Los Angeles. Then there were two German Professors, one from Munich who had a small goatee beard; the other from Dresden, with grey whiskers and gold-rimmed eyeglasses. Finally, there was a Frenchman, head of Medieval Studies at the Municipal Museum of Bordeaux, who sported a fine black, waxed moustache and walked with a limp. All claimed to be experts in some particular architectural style featured in the houses which were later burgled, from fifteenth-century stone mullions to Regency fireplaces.

'As for the objects which were stolen from the various premises, allow me to read a few items from the list I have compiled. "A jewelled fan which had belonged to Lord Maplewood's great-grandmother. A collection of eighteenth-century family silhouettes carved from ivory. A pair of silver salts given by Charles II to a female ancestor of the Duke of Medwater." I could go on, Watson, but I believe you may have grasped their significance.

'For my part, I am convinced that they were stolen on the specific orders of a private collector. Indeed, I am beginning to build up a picture of the man, stroke by stroke. He is undoubtedly very rich and almost certainly eccentric, for what normal man would go to such extremes to acquire these objects? In addition, I see him as a self-made millionaire with some doubt surrounding his own antecedents which causes him great personal shame and distress. He could be either a bastard or a foundling.'

'Oh, I say, Holmes!' I protested. 'You are reading too much into the situation.'

'I think not,' he replied with a quiet confidence which cut short any further objection. 'Consider the items which have been stolen by Vanderbilt on this man's behalf. They are all personal belongings once owned by some illustrious individual of historic interest or importance. I believe that our collector, whom for reasons of easy reference I shall call the Magpie, has ordered their theft in order to provide himself with the illusion that he can lay claim to the same eminent and wealthy forebears as compensation for his own doubtful pedigree.

'As you know, Watson, I am not normally a fanciful man. I prefer facts to speculation. And yet, I must confess that the Magpie has caught my imagination. I can picture him alone in a locked room, gloating over these family treasures as if they were his own.'

We were both silent for a few moments while we contemplated this image before Holmes continued more briskly, 'But let us return to the present reality and the facts of the case under investigation. What else do we know about Vanderbilt which we can add to our knowledge of him?'

'Well, he must be widely travelled,' I ventured, 'if he has sent letters from places as far apart as Los Angeles and Dresden requesting permission to look over the houses.'

I was pleased with this piece of deduction, only to be dashed when Holmes replied, 'Not necessarily. He could have acquaintances in all these different cities. Vanderbilt merely wrote to them, enclosing the letters, which were already addressed, and asked his colleagues to post them on his behalf. His associates may not even be aware that there was any criminal intention behind the request.'

'You did ask, Holmes,' I pointed out, a little piqued at his reply.

'The question was merely rhetorical, my dear fellow, and did not require an answer. Pray allow me to continue with my main theme. I have marked the dates of each burglary on an almanac and another interesting fact has come to light. All of them took place on a night when there was no moon. Bear that in mind, Watson, when we turn to the answers that I received from those owners of country houses which seemed likely targets for Vanderbilt's next foray.

'Not all replied but among those who took the trouble to write was Colonel Heath-Bennington of Huntswood Hall, Upper Tilney, in the county of Kent. If you would pass me once again my volume on country houses, I shall read out to you the relevant parts of the entry. Thank you. "Huntswood Hall, a Georgian mansion, possessing very fine eighteenth-century panelling in the main rooms. Among its superb collection of antiques and heirlooms" – and mark this, Watson! – "are the family christening basin, a rare example of the seventeenth-century silversmith's art, an exquisitely illuminated Book of Hours which belonged to one of the Heath-Benningtons' remoter ancestors, and a gold and emerald locket containing a piece of the Duke of Wellington's hair, the present head of the family having descended from the Duke on the maternal side."'

Putting down the book, Holmes picked up a letter.

'Colonel Heath-Bennington writes that last October he received a letter from a certain Professor Angelo Galiano of Turin University requesting permission to examine the panelling in the house. Professor Galiano was, it seems, an expert on the use of carved wood in eighteenth-century domestic interiors and was planning a series of lectures on the subject. Like Professor Vanderbilt, Professor Galiano had arranged to stay at a London hotel to which Colonel Heath-Bennington wrote granting permission, and the Professor duly arrived at Huntswood Hall in November of last year. He was, Colonel Heath-Bennington writes, a most charming and knowledgeable man; in his fifties, with a full brown beard and spectacles.'

'Good Lord, Holmes! That surely means – ?'

'Indeed it does, Watson. The question is, exactly when will Vanderbilt and his attendant yeggman return to Huntswood Hall?'

'Next month when there is no moon?' I suggested.

'That is precisely my opinion, my old friend. If we consult the almanac, a most useful volume of reference and indispensable on this occasion, we find that the likely date is July 14th.'

There was a ring at the front door at this point and Holmes broke off to announce, 'Ah, the telegraph boy has arrived!'

'How do you know that?' I inquired.

'Two reasons, Watson. Firstly, the peremptory nature of the summons. Only telegraph boys and bailiffs press a doorbell quite so imperiously. Secondly, I am expecting a reply to the telegram I sent off yesterday afternoon to Colonel Heath-Bennington after receiving his letter by the midday post.'

A few moments later, Mrs Hudson brought in the message and, having cast a reproachful glance at the row of saucers on the scientific bench, left the room.

Holmes eagerly tore open the envelope and, scanning its contents, exclaimed with evident pleasure, 'Excellent! The Colonel has agreed to my suggestions. He will send his carriage to meet the 11.25 at Chatham station. He also adds, "As CC no problem with local inspector. Gow good man."'

'What on earth does he mean by that, Holmes?' I asked, puzzled by the cryptic nature of the last part of the message.

'It means, Watson, that at the meeting tomorrow with Colonel Heath-Bennington there will also be present, as I requested, an Inspector from the local constabulary – which, in his capacity as Chief Constable, the Colonel has been able to arrange with no difficulty. I take it that this Inspector, Gow by name, is in the Colonel's estimation a competent police officer. But we shall judge that for ourselves when we meet him tomorrow.'

'"We", Holmes? You intend that I shall accompany you?'

'Of course, my dear fellow. I assumed you would wish to be included in the invitation. Surely you can arrange for a colleague to take over your practice for the day?'

'Unfortunately not, Holmes. I have a most important appointment which I cannot possibly postpone and which I myself must attend.'

'That is a great pity. I was looking forward to having your company. But no matter. I shall attend the meeting alone and report back to you tomorrow evening if you care to call round at eight o'clock. But please make sure you are free on July 14th, Watson. You must not be absent on that occasion for it is on that date, I believe, that we shall lay Vanderbilt and his yeggman by the heels.'

As Holmes had requested, I called back on the following evening and listened eagerly to his report. All had gone well, Holmes informed me. Colonel Heath-Bennington had been most co-operative, Inspector Gow both intelligent and efficient, and between the three of them the arrangements for July 14th had been completed to everyone's satisfaction.

'By the way, Watson,' Holmes concluded, 'when we return to Huntswood Hall on July 14th, please bring with you an overnight bag and a stout walking-stick. Vanderbilt and his accomplice may be armed.'

'Shall I pack my revolver?' I inquired.

'I think not on this occasion,' Holmes replied, a note of regret in his voice. 'We shall be acting in liaison with the official police and they may object to firearms. A stick will have to suffice. I shall bring my own favourite weapon, my lead-weighted riding crop.* As we shall catch the 5.24 from Charing Cross, please make sure you call here in good time.'

I saw nothing of Holmes in the intervening weeks, returning to Baker Street only on the afternoon of July 14th when, as Holmes had specified, we caught the 5.24 train to Chatham. There we were met by Colonel Heath-Bennington's brougham and were driven to Huntswood Hall, a charming Georgian mansion set in extensive grounds.

Holmes introduced me to the Colonel, a tall, vigorous gentleman, with a smart, clipped moustache, a former officer in the Rutland Light Cavalry, now retired and managing the family estates at Huntswood.

* Dr John H. Watson refers to a 'loaded riding-crop' as being Mr Sherlock Holmes's favourite weapon in 'The Adventure of the Six Napoleons'. (Dr John F. Watson)

From his conversation over dinner, I gathered that the arrangements for that night had been made with military precision. Inspector Gow would arrive in time to join us for coffee, accompanied by six police constables and a sergeant who would be conveyed to the house in a closed bread van, requisitioned for the occasion from a local baker, the ruse having been devised by the Colonel in order not to arouse the suspicions of Vanderbilt and his yeggman in case they should be watching the premises. The sergeant and the constables would be entertained in the servants' hall until the time when the household would normally retire for the night.

The servants having gone to bed and the lights in the house having been extinguished, the police officers would then take up their positions. Three, including the sergeant, would be posted in the grounds in case Vanderbilt and his accomplice attempted to escape, and two in the hall; while two more, together with Inspector Gow, would be stationed along with Holmes, the Colonel and myself in the drawing-room where it was assumed the attempted burglary would take place.

When dinner was over, we retired to the drawing-room, where coffee was served and where Inspector Gow shortly joined us.

I was a little disappointed on first being introduced to the Inspector. He was a large, slow-moving man with a shock of very fair hair and almost white eyelashes, but this appearance of a country yokel was belied by the intelligent expression in his pale blue eyes and the air of quiet efficiency with which he assigned to us the positions we were to take up in the room.

One constable, together with Holmes, was to be posted near the windows to cut off the burglars' retreat. The Colonel's place was by the door leading into the hall; I myself would be concealed behind a large sofa; while Inspector Gow would take up a position close to a flat-topped display cabinet in which were displayed those family heirlooms, such as the christening basin, the locket and the illuminated Book of Hours which, it was assumed, had already been selected by Vanderbilt as items to steal.

Inspector Gow went on to explain that no one was to move

until he gave the order. When he did so, the two constables in the hall, equipped with lanterns, would then rush into the room.

In the meantime, we were to wait in total silence and darkness.

At midnight, signalled by the bell in the stable clock-tower striking twelve, Colonel Heath-Bennington, accompanied by the Inspector, made a final tour of the house, the Inspector to make sure that his men were in position, the Colonel to check that the servants were safely upstairs and the house was in darkness.

On their return to the drawing-room, the Colonel extinguished the lamps and we took up our own positions, I crouching behind the sofa, my heavy walking stick in my hand.

There is a tension about waiting to which I have never become adapted although Holmes has mastered the art to perfection. I have seen him stand for hours in a doorway or a darkened room, all his senses alert and yet with no apparent strain or weariness. Perhaps his remarkable ability of seeing in the dark, which he has carefully cultivated and which I have commented on elsewhere,* helped to sustain him during such stressful periods.

For my part, I was incapable of relaxation and was soon aware of a numbed sensation in my limbs, particularly in the hand which gripped the cudgel, while the heavy beating of my heart seemed to my ears to echo like a drum through the muffled darkness.

Apart from this, the only other sound to break the silence and the monotony was the stable clock striking the hours.

One o'clock passed and then two.

I was beginning to doubt if Holmes had chosen the right date and to think that the burglary would take place on August 11th, the next night when there would be no moon, when I heard a sound outside in the garden, so faint that it was almost inaudible.

* Dr John H. Watson refers to this ability of Mr Sherlock Holmes in 'The Adventure of Charles Augustus Milverton'. (Dr John F. Watson)

A footstep perhaps? Or was it merely the night breeze stirring in the shrubbery?

It was followed by a silence so complete that I persuaded myself I had heard nothing.

Several minutes passed and then there came another noise, still soft but this time clearly recognizable. It was the unmistakable squeak of metal on glass.

The long curtains over the central window stirred gently in a sudden draught which I could feel against the side of my face. The next moment, there was a tiny click as the window catch was released, then the sound of the bottom sash being pushed softly upwards and two figures, one tall, one short, were silhouetted momentarily against the night sky as the curtains were parted and they climbed in over the sill.

As the draperies fell back into place, total darkness again descended and I would not have been aware of the burglars' presence nor of their silent advance into the room had they not opened the shutters on their dark lanterns and, by the forward motion of the glimmering spots of light, I was able to plot their progress.

The little cones of brightness proceeded step by step, past my own hiding-place, illuminating briefly the gilded legs of chairs and the pattern on the carpet until they reached the far side of the room where they paused to hover like two luminous moths above the cabinet.

As they did so, Inspector Gow rose from his place of concealment.

'Now, my lads! At them!'

There was a startled oath from one of the two figures, soon lost in the general outcry as we rushed forward, I among the *mêlée*, clutching my stick but hesitating to use it on the writhing mass of bodies on the floor in case I struck at friend instead of foe.

To my great relief, at this moment the two constables burst in from the hall with their lanterns, the lamps were lit and it was possible at last to discern what was happening.

Holmes, his face blazing with a look of triumphant exultation, was kneeling over the recumbent body of a man spread-eagled on the floor, his loaded riding-crop raised, while the Colonel and the Inspector held another struggling figure by the arms.

As the Inspector snapped on the handcuffs, I stood back to observe the captives.

The shorter of the two, who I deduced was the yeggman, was a small, rat-faced individual with black hair and so white-complexioned and undersized that it seemed he might have been raised in some dark cellar, well away from sunlight and air.

On the other hand, his companion, Vanderbilt, whom Holmes had been guarding on the floor, was a tall, well set-up man, broad in the shoulders and good-looking, with clever, mobile features which would have easily adapted themselves to the many identities he had assumed during his infamous career.

Unlike his yeggman, who cowered back, snarling like a cornered dog, Vanderbilt stood erect, a smile playing about his lips, as the Inspector placed the handcuffs on his wrists. He then bowed to the Inspector before turning to Holmes to make an even deeper obeisance.

'Mr Sherlock Holmes, I assume?' he inquired in a courteous, educated voice which bore a trace of a foreign accent. 'I have long wondered when I would find you on my trail. *Mes félicitations, mon cher monsieur*. Or, as Professor Galiano might have expressed the same sentiments, *Congratulazioni*! You have proved to be a worthy opponent.'

'And so, too, have you,' Holmes replied, returning the bow. 'It has afforded me the greatest pleasure to take part in the chase. But the hunt is, I think, not quite over. Before Inspector Gow takes you and your accomplice into custody, pray do me the kindness to answer me one question.'

'If I can, I shall be happy to oblige.'

'Then what is the identity of the man who is behind your series of burglaries and whom I call the Magpie for want of his real name?'

Vanderbilt laughed, throwing back his head.

'The Magpie! That is an excellent pseudonym which suits him perfectly! But, my apologies, Mr Holmes. I very much regret that I cannot reveal his identity; not for reasons of thieves' honour, you understand, but for a far more pressing consideration – money. I have discussed with the Magpie, as you call him, the possibility that I might one day be apprehended and have received his assurance that, should that contingency arise, a very large sum of money will be deposited in a bank account which, on my release from prison, I shall be able to draw on, provided I keep his identity secret. I am sure you can understand, Mr Holmes, that under those circumstances, my lips must remain sealed. And now, Inspector,' Vanderbilt added, turning to Gow, 'if you are ready, shall we complete the formalities?'

As Inspector Gow stepped forward to escort Vanderbilt and his accomplice from the room, assisted by the police constables, Vanderbilt bowed again in Holmes's direction but this time my old friend did not return the courtesy. Instead, he stood quite silent and immobile as the villains made their departure and the door closed behind them.

Nor would he agree to join the Colonel and myself at a celebratory supper of ham sandwiches and glasses of whisky which the butler had laid out in readiness in the study. Instead, Holmes excused himself and went upstairs to his bedroom, exhausted, I assumed, by his exertions and the nervous tension of the past few weeks.

He was in a similar subdued mood over breakfast the following morning and, when the time came for our departure, accepted the Colonel's congratulations and thanks in a reticent fashion.

It was not until we were in the train on our way back to London that I received any response from him.

As I settled myself in a corner seat, I remarked, echoing Holmes's own words after our visit to Whitestone Manor, 'A most satisfactory night's work!'

I was considerably taken aback when Holmes turned on me a most morose expression.

'Is it, Watson? I find nothing in it to be sanguine about. For my part, I confess I am bitterly disappointed.'

'But I do not see why, Holmes!' I cried in disbelief. 'After all, you have successfully arranged for the arrest of two professional criminals who will no doubt serve long prison sentences.'

'Yes, *two*, Watson. Two! But the third, the Magpie, who organized this series of thefts, has slipped our net and while he remains at large I shall count this case as one of my failures. No!' he added sternly, holding up a hand to cut short any further argument. 'Not another word on the subject, there's a good fellow. And you will oblige me by refraining from writing an account of the case unless it is for your own personal amusement.'

It was my turn to be bitterly disappointed.

'But, Holmes – !' I began.

'I am resolved. Do you wish to publish the story of my failure while at the same time – and worse still! – advertising to the Magpie my interest in his whereabouts together with my deductions concerning his identity? No, Watson. The public shall remain in ignorance of the case until such time as the Magpie is behind bars and I have restored to their rightful owners those family heirlooms which no doubt he is exulting over at this very moment.'

And with that, he shook out his copy of *The Times* and retired behind it, leaving me to come to terms with his refusal and to turn over in my mind how I might slip at least a brief reference to the case of Vanderbilt and his yeggman into the published canon in order to prevent that remarkable investigation from passing entirely into oblivion.*

* This Dr John H. Watson succeeds in accomplishing in 'The Adventure of the Sussex Vampire' where the case is listed among others under the letter 'V' in Mr Sherlock Holmes's encyclopedia of reference. (Dr John F. Watson)

THE CASE OF THE ABANDONED LIGHTHOUSE

Because of the recent attempts to obtain and destroy certain papers in my possession, in particular my notes and memoranda concerning one specific investigation, my old friend, the great consulting detective, Sherlock Holmes, has suggested that I write two accounts of the case, one which shall be deliberately kept among my files and which I shall threaten to publish should these outrages continue,* and this one, the true narrative of the events which took place and which I shall deposit with other confidential material at my bank, Cox and Co. of Charing Cross.

However, for reasons of the security of the realm, I shall refrain even in this secret account from referring to precise dates and facts in case it should, due to unforeseen circumstances, fall into the wrong hands.

Suffice it to say that the events occurred during the time when I had moved out of my former lodgings in Baker Street into my own rooms in Queen Anne Street and before Holmes's retirement to Sussex.†

One afternoon in early July, I received a brief telephone

* Dr John H. Watson makes this threat in the opening paragraph of 'The Adventure of the Veiled Lodger'. (Dr John F. Watson)

† As Dr John H. Watson was living in Queen Anne Street in September 1902, the time of 'The Adventure of the Veiled Lodger', and as Mr Sherlock Holmes had already retired to Sussex by July 1907 when he undertook the investigation known as 'The Adventure of the Lion's Mane', the events referred to must have taken place between these dates. (Dr John F. Watson)

message from Holmes, requesting my presence at Baker Street promptly at six o'clock. Having taken a cab to my old address, I found Holmes pacing up and down the sitting-room, impatiently awaiting my arrival.

No sooner had I entered the room than he thrust a sheet of paper at me, at the same time uttering the one word, 'Mycroft!'

I hardly needed to read the note, which had been sent round by special messenger, to understand the urgent and unusual circumstances behind Holmes's summons.

Mycroft Holmes, my old friend's elder brother, acted as a highly-placed ministerial adviser and had the confidence of some of the most powerful men in the country. As Holmes had once observed, there were occasions when Mycroft *was* the Government.*

The message read: 'I have a most urgent matter to discuss with you. Please present yourself at the Diogenes Club this evening at six-thirty sharp. Cancel all other appointments and do not accept any private clients for the foreseeable future. If you wish, Dr Watson may accompany you. Mycroft.'

'Do you know what this urgent matter involves?' I asked Holmes.

'No; except it must be Government business. Mycroft concerns himself with nothing else. It must also entail an inquiry of some nature. Otherwise, why should he request that I take on no other clients? It is fortunate I am free, having just completed, as you are aware, Watson, the case of Lady Violet Fitzmorgan and the bareback rider. I have ordered a cab which I believe I can hear drawing up outside at this very moment. So let us proceed without any further delay, my dear fellow. We shall no doubt discover the exact nature of this urgent matter when we arrive for our appointment.'

The Diogenes Club was situated in Pall Mall, not far from the Carlton and opposite Mycroft's own lodgings. As Holmes remarked as we alighted from the cab, his brother's life was conducted within a small and tightly drawn circle, consisting of

* Mr Sherlock Holmes makes this observation in 'The Adventure of the Bruce-Partington Plans'. (Dr John F. Watson)

his club, his private lodgings and his office which was just round the corner in Whitehall. It was rarely that he stepped outside its perimeter even to visit Holmes in Baker Street.

I was already familiar with the club, having visited it before, notably on the occasion when Mycroft had introduced Holmes and me to Mr Melas, whose case I later published under the title of 'The Adventure of the Greek Interpreter',* and, as on that evening, Holmes led the way into the Strangers' Room, the only part of the entire establishment where conversation was permitted.

We entered to find the portly figure of Mycroft Holmes already comfortably installed in an armchair by the bow window which looked out on to Pall Mall. Much larger and stouter than his brother, Mycroft Holmes nevertheless managed to convey, despite his corpulent frame and air of physical inertia, an impression of keen intelligence and sharpness of intellect, evident in the dominant brow and the alert expression in his light grey eyes.

Holmes had once informed me† that it was Mycroft's omniscience of mind, his ability to store facts and collate them, which had made his services indispensable to Government ministers, and that it was on Mycroft's advice that national policy had been decided on many occasions.

The greetings over, Mycroft Holmes subsided heavily again into his armchair, waving a languid hand in the direction of a side table on which were standing a whisky decanter, a soda syphon and a tray of glasses.

'As you are already on your feet, Sherlock, you may pour all of us a drink, thereby saving me the exertion. For my part, merely crossing the road to reach this establishment consumes enough energy for one evening. Thank you, my dear boy. You show a proper sense of fraternal duty. And now that we are all seated, our glasses charged, I shall come straight to the point.

* This case occurred before Dr John H. Watson's marriage although the precise date is unknown. (Dr John F. Watson)

† Mr Sherlock Holmes's information is recorded in 'The Adventure of the Bruce-Partington Plans'. (Dr John F. Watson)

The matter I shall lay before you concerns nothing less than the security of this nation.'

Pausing portentously to allow us to grasp the significance of this remark and also to refresh himself from his whisky glass, Mycroft continued, 'You are no doubt aware of the present state of diplomatic relations between this country and Imperial Germany. Since his appointment of Admiral von Tirpitz as his Minister of Marine in 1897, the Kaiser has set about creating a powerful German navy which, it is feared, will be used to attack our Empire, our trade, even the British Isles themselves. Although the Admiralty has ordered the reorganization and rearmament of our own fleet, it is nevertheless thought that our best defence against any enemy naval attack lies in the development of the submarine.

'It has therefore been decided to press ahead with research into a new prototype, based on the original Bruce-Partington design but much improved. There is no need, of course, to remind you of that particular invention and young Cadogan West's tragic death when he tried to retrieve the plans from Oberstein, the foreign agent. Both you and Dr Watson were closely involved in that affair.*

'Some time ago, the Admiralty set about enlarging and re-equipping the old secret research laboratory at Woolwich under the control of the eminent scientist, Roderick Jeffreys, who was instructed to recruit his staff from among the most promising young engineers and physicists he could find.

'This brings me to my reason for asking you here this evening.

'It concerns one of those young scientists, Maurice Callister, a brilliant man – a genius, one might say – who possesses a particularly inventive mind. You have probably never heard of him. He is something of a recluse and shuns publicity. However, his twin brother may be more familiar to you in the political field.'

'You are speaking of Hugo Callister, are you not?' Holmes

* This case, which occurred in November 1895, was recorded by Dr John H. Watson under the title of 'The Adventure of the Bruce-Partington Plans'. (Dr John F. Watson)

inquired. 'The Independent Member of Parliament for Dowerbridge and an excellent back-bench speaker on matters of defence?'

'Exactly so, my dear boy. As a pacifist and an opponent of rearmament, he is something of a thorn in the Government's flesh but I grant you his debating skills. In his own way, he is as gifted as his twin brother and shares with him certain eccentricities of behaviour although, unlike Maurice Callister, he goes out of his way to court attention.

'Maurice and Hugo are the only children of the late Sir Douglas Callister, the former diplomat, and their peculiarities of character and outlook may derive from their upbringing. Their mother died at their birth and, as children, they travelled extensively abroad with their father to various foreign embassies, mostly in the Far East, although Sir Douglas served for several years in Berlin where he and his sons became friends with a certain Count Rudolph von Schlabitz-Hoecker and his family. In particular, Maurice Callister was very close to the Count's son, Otto, with whom he shared an interest in scientific matters. Mark that fact, Sherlock! It has great significance.

'As a consequence of their unorthodox education, both the Callister boys became excellent linguists with a wide knowledge of foreign cultures which bred in them what I can only describe as an international outlook. In Hugo Callister it takes the form of advocating political and economic co-operation, in addition to his well-known support of pacifism. He would, for example, dispense altogether with passports, abolish all frontiers and trade barriers and establish some kind of grand central committee which would govern the entire planet. Mere pipe dreams, of course,' Mycroft added, with a sad shake of his head, 'as we who live in the real world can testify.

'As for his brother, Maurice, while he appears to have no particular party political beliefs, he nevertheless while at Oxford expressed the opinion that all knowledge and information, especially in the areas of scientific research, should be freely communicated between scholars regardless of their nationalities. That fact, too, is highly relevant.'

Holmes, who had been listening to Mycroft's account with great attention, interposed a question of his own.

'Was not Sir Douglas Callister something of a scholar himself?'

'I believe he published several monographs which tended to be on artistic subjects, such as Chinese porcelain or the use of masks in Noh drama. No doubt his sons inherited their intellectual curiosity from him. However, to continue my account, Sir Douglas returned to England and the two boys were sent to Oxford where Maurice gained a double first in mathematics and physics. Later, he was awarded a Fellowship at St Olaf's, the youngest man ever to have been given such a distinction. It was at this time that he came to the attention of Roderick Jeffreys and it was on Jeffreys' recommendation that Callister was offered a post at the Woolwich laboratory to assist with the development of the new submarine, where he has access to all the plans and is involved in every stage of the research.

'I come now to the nub of the affair. We have reason to believe that Callister is passing that information to his boyhood friend, Otto von Schlabitz-Hoecker, who is engaged in similar research on behalf of the German Admiralty.'

'How do you know this?' Holmes asked.

Mycroft lifted a broad hand, like a flipper.

'Is it not obvious, my dear Sherlock? We have our own agents in Germany who keep us informed of all aspects of the Kaiser's rearmament plans. As soon as His Majesty's* Government was alerted, I was asked to establish a team of experienced men who have been investigating Callister's activities, at the head of which I have placed a Scotland Yard officer, Inspector Drury, whom I believe you have already met.'

'Indeed I have. He is an excellent man,' Holmes agreed warmly. 'Watson and I worked with him only a year ago on the unfortunate affair involving the bishop and the actress.'

'Exactly so. For the past three months, Drury and his men have been keeping a strict watch on Maurice Callister in order

* King Edward VII succeeded to the throne on 22 January 1901 and was crowned on 9 August 1902. (Dr John F. Watson)

to discover the method by which he passes on details of the submarine to Otto von Schlabitz-Hoecker, so far without success. Callister is a strange, solitary individual who appears to have no acquaintances outside his place of work, owing possibly to the fact that he was born with a deformed shoulder. As far as the Woolwich side of the investigation is concerned, all reports are negative. He has modest lodgings close to the laboratory but receives no visitors. He walks to and from the research station but meets no one on the way. Since starting work on the Admiralty project, he has not even been in contact with his brother. I gather from sources inside the House of Commons that Hugo Callister disapproves strongly of any research into armaments, which is only to be expected, given his pacifist beliefs.'

'Is there a possibility that Maurice Callister passes on the secrets from inside the laboratory itself?'

'No, my dear Sherlock, there is not. We learned that lesson from the Cadogan West affair. All the plans of the submarine are kept in a safe to which only Jeffreys has the key; not that this need discourage Callister. He has a phenomenal gift of almost total recall and could easily memorize details of any of the designs he was working on. Two of Inspector Drury's own men have been placed inside the laboratory and monitor all Callister's movements. No one is allowed inside the building without a pass and, as the only telephone is in the main office where one of Drury's men acts as chief clerk, Callister cannot use that to communicate with anyone outside.'

Holmes observed drily, 'You would appear to have stopped up all the earths. How is it possible that your fox still manages to elude you?'

'Through the only bolt-hole which is left open to him, I assume. Every Friday evening for the past few months, Callister has been in the habit of travelling down by train to Cornwall, returning to town on Sunday. And no,' Mycroft added, anticipating his brother's query, 'he communicates with no one on the way, either at Paddington station or on the train itself. Drury's men who travel with him make sure of that. While in Cornwall, he stays at a small villa, "The Firs", which his father,

Sir Douglas, had built on his own retirement and where he lived until his death.

'"The Firs" is remote, isolated on top of a rocky headland, called Penhiddy Point, on the north coast of Cornwall and some distance from the nearest habitation. The whole area was notorious in the past for shipwrecks and the property includes an abandoned lighthouse, known as Penhiddy Beacon, which fell into disuse some time ago when a new lighthouse was built on another, more convenient headland. A set of steps has been cut into the cliff, giving access to a small landing-stage from which the lighthouse can be reached by rowing-boat in calm weather.

'I give you these details because, since Callister has been spending each weekend in the villa, he appears to have set up his own laboratory in the lighthouse, part of which was converted by his father into a studio. Drury's men have observed him taking equipment and supplies there by boat and, when he is in residence at "The Firs", he spends most of the day at Penhiddy Beacon.

'There are two mysteries surrounding Callister's trips to Cornwall which make me believe he uses them to communicate with his German friends. The first concerns an elderly housekeeper, a Eurasian woman, Miss Mai, who lives permanently at "The Firs". She is an old family servant of the Callisters, having acted as *ayah* to the two boys when they were young and later as nurse to Sir Douglas during his last illness. The enigma involves her weekly grocery orders which are delivered to the house from the nearest town, Portswithin, a small fishing port, by the suppliers and shopkeepers. The point is, Sherlock, the quantities of food are too great for one elderly lady to consume, even allowing for the fact that Callister spends every weekend there. We suspect another person must be living permanently at the villa in addition to Miss Mai but no one has seen who it is, not even Drury's men who have acted on occasion as delivery men. Nor are any messages passed to and from the villa in the baskets. They are vigorously searched and there is no reason to suspect the local butcher, baker or candlestick-maker, all loyal Cornishmen, of being German spies.

'The second mystery concerns a fishing-boat, the *Margretha*, which since the time Callister has been kept under observation has been seen close to the headland at irregular intervals; not every weekend. I stress that point. Having spent several days out at sea at the fishing-grounds off the Irish coast, it anchors near a small, uninhabited island near Penhiddy Point, less than an eighth of a mile from the lighthouse. Drury's men have kept it under close observation both day and night but the activities on board appear to be perfectly innocent. The crew spend the time sorting fish, cleaning decks, mending nets. As far as can be ascertained, no communication of any nature passes between Callister and the men on board the boat; no signals; no flashing lights; no secret rendezvous at night.'

'And yet you believe that this boat is the means by which Callister passes details of the submarine plans to von Schlabitz-Hoecker?'

'I am convinced of it. Its mere presence there is suspicious.'

'Could you not find an excuse to board and search her?'

'The boat is Dutch-registered and we do not wish to take such action until we have positive evidence of Callister's guilt. But you take my point, Sherlock? It would be easy enough to pass on any papers to Germany once the boat returns to Holland.'

'What activity does Callister engage in while the boat is anchored off the island?'

'Exactly the same as every other weekend when it is not there. He rows out to the lighthouse quite early in the morning, taking a picnic basket with him, enters the beacon and presumably spends the day working in his laboratory. In the evening, he re-emerges, feeds the seagulls, and attends to his fishing-lines before rowing back to the steps and returning to "The Firs". His routine never varies.'

Holmes's lean features took on an expression of even keener attention.

'Fishing-lines!' he exclaimed.

'He has set up two fixed rods on the lighthouse rocks which he baits in the mornings when he first arrives. Later, before leaving, he examines them, removes any fish from the hooks and places them in the basket. That is all. I assume the catch is cooked and eaten that evening for supper. You consider the fishing-lines might be significant?'

'It is possible. In so unusual a case, any fact could be relevant. What other information can you give me about Callister?'

'Very little. As I have said, the man is a recluse. However, last summer he broke his usual pattern of behaviour and requested a month's leave from the laboratory, during which he visited France. Jeffreys acquainted me with this fact when we were building up a dossier on Callister. It seems he sent picture postcards to Jeffreys' young daughter for her album from each town where he stayed. If you wish, I could send Callister's file to Baker Street this evening by Government messenger.'

'Pray do. When a man of strict habits breaks the pattern . . .'

'. . . one has cause for suspicion,' Mycroft Holmes agreed. 'Quite so. Am I to assume from your reply that you are willing to take up the investigation in Cornwall? Yesterday, I received a report that the *Margretha* has been observed fishing off the Irish coast which leads one to believe that on Friday she will anchor once again in Penhiddy Bay. I am much too fixed in my own habits to go scrambling about on cliff-tops. Besides, there is an urgent meeting with the Japanese Overseas Trade Minister I must attend to.'

'I shall certainly accept. The case has some remarkable and challenging features. I take it the invitation includes my old friend, Dr Watson?'

'Of course, my dear boy! Who would dare separate you? You are the Castor and Pollux of the investigative world. And now that I have your acceptance, which, knowing your disposition, I must confess I had expected, let us attend to the practicalities. Here are two first-class return tickets for the morning express from Paddington on Friday. By catching this train, you will avoid Callister who always travels down in the late afternoon. Inspector Drury will meet you at Penzance with an official car and will escort you to his headquarters which he has set up in an old coastguard cottage. Take only a minimum of luggage with you but be certain to pack your field-glasses. They will be most necessary. Should there be any difficulties you may contact me by telephone from the police house at St Auban, a small village only a short distance away. Rest assured that you have full Government support for any action you may undertake. However, I should warn you that I want Callister taken cleanly, with proof positive of his guilt which will satisfy a court of law. Any mistake will be seized on by the Opposition, especially the disarmament lobby led by Hugo Callister, to discredit the Government, which could bring about its downfall. The Prime Minister has personally requested me to stress that point.'

'I understand,' said Holmes quietly. 'There is one question I should like to ask before Watson and I take our leave. Is Maurice Callister aware he is under observation?'

'Probably so; he is, after all, highly intelligent. But he shows no sign. It is possible that he considers his method of passing the secret plans to Germany so clever as to be undetectable.'

'He seems a worthy opponent. There is nothing else you can tell me about him?'

'Only that he once had an interest in the circus, a hobby he appears to have abandoned since he began work at the Woolwich laboratory. You will see it is remarked on in his dossier which I shall send round to your rooms tonight.'

I was not present when Callister's file was delivered at Baker Street, Holmes and I having parted outside the Diogenes Club to return separately to our different lodgings, and I did not, in fact, see my old friend again until we met at Paddington station on Friday morning to catch the express train to Penzance.

However, the contents of the dossier were clearly in the forefront of Holmes's mind, for no sooner had we settled ourselves in our first-class compartment than he remarked, 'The circus, Watson. What does that word convey to you?'

'Clowns. Acrobats. Trapeze-artistes.'

'Ah!' said he thoughtfully. 'And Chateaurenard, Claircourt and Montcerre?'

'Nothing at all, Holmes; except they sound French.'

'Quite so, my dear fellow. They are all small provincial towns in the Midi which Callister visited last summer. A strange choice, would you not agree?' Then with an apparent change of subject, he continued, 'I have spent two days researching into

Sir Douglas Callister's monographs at the Reading Room of the British Museum. What a remarkable family they are! Their interests cover so many widely differing subjects. Noh drama! Pacifism! Submarines! Such intellectual curiosity and such curious intellects!'

With that, he opened the small portmanteau he had brought with him and took out a book, the title of which he showed me. It was *British Birds of Coasts, Estuaries and Lakes*.

'And now, Watson,' he announced, 'I shall satisfy my own intellectual curiosity.'

'You are interested in birds, Holmes?'

'As we are to stay on the north Cornish coast, it seemed an apt subject.'

His book, the morning newspapers and exchanges of conversation on general matters kept us both occupied until the train arrived at Penzance, where we alighted and where we were met by Drury, the tall, ruddy-faced Scotland Yard Inspector, dressed in shabby, unofficial tweeds, who conducted us to the waiting car.

The journey by road across the peninsula to the north coast took us through some of the most beautiful of English scenery until we reached our destination, a narrow, high-banked road about a quarter of a mile past the small village of St Auban.

'We shall have to approach the coastguard's cottage on foot, gentlemen,' Drury informed us, leading the way towards a high-stepped stile. 'The road, which continues on round the headland, passes Callister's house and leads eventually to the small fishing town of Portswithin, about three miles away. If you would care to follow me.'

Having climbed the stile, we found ourselves on a stony track which led across a field of rough grass and which gradually grew more steep and enclosed. Low trees and bushes, stunted by the wind, grew on either side between rocky outcrops, obscuring the view although from time to time we caught glimpses of the ocean glittering ahead of us.

The cottage, a small, single-storey building of stone, stood in a natural clearing between these rocks and at first sight appeared derelict, its slate roof partly collapsed and all its windows closely boarded in.

To avoid being observed, we entered through a rear door into a small room, once a kitchen, judging by the rusted cooking range standing in the fireplace opening, and from there Drury showed us into the main living-room at the front of the building where he introduced us to Sergeant Cotty, a heavily-built and moustached man, who was in charge of the night-watch.

The introductions over, we were free to examine the room which would be our living quarters for the next two days. Because of the screens covered with black felt which had been nailed over the window to prevent even the smallest crack of light from being seen, the interior was lit by two hurricane lamps which hung from the ceiling. Folding canvas beds, of the type I had been used to sleeping on when serving in India, were placed in a row against the further wall, while a wooden table and four upright chairs occupied the centre of the room.

The Inspector seemed as proud of these living arrangements as a new bride, showing us the simple kitchen, comprising a paraffin stove and some boxes for storing food and cooking utensils which had been set up in one corner, and the washing facilities, a tin basin placed on top of a crate in the small rear room. Fresh drinking water, he informed us, was still available from an outside pump.

I had the impression that Drury who, as far as I knew, had been born and brought up in London, was enjoying the primitive and challenging nature of his new surroundings.

It was with equal pride that later, when we had stowed our belongings, he demonstrated to us the observation post which had been set up at the edge of the cliff and where he introduced us to the third member of his team, Sergeant McGregor, a keen and alert-looking young officer.

The post itself was a dense clump of furze bushes, the interior of which on the landward side had been carefully cut away to form a horseshoe-shaped hide or cover, such as are used on grouse moors to conceal the guns. Crates served as seats for whoever was keeping watch.

'Comfortable, isn't it?' Drury asked, his eyes positively sparkling with delight at the simple ingenuity of these arrangements. 'Quite a little home from home!'

Seated on these boxes, we had a clear view on the seaward side through small gaps in the bushes of the vista which lay before us. Immediately in front, a mere few feet away, the cliff plunged precipitously down to a narrow shore, composed of tumbled rocks over which the waves broke in scatters of white foam. Beyond lay a small, semicircular bay, less than half a mile in width and surrounded by more cliffs which swept round to form on the far side another headland – Penhiddy Point, as Drury informed us – which extended out to sea like an arm at the end of which stretched a long, bony forefinger of rock. This finger seemed to be pointing to an isolated outcrop which thrust itself up from the waves, its irregular and broken outline crowned by the tall, white, slender tower of a lighthouse which stood sentinel over the entrance to the bay.

I could understand the necessity for its presence for the surface of the cove was scattered with granite needles and small, submerged islets, their presence only apparent from the surge of water and spray as the sea broke over them. Any ship attempting to seek shelter in the bay, especially after dark, would run the risk of foundering on any one of these hazards.

A larger island lay between us and Penhiddy Point although its total area could not have been more than a few dozen square yards. It rose to a high peak and appeared to be inhabited solely by sea-birds which swooped and circled above it or gathered in squabbling groups on every ledge and crevice, the rocks whitened by their droppings.

Anchored on the leeward side of this island was a fishing-boat. With the aid of our field-glasses, we were able to read the name, *Margretha*, painted on its hull and to distinguish two members of its crew, one inside the wheelhouse, the other lounging on the after-deck, his arms folded along the rail as he smoked a short pipe, apparently enjoying the last of the evening sunlight.

As we watched, a third man appeared on deck to empty a bucket over the side which he then filled by lowering it into the sea and hauling it back on board by means of a rope. Having done this, he disappeared below deck.

On Drury's instructions, we next turned our glasses towards Penhiddy Point and to a small coppice of densely planted trees on its summit which marked the position of 'The Firs' although the house itself was hidden by the branches.

However, the rock-hewn steps leading down from the cliff were clearly visible. So, too, was a rough wooden landing-stage at their foot where a rowing-boat was made fast.

Also just visible in the low dazzle of the setting run was a further headland, Portswithin Point, stretching further out to sea where the new lighthouse had been built to replace the old Penhiddy Beacon.

As the light faded, we returned to the cottage, leaving McGregor to complete his watch. Here a meal had been prepared for us by Cotty who left shortly afterwards to relieve McGregor at his post.

Callister, Drury told us, would arrive later that night from London and we could expect no further action until the following morning when our suspect would begin his two-day visit and our own surveillance of him would start in earnest.

We were wakened at half past six the next morning by Drury who was evidently still enjoying his rustic surroundings and who, by the light of the lamps, was preparing a huge fried breakfast of sausages, eggs and bacon for us on top of the paraffin stove.

Once that was eaten, the four of us, Holmes, Drury, McGregor and I, emerged from the lamplit cottage into the full brilliance of an early July morning, a little dazed by the sunlight which glittered on every surface of rock, leaf and grass-stem and especially on the wide, restless expanse of the sea which, like a vast prism with a million facets, flashed the light back at us, forcing us to shade our eyes as we made our way to the observation post. Here we relieved Cotty who, having assured us that there was nothing to report, returned to the cottage, leaving the four of us to take his place inside the hide.

The *Margretha* was still anchored off the small island but there was no one on board and it was not until shortly before eight o'clock that we observed any movement.

It was then that we caught sight of a figure which emerged from the coppice on top of the headland and began the descent of the cliff-steps; our first glimpse of our quarry, Maurice Callister.

Through our field-glasses, it was possible to pick out certain details of his appearance. He was slight in build and dark-haired, not more than in his early thirties, and was wearing a loose cape, a curious choice of garment considering the warmth of the morning. Because of the deformed left shoulder, which was thrust higher than the right, he moved with a strange crab-like motion, awkward but surprisingly agile. With one hand, he steadied himself on the wooden rail which ran alongside the steps; in the other, he carried a picnic basket.

Having reached the bottom of the steps, he crossed to the landing-stage, climbed into the rowing-boat and, casting off, started to pull with strong, even strokes towards the lighthouse.

Turning my glasses momentarily towards the *Margretha*, I observed that no one was on deck and the craft appeared deserted. I also noticed that Callister appeared uninterested in its presence, not so much as turning his head in its direction and, once he had landed on the lighthouse rock, seemed totally absorbed with mooring his own boat and scrambling up the granite boulders, basket in hand, to a flat expanse of rock which immediately faced the lighthouse entrance. Here he paused, setting the basket on the ground, and squatted down over two fishing rods which had been wedged into crevices between the rocks.

As we watched, he reeled in the lines, baited them and cast them back into the sea before, picking up the basket, he climbed rapidly up the flight of stone steps that led up to the lighthouse door, which he unlocked. Seconds later, he had disappeared inside the tower.

Drury consulted his pocket-watch.

The whole action, from the time Callister had appeared on

top of the cliff to the moment he had entered Penhiddy Beacon, had taken exactly twenty-three minutes and five seconds.

'And, gentlemen,' Drury added, 'we shan't see him again today for another twelve hours when the sun sets.'

Drury was correct. We were awarded no further sightings of Callister although signs of activity occurred from time to time on board the *Margretha*. Members of its crew could be seen on deck cleaning and sorting fish, discarded scraps of which were thrown overboard to the gulls; gear was attended to, decks scrubbed. As Mycroft had observed, it all seemed perfectly innocent.

As for ourselves, we passed the hours as best we could in reading or talking in low voices, these periods of inactivity interrupted by short walks to relieve our cramped limbs. Holmes spent most of the time either studying his book of birds or observing the living examples as they wheeled and gathered about the cliffs, marking off on the page each individual species of gull, tern or shearwater as he recognized them.

It was past eight o'clock and the sun was just beginning to dip towards the horizon before Callister reappeared.

In the meantime, the man whom we had observed lounging on the deck of the *Margretha* the previous evening had again taken up his position on the after-deck where he stood, as before, pipe in mouth and leaning his forearms on the rail, it being his habit, it appeared, to enjoy this brief respite before dusk descended.

He seemed to take no notice, not even glancing up, as Callister emerged from the lighthouse and, locking the door, walked across to the water's edge a little distance from the place where the rods were positioned, where he again squatted down on his heels and, opening the basket which he had set down beside him, took something from inside it which appeared to be bread.

I use the word 'appeared' because his back was towards us and the folds of the loose cape he was wearing hid his hands and arms. But there was no mistaking the handfuls of white morsels which he flung into the air towards the flock of sea-birds which, as if well used to this evening ritual, had begun to gather about him screaming excitedly, some circling above his head, some diving to scoop up the fragments before they fell, while others of a more sedate and temperate nature, if such human characteristics can be attributed to birds, bobbed about in the sea close to the rocks, waiting for those pieces of bread which would inevitably fall into the water.

The feeding over, Callister brushed the last crumbs from his hands and, still with his back to us, crossed the few feet to his fishing-lines and, again squatting on his heels, reeled them in and removed two fish from the hooks which he placed inside the basket before once more casting the lines out to sea.

Callister then picked up the basket and, clambering down the rocks to his boat, began to row back to the landing-stage, thus completing the pattern of actions which Mycroft had described to us.

The activity on board the *Margretha* also followed the same routine which we had observed the previous evening.

The lounging figure remained on deck, to be joined after a short interval by another crew member who, as before, emptied a bucket overboard before lowering it on its rope and filling it with clean water, inadvertently banging it against the hull as he did so. The bucket was then hauled back on board and the man disappeared with it below deck.

In the meantime, Callister had regained the landing-stage and, having moored his boat, had begun the ascent of the cliff-steps, basket in hand, to disappear shortly afterwards into the coppice of trees which surrounded 'The Firs'.

Shortly afterwards, Cotty arrived to take over night-watch, relieving us of our duties.

As Holmes, Drury, McGregor and I made our way back to the cottage, I remarked, 'Everything appeared perfectly normal. As far as I could see, nothing unusual occurred.'

Drury agreed with me.

'It is the same every weekend, doctor. Callister repeats the same actions, in the morning baiting his hooks, in the evening feeding the sea-birds and removing his catch from the lines. The same can be said of the men aboard the *Margretha*. I cannot for the life of me see how any communication is made between Callister and its crew.'

Holmes, who had been strangely silent during this exchange, broke in at this point to ask abruptly, 'Can you not, Inspector?'

Drury looked utterly astonished.

'You believe some message was passed? How was that achieved?'

'You observed the man on deck, the one smoking the pipe?'

'Of course I did, Mr Holmes. He is there every evening when the *Margretha* is anchored off the island. But he does nothing except stand with his arms on the rail.'

'*Arm*, Drury,' Holmes corrected him. 'This evening you may have observed that he had only *one* arm on the rail. The other, the one furthest from us and therefore hidden, was by his side. Then there is the man with the bucket to consider.'

'But surely he is only emptying slops over the side!' I protested.

'And filling the bucket with clean water,' Drury added.

'He is certainly filling the bucket with *something*,' Holmes conceded. 'By the same token, Callister's picnic basket is used to convey some object to and from the lighthouse. However, should we examine it, which I propose to do tomorrow morning, I dare say we shall find it contains more than a packet of ham sandwiches and some stale bread for the gulls. And speaking of which, my dear Watson and Drury, may I recommend Saint Matthew, chapter six, verse twenty-six, which advises us to observe the fowls of the air? While you are so doing, spare a thought also for the birds of the sea.'

As he finished speaking, we reached the door of the cottage and, thrusting it open, Holmes strode ahead, leaving the rest of us, after a bewildered exchange of glances, to follow.

Once inside, Holmes, whose mental energies seemed to be running at a high pitch of excitement, threw himself down on one of the chairs and, taking out his notebook, began writing in it at great speed. Drury and I waited in silence as his pencil raced across the paper. Then, tearing the page from the book, he tossed it across the table towards us before, folding his arms, he flung himself back in his chair.

'There!' he declared. 'That is my chain of reasoning, the final link of which is now in position. Follow that for it is the line which leads directly to the centre of Callister's treachery.'

With Drury leaning over my shoulder, I eagerly scanned the sheet of paper.

It read:

1. Japan
2. France
3. The circus
4. Miss Mai's grocery orders
5. The abandoned lighthouse
6. The *Margretha*
7. The picnic basket and the bucket
9. The fishing lines
10. The feeding habits of sea-birds, especially the species Phalacrocorax carbo.

'Holmes,' said I, laying down the sheet, 'I have to confess it means nothing to me. It is a mere enigma.'

'No enigma is ever mere to those who cannot solve it. Nor is any mystery quite as complex as one imagines. You do not follow my reasoning? It is perfectly straightforward. I set it out under those ten simple headings so that the links between them could be more easily grasped. Well! Well! You disappoint me, my dear fellow. You, too, Inspector Drury, for I can see by your expression that you also have failed to follow the logic. Nevertheless, are you prepared to act upon it, even if you do not understand it?'

'Act upon it, Mr Holmes?'

'Yes, act upon it! Put a series of actions into motion! You could acquire the use of a rowing-boat, could you not?'

Drury, who seemed mesmerized by the speed of Holmes's mercurial mind, could only nod dumbly.

'And warrants for the arrest of Callister and any of his accomplices?'

'They could be drawn up but would need the signature of a magistrate.'

'Which no doubt could be easily arranged if the right influence is brought to bear. As could a coastguard cutter to board and search the *Margretha*. I suggest I telephone my brother Mycroft immediately so that he can begin to pull the necessary strings and set his puppets dancing.'

Without any further delay, we started off on foot for the nearby village of St Auban where we parted, Holmes and Drury to the police house to use the telephone, I to the Fishermen's Arms inn where Holmes later joined me in the privacy of the snug where our conversation could not be overheard.

I could tell by the light in my old friend's eyes that he had been successful.

'I have spoken to Mycroft,' he told me in a low rapid voice, 'and everything is in hand. A coastguard cutter will be standing by tomorrow morning to board and search the *Margretha* on suspicion of smuggling, once we have made our own move. Drury is at this moment arranging for a rowing-boat to be placed at our disposal in a small cove near the coastguard's cottage, out of sight of the lighthouse. This will convey us to the beacon where we shall land once Callister is safely inside his laboratory. Drury will have in his pocket warrants for Callister's arrest and any accomplice on a charge of treason as well as an authorization to search "The Firs". Mycroft will see to it that a magistrate in Penzance is immediately alerted by telephone and will be ready to sign the warrants later this evening.

'Meanwhile, Drury will contact the police station in Portswithin to arrange for an official motor car to take him to Penzance to obtain the necessary signatures. Drury will also ask for the same car and driver to be standing by tomorrow morning at half past nine on the road outside "The Firs" to convey Callister and his accomplice to London for questioning. What a remarkable instrument the telephone is, Watson! Remember the old days and how we were forced to communicate by telegram? How cumbrous a method it now seems!'

'Indeed it does, Holmes. And speaking of communicating, will you now have the goodness to explain your "chain of reasoning"?' said I, taking from my pocket the sheet of paper on which he had written down his ten headings and laying it flat on the table in front of him.

But Holmes was in a mood to tease.

'There is barely time,' he replied with a twinkle. 'Inspector Drury will be joining us shortly to wait for the car to take him to Penzance. Besides, my dear fellow, think of the intellectual pleasure it will give you to cudgel your brains a little longer over its solution!'

I was no nearer solving Holmes's 'chain' when the following morning the four of us, Holmes, Drury, McGregor and I, set out once more for the hide. Nor could I understand my old friend's evident satisfaction at what we witnessed there.

As before, Callister descended the cliff-steps and began to row out to the lighthouse. Shortly after he landed, the man with the bucket again appeared on the deck of the *Margretha* and lowered it overboard to fill it with sea-water. There were only two divergènces from this normal routine, as far as I could ascertain. One was the presence on deck of the pipe-smoking member of the crew who, on this occasion, was seated on an upturned fish-crate and appeared to be mending a net. The other was the time it took Callister to bait his hooks. One of the lines seemed to have become entangled for he crouched over it for five minutes or more, alternately tugging it in and paying it out, until at last it was freed. Then, reeling both of them in, he took bait from the basket, fastened it to the hooks and, casting out the lines, retreated once more inside the beacon, taking the basket with him.

Holmes, who had been watching these activities with great absorption, let his field-glasses fall on their strap around his neck with a chuckle of pure pleasure.

'We have him!' cried he. 'The rowing-boat is waiting for us, is it not, Drury? Then let us go! It is time we drew in our own line and landed this prize catch of ours.'

With Drury leading the way, we set off towards the far side of the headland where a steep path descended the cliff to a small cove. Here a rowing-boat, ordered by the Inspector the previous evening, was waiting for us.

Dismissing the constable who had brought it round from St Auban, the four of us climbed into it and, with McGregor and Holmes at the oars, we rounded the point into Penhiddy Bay.

It was a bright clear morning with only a light breeze barely ruffling the surface of the sea, which aided our progress. Within a short time, we had passed the small island where the *Margretha* lay at anchor, taking care to keep well clear of the vessel although by that time the two men had gone below and the deck was deserted.

There was no sign, either, of the coastguard cutter which had orders to keep out of sight beyond Penhiddy Point until nine o'clock, by which time, Holmes had estimated, we should have landed at the beacon and it would be too late for the crew of the *Margretha* either to warn Callister of our presence or to make their own escape out to sea.

Holmes's estimation of the time of our arrival was accurate to within a few minutes for it was five to the hour when we landed, secured our own boat close to Callister's and, scrambling over the boulders, gained the rocky plateau on which the beacon stood. A quick dash of about twenty yards took us to the foot of the steps leading up to the door which yielded silently on well-oiled hinges and gave us access to a small vestibule.

To our left lay a room, its door swinging loose and allowing us a glimpse of an ill-lit chamber full of discarded lumber. Ahead of us, a spiral staircase ascended, its flight of stone steps hugging close about a central pillar and disappearing into the upper reaches of the tower. We ascended these as rapidly and as quietly as we could, confident that our footsteps could not be heard above the surge of the sea beyond the walls.

On the ascent we passed several more disused rooms until we reached a landing about half-way up the beacon where freshly whitewashed walls and a new, secure door warned us that we had arrived outside Callister's laboratory.

Here we halted, crowded together into the small space, while we regained our breath and then, as Holmes raised his hand, a pre-arranged signal, we flung our combined weight against the door.

Our entry took Callister totally by surprise.

He was bending over a work-bench on the far side of the room and, as we burst in, he spun about, his face expressing shock and consternation.

I still have in my mind an impression of that curious chamber, fitted into the rounded tower of the lighthouse and therefore possessing semicircular walls against which a number of curved lockers and cupboards had been built with great ingenuity.

Facing us was a window looking seawards, its upper light open allowing plenty of air and sunlight to flood in and giving an incomparable view of a vast expanse of sky and ocean until they fused together into the haze of the distant horizon. Through it, I also caught a glimpse of the coastguard cutter, which had rounded Penhiddy Point and was bearing down on the *Margretha*.

Apart from these fleeting impressions, I have no clear recollection of what else the room contained or what objects lay scattered about on the bench where Callister was standing, except that they included lengths of wire, parts of an engine or dynamo and several open books.

It was Callister I recall in greatest detail, especially the awkward lurch of his misshapen shoulder as he swung round to face us. But more memorable even than that was his head which, because of his small, twisted frame, seemed larger than normal. It was noble in its features, particularly the huge, brilliant eyes and the high arch of his forehead, distinguished by a deep widow's peak of dark hair which gave the impression of a curious cap, such as medieval scholars wore, fitting close about the head.

Beside him on the bench stood the picnic basket, a large wicker receptacle fastened with two leather straps, near which lay several small squares of fine, oiled silk.

Callister, who had recovered some of his composure after the first shock of our precipitate entry, appeared quite calm as Holmes and Drury stepped forward, Drury to make the arrest, Holmes to search the bench and to remove one of the oiled silk squares and a little tube of paper, in shape not unlike a small, squat cigar, which he unrolled and, having read its contents quickly, passed to Drury.

'I think you will find in there all the evidence you need for the charge of treason, Inspector. The rest,' said he, laying his hand on the picnic basket, 'is contained in here.'

It was Callister who spoke first. Before Drury could reply, he said, addressing Holmes, his voice light and courteous, 'Mr Holmes, is it not? I have long admired the quality of your intellect which, if I may say so, is wasted on the criminal world. Allow me to show the Inspector the evidence to which you refer.'

Turning aside, he began to unbuckle the straps which fastened down the lid of the basket, at the same time glancing back over his shoulder with an amused smile as we crowded forward to see what it contained.

It was at this moment, when our guard was down, that Callister acted.

Before Holmes could shout a warning, he had flung back the lid with one hand, with the other sweeping the books and pieces of machinery off the bench and sending them crashing to the floor. As they fell, a large bird, terrified by the noise, burst from the basket with the velocity of a bullet in an explosion of wings and feet and feathers, beating at our hands and faces and causing all of us, even Holmes, to start back in alarm at its sudden eruption.

Our confusion was only momentary but it was long enough for Callister. Thrusting us aside, he darted for the door which opened on to the landing and disappeared up the spiral staircase.

Holmes was the first to recover. With a shout to us to follow, he sprinted off in pursuit, leading the way as we raced up the steps after him.

We emerged at the very top of the lighthouse, into a small circular chamber, completely enclosed with glass, which housed the lantern and its reflectors and where another door gave access to an open gallery which ran round the exterior of the beacon, guarded on the seaward side by a waist-high iron railing.

Callister sat crouched on its topmost bar, balancing himself with hands and feet. He remained perched there for no more than two or three seconds although to us, standing immobilised with horror in the doorway, it seemed an eternity of time.

The next instant, he had vaulted into the abyss.

Galvanized into motion by the energy of that leap, we rushed to the rails to watch as he plunged downwards, powerless to save him.

The breeze had caught his cape, billowing it out round him so that he had the appearance of a bird swooping on huge, black wings as he rode the air until it seemed to dissolve under him and he crashed on to the rocks below.

At that very moment of impact, the sea-bird which Callister had released from its captivity and which must have escaped from the open window in the laboratory, suddenly flew free and circled three times over the shattered body before soaring away in the direction of Penhiddy Point.

I am sure Holmes would consider it fanciful on my part but I confess when I saw that bird, it came to me that it was Callister's soul breaking free from its own mortal captivity.

There was no time, however, for any such metaphysical speculation. Turning swiftly on his heel, Holmes had already begun the descent of the lighthouse stairs, the rest of us behind him, our feet pounding on the stone steps.

Having witnessed Callister's fall, none of us expected to find him alive and one glance at the shattered remnants of his head was enough to persuade me that he was beyond all medical help. Nevertheless, as a doctor, I felt obliged to lift one lifeless hand and feel for a pulse.

Holmes stood silently beside me, arms folded, chin sunk on his breast, a look of such fierce concentration on his face that, even as I knelt by Callister's body, I could feel the mental energy pouring from him in almost palpable vibrations.

Then he said curtly, 'Callister's death was an accident of which you, Watson, are the only witness. It is essential that neither Drury, McGregor nor I should be involved. We shall carry the body to the boat and take it back to the landing-stage, where it will be left. At the top of the cliff steps, we shall separate. McGregor, you will make your way to the road and warn the driver of the official motor car to keep out of sight until we are ready for him. In the meantime, Drury and I will conceal ourselves in the garden of "The Firs" while you, Watson, go up to the house alone to report what has happened. And remember, my dear fellow, it was an accident.

'You are on holiday and you were rowing in the bay when you saw someone fall from the top of the lighthouse. On disembarking, you found the man was dead. You have brought the body back to the landing-stage but you were not able to carry it up the steps alone.

'Miss Mai will answer the door to you. You must use some pretext to get her away from the house for as long as possible.' He turned to Drury. 'Where is the nearest residence which has a private telephone?'

'The vicarage, which is in the small hamlet of Trebower. There is a short cut across the fields.'

Holmes turned back to me.

'Then persuade Miss Mai to accompany you. You are a stranger and might lose your way. Once at the vicarage, telephone the police station at Portswithin and report the accident, making sure you keep Miss Mai with you. Then accompany her back to the house, again taking your time, to await the arrival of the constabulary.

'In your absence, Drury, McGregor and I will enter "The Firs" with our search warrant, arrest whoever is living there as Callister's accomplice and remove what evidence we can find. By the time you and Miss Mai return, we shall have left in the official car.'

'Is all this subterfuge really necessary, Holmes?' I protested.

'You remember my brother's warning that Callister should be taken cleanly? To my infinite regret, I have failed to do so. Our chief concern now must be to limit the damage by avoiding any scandal which could discredit the Government.'

'But will not Miss Mai be suspicious if, when we return,

Callister's accomplice, who you say is hiding in the house, has disappeared?'

'Leave that to me,' Holmes said tersely. 'I shall contrive some excuse when the occasion arises. And now we must hurry. Time is limited.'

We carried out his orders, placing Callister's body in our own boat and rowing it back to the landing-stage where we left it as together we climbed the cliff steps. At the summit, where McGregor departed to warn the driver of the official car, Holmes paused to give me his last instructions.

'When it is all over, Watson, meet me at the coastguard's cottage. I shall then lay all the facts before you and give you a full account of the affair. Now go up to the house and take care to keep Miss Mai away from the place for as long as you can. I am relying on you.'

With that parting remark, he and Drury withdrew into the coppice, leaving me to set off alone along the narrow path which twisted its way between the trees.

As I walked, I turned over in my mind what ruse I could employ to delay Callister's housekeeper, as my old friend had requested. A sprained ankle seemed a likely ploy and thus it was that, limping heavily, I reached the house.

It was a gloomy building, no doubt named after the fir trees which had been planted close about it, perhaps to serve as a wind-break but which over the years had grown so tall and dense that they shut out both light and air, giving the house a closed-in, melancholy air.

A wide wooden veranda faced me and, still limping, I mounted the steps to knock at a green-painted door. After a short interval, it was opened by a tiny, white-haired woman whose broad, wrinkled features and yellowish-brown skin spoke of her Eurasian origins. It was a face which also demonstrated that impassive, Oriental lack of expression, for when I had blurted out my story of the accident, she betrayed no emotion apart from a widening of the eyes and a small tremble of the lips.

'Is there a telephone?' I concluded. 'I shall have to inform the police.'

'Not in the house,' she replied in good English, her voice betraying only a slight accent. 'Wait here.'

She made no attempt to ask me inside, leaving me on the doorstep where I had a view of a dark, panelled hall, its walls hung with Chinese water-colours and porcelain plates. I thought, but could not be sure, that I heard the sound of voices, hers and a man's, from somewhere deep inside the house.

As the event proved, there was no need for me to persuade her to accompany me for, when she returned within a few minutes, a shawl about her shoulders, she announced, 'I shall come with you to show you the way.'

It is not necessary for me to describe in detail what happened afterwards – the walk to the vicarage at Trebower over the fields, my telephone call to Portswithin to report the accident, and the return to 'The Firs' – except to record that, because of my supposedly sprained ankle, I contrived to remain away for three quarters of an hour, enough time, I fervently trusted, for Holmes and Drury to carry out their own part in the plan.

There was no sign of them when we eventually arrived back and the house appeared deserted.

On this occasion, I was invited into a small drawing-room, furnished with Far Eastern objects and with a view of the fir trees which crowded close up to the windows. Here Miss Mai left me to wait alone and I did not see her again although once more I heard noises; not voices this time but the sound of doors opening and closing and feet moving rapidly about, as if someone were searching every room in the house, an explanation for which I was to learn later from Holmes.

After about half an hour, two policemen arrived by motor car from Portswithin and I told my story, giving my name and my Queen Anne Street address with the excuse that, as I was on a walking holiday in the area and would be returning that evening to London, I had no settled residence in the area.

My 'sprained' ankle also served as an excuse not to help the officers to carry Callister's body up from the boat and, after my statement was taken down, I was allowed to leave.

Once I was out of sight of the house and my subterfuge was no longer needed, I set off at a brisk pace to walk back to the coastguard's cottage, there to await my old friend's return with considerable impatience, eager to learn what had happened at 'The Firs' during my absence and to hear the full account of Callister's treason.

I did not have long to wait.

Within the hour, Holmes arrived and, at his suggestion, we carried two of the chairs into the overgrown garden where we sat in the sunshine and where, on his insistence, I told my part of the account first.

'And now, Holmes,' said I, when I had finished, 'I have been patient for long enough. It is time you explained your "chain of reasoning" and the meaning of your ten enigmatic headings.'

'Indeed I shall, Watson,' he replied, lighting a cigarette, 'although I feel I owe you far more than that. However, if an explanation will suffice, let me begin.

'First there was Japan, where Sir Douglas Callister served for a time as a diplomat. Mycroft gave me this first link in my chain when he referred to the monograph which Sir Douglas had written on the use of masks in Noh drama, an entirely Japanese art form. As you will recall, Watson, I spent a morning in the Reading Room of the British Museum where I discovered that Sir Douglas had published other monographs, including one on the fishing communities on some of the Japanese islands, the relevance of which I shall shortly make clear to you.

'My second heading concerned France and referred to Maurice Callister's curious visit to that country last summer in which he moved from one provincial town to another. What, I asked myself, could Callister find to interest himself in such places and was there any link between them? A telegram to an old acquaintance of mine in Paris soon provided the answer. A search by him in the provincial newspaper records established the fact that a small touring circus had visited each of those towns during the relevant period. Among the performers was a certain Pierre Leblanc with whom Callister struck up a friendship and for whom the second arrest warrant was drawn up.

'Leblanc was the link with my third heading, Callister's interest in the circus, and led to the fourth, Miss Mai's weekly grocery orders – too large for one elderly lady to consume on her own. I assume you do not need me to explain that connection?'

'Oh, that part is simple! The extra food was bought for Pierre Leblanc who was living in hiding at "The Firs" and whom Callister had met in France and had brought back to this country. But I still fail to see the connection between Leblanc and Japan.'

'Do you, Watson? Then let us pass on to links five, six and seven – the lighthouse, the fishing-boat, and the contents of the picnic basket and the bucket.'

'The picnic basket contained a sea-bird, as we found to our cost.'

'Exactly, my dear fellow. But it was a very particular type of sea-bird; a member of the Phalacrocorax carbo species; a cormorant, in short. And there lies the connection between France, Japan, the circus and the last two links in my chain. On certain of the Japanese islands, cormorants are trained by the local fishermen to assist with the catch. They are naturally endowed with a small gular sac or pouch in the throat in which they can retain a fish. Before the bird is put over the side of the boat, a ring is placed round the neck to prevent it from swallowing the fish once it has caught it. Then as soon as the cormorant has done so, it is taken back on board and disgorges its catch.

'Now we have already established the fact that Leblanc was a performer in the circus which Callister followed so assiduously from one small French town to the next. His act? Surely you can deduce that for yourself, my dear fellow? No? Then allow me to explain. He worked with birds – doves, in that particular instance, which were trained to remain hidden inside different receptacles and to perform tricks at given signals.

'Watching Leblanc's act must have given Callister the idea of how he might smuggle information concerning the secret Admiralty research he was engaged on to his old boyhood friend and fellow scientist Otto von Schlabitz-Hoecker in Germany, believing, as Callister did, that all scientific knowledge should be freely available, regardless of national boundaries. If Leblanc could train a dove, why not a cormorant, a sea-bird* with a natural capacity for holding a fish in its throat sac and later disgorging it?

'He had all the necessary props for such an act, the isolated house, the abandoned lighthouse and an abundance of wild cormorants which nest about the headlands. For a financial consideration, Leblanc proved willing to co-operate and the plan was put into operation.

'While in France, Callister contacted von Schlabitz-Hoecker, explaining the scheme and suggesting that a Dutch-registered boat should be made available at a later date. Leblanc was then brought secretly to England last summer and kept hidden at "The Firs" where he was set to training a young cormorant which was no doubt trapped in some way and hand-reared.

'The rest of my chain surely needs little explanation. You yourself witnessed the method by which Callister carried out his plan. He took the cormorant, by now trained to obey certain signals, to the lighthouse concealed inside the picnic basket and carried it up to his laboratory where, later that day, he fed it with a small packet containing a piece of paper on which were written details of the latest development of the submarine and which was wrapped in several layers of oiled silk. A ring placed round the cormorant's neck prevented the bird from swallowing the package. The basket was then carried down to the water's edge where Callister opened the receptacle ostensibly to take out some bread which he fed to the gulls.

'You will recollect that the cape he was wearing conveniently hid his hands and arms, thus concealing his exact movements, which, at the same time as he removed the bread, were to release the cormorant into the water where its presence would pass unnoticed among the other birds waiting to be fed.

'His next action, you will recall, was to cast the lines of his fixed fishing rods into the water, a signal to the cormorant to begin to swim out to sea, lured towards the *Margretha* by the man who stood on deck smoking the pipe.

* This is not the only instance of a sea-bird being used for a special mission. During the First World War, it was suggested that seagulls should be trained to defecate on the raised periscopes of German submarines, thus rendering them inoperative. (Dr John F. Watson)

'You recollect my remark that, on this occasion, the man had only one arm on the rail? The other was at his side, out of sight as he reeled in the line to which the lure, in the form of a brightly-coloured, artificial fish, was attached and to which the cormorant was trained to respond. As the bird neared the boat, the second man appeared on deck with his bucket, apparently to empty it overboard and fill it with sea-water. You may also recall that as he lowered the bucket into the water, he banged it against the side of the boat, another signal to the cormorant to dive under the water, swim into the bucket and be hauled on deck. Once it was on board, the bird was carried down to the cabin where it disgorged the small packet containing details of the plans.

'The following morning, the procedure was put into reverse operation. The bucket containing the cormorant was lowered over the side, only this time it was carrying in its pouch a message from one of von Schlabitz-Hoecker's colleagues who was on board the *Margretha*, requesting further clarification of one of the submarine engine parts.

'Meanwhile, on the lighthouse rock, Callister, who was apparently baiting his fixed fishing rods, reeled in the line to which another similar lure was attached. If you recollect, he appeared to have difficulties disentangling one of the lines, a pretext to give him time to attract the cormorant towards him. Once he had done so, he took the bird from the water and placed it inside the basket, his actions again hidden by his cloak. He then carried the cormorant back to his laboratory where it disgorged the message. That was the piece of paper I found rolled up on Callister's work-bench. The system of the lures had, of course, been set up much earlier, before Callister was suspected of treason and was placed under observation.

'Had we not surprised him this morning, I have no doubt that the cormorant would have later been taken back to "The Firs" inside the basket to be kept there until the next occasion when the *Margretha* anchored in the bay. Callister would then have answered the message, sending the further clarification of the engine part which von Schlabitz-Hoecker had requested, together with fresh information on any other research which had taken place in the meantime.

'Ingenious, was it not? I have Leblanc to thank for confirming the details of exactly how the operation was carried out when we interviewed him this morning at the police station in Portswithin.'

'How did you manage to contrive his disappearance from "The Firs"?'

'Oh, quite easily, my dear fellow. Once he learned of Callister's death and knew we had evidence of the treason, it did not take much to persuade him to write a letter to Miss Mai, explaining that he was frightened about the police inquiry which would follow and that he was leaving immediately to walk into Portswithin where he would try to take passage on a boat back to France.'

'Ah, yes; I see, Holmes,' I said. 'This accounts for Miss Mai's search of the house when I returned with her to "The Firs" this morning. And what will happen to Leblanc?'

Holmes took out his pocket watch.

'At the moment, he is being driven back to London in an official car, accompanied by Inspector Drury and Sergeant McGregor. On arrival, he will be taken to Mycroft's office in Whitehall where he will be questioned further and a statement drawn up. After that, the matter is in Mycroft's hands. No doubt Leblanc will be held for a time in prison until some agreement can be arranged between the English and French governments, after which he will be deported to France as an undesirable alien who was in this country unlawfully.'

'Supposing he talks? Could he not sell his story to the newspapers?'

Holmes smiled sardonically.

'It is quite obvious, my dear Watson, that you have no understanding of the way in which governments work. They can be quite Machiavellian in the conduct of their affairs. Leblanc will not talk. He will return to France with some threat hanging over his head which will ensure his silence. You may trust Mycroft on that.

'As for the *Margretha*, after she was boarded and searched

this morning and the crew questioned, including von Schlabitz-Hoecker's agent, a man called Zeiss, she was allowed to return to Holland, after certain papers were removed which are also on their way to London in the good Inspector Drury's pocket. No charge of smuggling will be preferred. His Majesty's Government, anxious to avoid an international incident with its Dutch counterpart, will let the whole matter quietly drop.

'We come now to your part in the affair. You are prepared, are you not, Watson, to stand as witness at the coroner's inquest which will have to be held on Callister's unfortunate death?'

'Well, yes, I suppose I shall have to, Holmes.'

'There is no need for you to feel any anxiety, my dear fellow. Mycroft will see that everything is so arranged that no awkward questions are asked.'

Holmes was correct in this prediction. In Mycroft's hands, action was swiftly taken to cover up the truth.

Holmes, who was too well-known to have his name connected with the case, quietly disappeared from the scene, together with Drury and the other police officers, while I, plain Dr Watson, who had happened to be in Cornwall for a short holiday, was the only witness to Callister's death.

My story, in which Mycroft himself coached me in his office at Whitehall, was quite straightforward. As he explained, the simpler the deception, the more likely it was to be believed, especially as I was clearly a poor liar.

I had been rowing in Penhiddy Bay, intending to indulge myself in a little solitary bird-watching, when I had seen a figure plunge to its death from the top of the lighthouse. Mooring my boat, I had landed and tried to give medical aid. Unfortunately, the man, who was a stranger to me, was dead.

The last three facts had, at least, the merit of being true.

My account must have been convincing because it was accepted without question by the coroner's court at Portswithin and a verdict of accidental death was recorded.

As soon as my evidence was heard, I left discreetly by a side door and was taken straight back to London by official car.

This subterfuge proved necessary for present in court were

not only Hugo Callister, Member of Parliament for Dowerbridge, but several Fleet Street journalists, including Archie Beal, chief reporter of one of the so-called popular newspapers, the *Daily Planet*, which specialized in the more sensational and scandalous stories.

Someone, no doubt Hugo Callister, had informed Beal that Maurice Callister was a scientist who had worked on clandestine Admiralty research for the following morning the *Daily Planet* carried the story on its front page under the headline: 'Secret Scientist In Mysterious Death Plunge', while the report itself hinted that the fall was not accidental and that the Government had conspired to cover up the truth.

Nor did the affair stop there.

As Mycroft had feared, Hugo Callister raised the matter of his brother's death in the House of Commons, demanding a full official inquiry and, although the Prime Minister, with characteristic aplomb, managed to brush the whole affair aside with a slighting reference to the unfortunate influence of the 'yellow' press on back-bench members, Callister's action added fuel to the fire.

It was for me a most uncomfortable time. My rooms in Queen Anne Street were besieged by journalists and, on Mycroft's advice, I moved out temporarily into a quiet Bayswater hotel under a pseudonym.

It was while I was staying at the hotel that my rooms were broken into and my papers searched.

As no attempt was made to take anything of monetary value, I can only assume that the outrage was the work of no ordinary burglar even though the felony was carried out with professional skill. A window at the back of the house was forced open, the lock on my desk was picked and certain pages from one of my note-books were torn out. As these covered my activities during the Cornish trip, the connection with the Callister affair should need no further clarification. Fortunately, the memoranda contained nothing more significant than train times, details of the weather and short descriptions of the countryside, notes I had intended using should I ever write up a full account of the case.

I have discussed the whole matter with both Sherlock and Mycroft Holmes and we have come to the conclusion that someone must have paid an experienced criminal to perpetrate the deed.

It was Mycroft Holmes who suggested that Hugo Callister might be behind the burglary. I consider this a little far-fetched on Mycroft Holmes's part and that he has become obsessed with Hugo Callister's attempts to discredit the Government. It may be naïve of me but I find it difficult to believe that a Member of Parliament, who is distinguished by the title of 'Honourable', should behave in so discreditable a manner and I am more inclined to see in the attempt to tamper with my papers the grubby hand of the gutter press.

However, as I am in no position to judge these matters, I have been forced to accept Mycroft's explanation and to acquiesce in his handling of the situation.

From his Whitehall office, Mycroft has put a rumour into circulation among the West End clubs, the Royal Enclosure at Ascot, the more exclusive Turkish baths and the dinner-tables of the most distinguished society hostesses – anywhere, in short, where people of influence and power are likely to gather – which purports to be the true account of Maurice Callister's death. By making sure that this story is supposed to be strictly confidential and must under no circumstances be repeated, he has guaranteed its widest dissemination.

Mycroft's version of the events is as follows: Maurice Callister had unlawfully smuggled into this country a French circus performer, a young man with a most disreputable past, whom he had kept concealed in 'The Firs' and with whom he was conducting an unnatural relationship. Blackmailed by his lover and fearful of his own good name and his family honour, Maurice Callister had committed suicide by jumping from the top of the lighthouse.

As a final touch, Mycroft Holmes, who shares with his brother Sherlock a rather strange sense of humour which I have remarked on elsewhere,* added a detail about the cormorant,

* In 'The Disappearance of Lady Frances Carfax', Dr John H. Watson refers to Mr Sherlock Holmes's ideas of humour as being 'strange and occasionally offensive'. (Dr John F. Watson)

embellishing his tale with a description of how Callister made his death-leap carrying in his arms his French lover's favourite pet, a tamed sea-bird, which symbolized for him his own entrapment in the tragic relationship.

Mycroft Holmes also prevailed on me to include a cryptic reference to this account in 'The Adventure of the Veiled Lodger', coupled with the threat of its exposure. This was directed specifically at Hugo Callister with the intention of dissuading him from pressing for an official Parliamentary inquiry, Mycroft being of the opinion that, as the popular press would soon lose interest in the story of Callister's death and would pass on to other scandals, his chief adversary in the affair was the Honourable Member for Dowerbridge.

Mycroft Holmes's assessment of the situation was perfectly sound.

Shortly afterwards, the attention of the editor of the *Daily Planet* was directed towards a most regrettable rumour concerning His Majesty, King Edward VII, and a certain countess who shall be nameless, and the reports on Maurice Callister passed from its pages.

As for Hugo Callister, the threat of the publication of the so-called 'true' account of his brother'd death and the subsequent scandal it would cause was sufficient to make him withdraw his charges of a Government conspiracy and the whole matter was discreetly forgotten.

However, Holmes and I have been seriously troubled by the deception, necessary though it may have been for the security of the realm; I on the grounds that any untruth, even from the very best of motives, is not the manner in which His Majesty's Government should conduct its affairs.

Holmes's concern is of a less narrowly political nature. Despite his deep patriotism, his sympathies have become more and more engaged by Maurice Callister's belief that all knowledge, particularly that concerning research into weapons of war, should be openly discussed at international level. His argument runs that if all nations shared the same information, it would be futile for any individual country to develop its own weapons, the armaments race would therefore become unnecessary, war unlikely, and the huge sums of money thus saved could be spent on more peaceful research for the good of mankind.

It is in this belief, he avers, that true patriotism lies.

He expounded his theory for several hours only yesterday evening as we sat together by the hearth in the sitting-room at Baker Street, Holmes's austere features lit up not only by the firelight but by the warmth of his convictions.

'But what can be done?' I asked.

It was then that Holmes made the suggestion which I referred to at the beginning of this narrative.

'Write up the true account of the politician, the lighthouse and the trained cormorant,' said he, 'and deposit it in some safe place where no one can gain access to it. Although its publication is out of the question for the foreseeable future, let us hope, my dear Watson, that attitudes will change and that a saner generation in years to come will have cured itself of this madness and that the true story can at last be placed before the public.'